SOMAN CHAINANI

RISE OF THE SCHOOL FOR GOOD AND EVIL

Illustrations by RaidesArt

HarperCollins *Children's Books*

First published in the United Kingdom by
HarperCollins *Children's Books* in 2022
HarperCollins *Children's Books* is a division of
HarperCollins*Publishers* Ltd
1 London Bridge Street
London SE1 9GF

www.harpercollins.co.uk

HarperCollins*Publishers*
1st Floor, Watermarque Building, Ringsend Road
Dublin 4, Ireland

1

ISBN 978-0-00-850802-9

Soman Chainani and RaidesArt assert the moral right to be identified
as the author and illustrator of the work respectively

A CIP catalogue record for this title is available from the British Library

Typeset by Amy Ryan

Printed and bound in the UK using 100% renewable electricity at CPI Group (UK) Ltd

MIX
**Paper from
responsible sources**
FSC™ C007454

www.fsc.org

This book is produced from independently certified FSC™ paper
to ensure responsible forest management.

For more information visit: www.harpercollins.co.uk/green

RISE OF THE SCHOOL FOR GOOD AND EVIL

Soman Chainani is the *New York Times* bestselling author of The School for Good and Evil series. The fairy tale saga has sold over three million copies, been translated into 30 languages and will soon be a major motion picture from Netflix, which Soman will executive produce. His most recent book, *Beasts and Beauty: Dangerous Tales*, was also an instant *New York Times* bestseller. Soman is a graduate of Harvard University and received his MFA in film from Columbia University. Every year, he visits schools around the world to speak to kids and share his secret: that reading is the path to a better life.

You can visit Soman at www.somanchainani.com

ALSO BY SOMAN CHAINANI

RISE
OF THE
SCHOOL
FOR
GOOD AND EVIL

The Pen writes the new School Master's name.

But this time it doesn't write one name.

It writes two.

The Pen is called the Storian.

Long and steel, sharp at both ends.

It floats into the air over the two boys, its tip like an eye.

Then it speaks.

The voice warm and ageless. Neither male nor female.

> *In exchange for immortality*
> *In exchange for eternal youth*
> *I choose you.*
> *Two brothers.*
> *One for Good.*
> *One for Evil.*

Your loyalty to your blood greater than the loyalty
    to your side.
As long as you love each other, the world stays in
    balance.
Good and Evil.
Brother and brother.
But every School Master faces a test.
Yours is love.
Betray that love and the test is failed.
You will wither and die.
You will be replaced.
Raise your hands to seal this oath.

The boys do, twins who wear the same face.

Rhian, skin golden, hair wild, lifts his hand.

The Pen glows hot and slashes his palm, Rhian crying out.

Then Rafal, skin milky-white, hair like silver spikes.

It stabs his hand and Rafal doesn't flinch.

The Pen's glow fades, its steel growing cold.

The twins glance at each other, burning with questions.

But in the end, they ask only one.

"What happened to the last School Master?"

The Pen doesn't answer.

Instead, a trembling voice rises from the shadows.

A withered old man.

"I failed," he says.

PART 1

BAD MAGIC

1.

If not for a boy named Aladdin, the School for Good and Evil might never have started kidnapping Readers like you.

You'd be safe in your beds instead of stolen to a world where fairy tales come true for some . . . and end in death for others.

But Aladdin is where the tale starts.

The tale of what happened between the School Masters.

Two brothers, Good and Evil, who ruled the legendary school.

But Aladdin hasn't the faintest clue he's part of a larger story.

He's too busy thinking about his magic lamp.

He should have been working at his family's tailoring shop, but like usual, he'd slipped away the moment his father turned his back, bounding off to Mahaba Market, on the hunt for good fortune. Mahaba sparked him to life—the smells, the sounds, the *girls*—and an hour there was worth a thousand days in his family's shop. He knew he should work in the shop, of course, that a good boy would do as he's told . . . but tailors don't marry the Sultan's daughter and that's what he dreamed of, a princess and a crown and the respect of the people, the kind of respect that no one gave him.

"Good morning, Raja! Busier than usual today!" Aladdin greeted the fruit seller.

Raja gave him a dirty look.

"Lovely day, Shilpa! Look at all the crowds!" Aladdin said to the fish vendor.

Shilpa spat in his direction.

"Shall we play a game of dice, Bassu?" Aladdin asked a skinny man at the corner.

Bassu fled.

Aladdin sighed, his hands in the pockets of his ragged blue jacket. He had a reputation as a thief, cheat, and loiterer, but what choice did he have? He had no money, status, or name in this world, and to earn those things, sometimes you have to take shortcuts. And today was the perfect day for action, the market bustling like it was a holiday, full of kids with parents fussing over them, buying their favorite treats. Aladdin had never seen

Mahaba like this, not even at New Year . . .

That's when he heard two men talking in an alley as he passed. Two men he knew well: Salim and Aseem.

"It's *the* magic lamp!" Salim was saying.

"How did you get it?" asked Aseem.

"The Sultan found the Cave of Wishes, but his caravan was robbed by thieves on the way back to the palace," Salim confided. "The thieves didn't know it was the treasured lamp and sold it right to me."

"Make your three wishes, then!" said Aseem.

Aladdin's ears perked up. The magic lamp had been the source of legend for thousands of years, but no one had ever found it. And now these two goons had it in their hands?

"A likely story," Aladdin said, turning into the alley.

Salim instantly put the lamp away—

"I already saw it. No doubt a fake," Aladdin scoffed, puffing at his mop of black hair. "But go ahead. Prove it's the magic lamp. Prove it has any value at all."

Salim and Aseem peeked at each other.

Then Salim held up the lamp and rubbed it with his palm . . .

Suddenly the lamp glowed and thick red smoke billowed from its tip, before Salim stoppered it with his finger and the lamp went dull once more.

"Don't want to set the genie loose here or we'll all get put in the Sultan's jail," Salim warned.

Aladdin's eyes flared. The lamp was . . . *real?*

He rushed forward. "Sell it to me!"

Salim laughed. "It's not for sale, you fool."

"Everything in this world is for sale," Aladdin insisted.

"Not this," Aseem scorned. "Not to a rat who cheats me and Salim out of our hard-earned money."

"A rat who is a worthless stain on his family," Salim added.

Aladdin smiled through his teeth. They could insult him all they wanted. In a negotiation, whoever wants something more wins and Aladdin didn't just want the lamp. He *needed* it. Imagine the princess he could wish for . . . imagine the man he could be, finally worthy of respect . . .

"I'll roll you my dice for it," Aladdin insisted. "If I win, I keep the lamp. If you win, I'll pay you back everything I've ever taken from you and I'll never step foot in Mahaba Market again."

He assumed the two men would mock this offer since he hardly had enough for lunch, let alone a chest of savings lying around . . . but to Aladdin's surprise, Salim and Aseem flashed each other mysterious looks.

"Hmm," said Salim. "He's cheated enough from us that if he

pays us back, we can each buy a house near Bahim Beach . . ."

"Plus the thought of never seeing his dirty, rotten face again . . . ," said Aseem.

The two men turned to Aladdin. "We have a deal."

"We do?" Aladdin said, stunned.

"Over six you win, under six we win," said Aseem.

Aladdin knew better than to waste more words. In his left pocket, he had dice carved to land over six; in his right pocket, he had dice carved to land under. He drew the ones from his left pocket and threw them down in the grimy street.

"I win," Aladdin gloated, holding out his palm. "Give me the lamp."

"You cheated—" Salim protested.

"A deal's a deal," Aladdin said firmly.

The two men glanced at each other. With a heavy sigh, Salim handed over the lamp.

Aladdin whistled as he walked away, stuffing his treasure under his jacket.

He couldn't see the grins spreading across the faces of the two men he'd just beaten.

2.

There were wishes to be made. A princess bride. A sultan's crown. His name remembered forever . . .

But first he had to clean toilets.

That was the price for skipping work, which was better than no supper, the punishment his mother had decreed for a few nights, before she realized he would happily starve and die instead of toil in a shop, so she had to try something else.

"What good are you?" she bellowed from the kitchen as he scrubbed the bathroom, but Aladdin was too full of her chicken stew and sour cherry rice to be bothered. He'd stuffed the lamp under his bed when he came home. As soon as his parents were asleep, he would take it to the garden and make his first wish, because it didn't seem wise to unleash a genie in a house with such thin walls. His mother raised her voice. "Hagrifa's son will surely get taken to the School for Good and become famous and rich and here my son is, stealing *paani poori* and cheating people in Mahaba Market. You think I don't know! Everyone knows!"

Aladdin stiffened. He'd forgotten it was Kidnapping Night. He glanced out the window at the row of houses down the lane, plates of *halva* and honey biscuits laid out on the windowsills to entice the School Master. No wonder it had been so crowded in the market! All those mothers and fathers, bringing their children to Mahaba, thinking—and hoping!—that it would be their last day together. That tonight the School Master would come and whisk their sons and daughters to the place where legends are born. After all, if a child was taken as an Ever or a Never, their parents would be celebrated in Shazabah, invited to the poshest parties, offered the best table at Giti's restaurant, even sent flowers by the Sultan himself. Of course, most children taken from Shazabah were for the Good school, since Shazabah was one of the Ever kingdoms in the Endless Woods. But over the years, there had been a handful of Nevers taken too, since regardless of whether a kingdom labeled itself Good or Evil, rogue spirits always slipped through.

Not that any of this applied to Aladdin. He was selfish, thieving, but he wasn't Evil, not down to his core like the souls the School Master wanted. Remember that stray dog he'd shared his pistachio tart with? (Yes, the tart was stolen, but who cares.) Or that girl at the schoolhouse that he'd helped with her homework? (Her being pretty had nothing to do with it.) Then again, he wasn't Good either. Even his parents would agree. The Good school was for other kids. Ones born to clearer paths. Ones who didn't struggle like him to find their way. But at last, that struggle had been rewarded. He didn't need to go to the School for Good and Evil to achieve his dreams. He had the lamp now, *the* magic lamp, that would give him more riches and power than the School Masters themselves. Finally, people would pay attention to him. People would know his name. But how to make the lamp work? Salim had just rubbed it, hadn't he? Or was there a magic word? He'd sort it out. First, he needed to finish his cleaning and pretend to sleep before his father came home, otherwise it would be an hour of lectures—

Downstairs, the door swung open.

"Aladdin!" a voice boomed.

The boy slumped.

It wouldn't have been so bad if his father hadn't plopped down on Aladdin's bed, right where the lamp was stuffed under the mattress, and his dad was so large that the boy worried the lamp would get crushed, along with the genie inside.

"What is it you're searching for, Aladdin?" his dad started, still sweating from his trip up the stairs. "What is it that takes you so far away from my shop?"

Aladdin imagined he and a beautiful princess living in a palace a thousand times the size of this house with locks on every door so no one could enter without his permission, a palace he'd wish to life once his dad left his room.

"Aladdin?"

"Hmm?" the boy said.

His father gazed hard at him. "I think you don't want to work in my shop because you think that you can do better. That you will be a big shot who will live in a castle and marry a king's daughter instead of working humbly like the rest of us. You go chasing after phantoms, when you have a perfectly good life in front of you. That never ends well. Anyone who knows the Storian's tales can tell you."

You don't believe in me, Aladdin thought. *You think I can't win a girl like that and make something of myself. You and Mom think I'm worthless, just like Salim said.*

But he didn't voice any of these things.

Instead he yawned. "Yes, Dad."

"So tomorrow I'll see you bright and early in the shop?"

"Yes, Dad."

"Good boy."

He gave Aladdin a hug, then closed the door behind him, and the boy promptly pulled the lamp from beneath the mattress. It was small and bronze, like a teapot with an elongated tip, carved with an intricate pattern of stars and moons. Though there were no scratches or flaws in its surface, Aladdin supposed it was very, very old. How long had it been sitting there in the

Cave of Wishes, the genie stuck inside, waiting for a new master to command him? How long had destiny anticipated this day, when *he*, Aladdin, would be that new master? He held it close, studying his big nose and thick eyebrows in the lamp's reflection. Inside this lamp was the life he was meant to live. The love and respect he deserved to find. Slowly, his palm reached for its surface—

Loud pounding shuddered his door.

"Hagrifa and Moorli and Roopa are putting out their best *ladoos* for the School Master!" his mother barked. "They asked what I was doing to welcome him. You know what I said? Hiding in shame!"

Aladdin blew out the candle and snored, pretending to be asleep. He hugged the lamp under his shirt, the metal cold against his skin. Soon his parents would be in bed and he'd have his chance. Until then, he'd stay awake, rehearsing his wishes . . .

3.

He woke to a sharp chill and hissing wind.

Aladdin lurched up in bed and saw the window latch had opened, the November night leaking through. The lamp had rolled onto the floor, near a pile of dirty clothes.

How long had he been asleep? Surely his parents were in bed by now. He grabbed the lamp and put on a coat, angling to get out to the garden and summon the genie. But first, he redid the window latch, glancing out at the moon over the dark lane—

Aladdin jolted backwards.

Something was in the window.

A shadow with shiny blue eyes.

Pressing against the glass.

Undoing the latch.

Aladdin tried to run for the stairs, but the shadow hooked him by the collar and yanked him outside, dragging him through the garden, the boy too stunned to scream. But then he gathered his wits and realized a monster was kidnapping him, a monster that had no *face*. He grasped at the shadow, but his hand went straight through, which left Aladdin even more scared, flailing and kicking, before the shadow shot him a harsh glare and pulled him quicker through the grass, faster, faster, its grip sealing on Aladdin's collar and swinging the boy like a hammer, a hundred feet into the air . . .

A bird caught him.

If one could call a creature with *fur* a bird.

It had skin like black velvet, its head blanketed in shiny black feathers, ending in a sharp beak, as if a bat had mated with a crow and spawned something much larger. With a furious screech, it bucked Aladdin onto its spine. Then it stretched its wings, drawing quick shallow breaths, before it revved forward and slammed into thunderclouds, lightning detonating all around like fireworks.

He had to be dreaming, Aladdin thought, shielding his ears from blasting thunder. Surely he was still in bed, conjuring this madness—

But then the bird swooped, slashing out of clouds, and Aladdin saw the sky filled with these sleek, furry creatures, all carrying menacing-looking children on their backs. Beneath them was a pockmarked manor that looked like it had been dipped in mud.

The School for Evil.

One by one, the birds flung the children off, dropping them into hellish darkness.

Aladdin's heart seized.

So it had happened.

He was Evil after all.

Now he would be condemned to a life of villainy. That is, if he could survive his time at school with murderers and monsters . . .

But then something peculiar happened.

His bird didn't drop him in the Evil school.

Instead, it flew past it to the *other* side of the same manor, leaving all the other Evil children behind. This side of the house was ivory white, with a grove of cherry blossoms shedding petals in the sun.

With a disgusted screech, the bird threw Aladdin down. The boy screamed in shock, freefalling to certain death—

Until a tree caught him in its branches.

Dazed, Aladdin poked his head up.

All around, boys and girls were rising from the ground, clean-cut and luminous.

The new students of this school.

Good students.

Aladdin blinked. *Impossible,* he thought. *Me . . . Good?*

But then he felt the metal outlines of something in his coat pocket and slowly a smile crept across the boy's face.

The lamp.

It had to be.

He hadn't even made his first wish yet and already his luck had begun to change.

4.

Just before noon, the two School Masters came out of their study and headed to the theater to welcome the new students.

"If Aladdin was on your list for Evil, how did he end up in *my* school?" Rhian asked, broad and tan with messy curls.

Rafal glanced at him, his spikes of snow-colored hair as pale as his skin. "Ask the stymphs."

"They're your birds and under your control," his Good brother reminded.

"Until today," Rafal groused. "They insist they put Aladdin where he belongs."

"That cheating thief? An Ever?" Rhian said.

Rafal nodded. "I tried changing him in the ledger too, but the Storian erased his name on the Evil roll and switched him back to yours."

The Good School Master stared at his twin. "So it's the Storian's doing, then."

"Apparently the Pen has overruled our judgment for the first time," Rafal surmised.

"It thinks we made a *mistake*?" Rhian replied. "We don't make mistakes on souls."

"One of the few things we agree on," said Rafal.

He grinned at his brother, but Rhian was pensive as they made their way through the school, a modest chateau no bigger than an estate house or a country villa. The brothers liked it this way, an intimate school that favored community rather than grand or selfish ambitions. Good students bunked in the east wing, Evil students in the west. Evers and Nevers shared most of their classes together, along with common rooms that served Good and Evil both. At first, they'd considered separating Good from Evil more intently, but just as Rhian and Rafal protected the school together, despite their opposing souls, they wanted the students to keep a healthy rivalry while respecting the balance of the Woods. It is why the Storian had named the twins as School Masters. Because their love for each other was greater than their loyalty to a side. As long as their love stayed strong, Good and Evil in balance, then the Storian reflected this balance in its fairy tales. Sometimes Good won at the end of a story. Sometimes Evil. And it was these victories and losses that made each side strive to do better. In this way, the Pen moved the world forward, one story at a time.

As for the school's place in all this, the Storian's tales tracked the students who had graduated from the famous academy, which is why young Evers and Nevers worked so hard in their classes, hoping the Pen would one day tell their story after graduation and make them into legends. The walls of the School Masters' study were lined with cases of these stories—*The Frog Prince*, *Tom Thumb*, *Clever Maria*, *Goldilocks*, and more—every fairy tale ever told, each book a tribute to a former student.

As they neared the Supper Hall, Rafal noticed his brother still quiet. "Surely that thief boy isn't worth this much thought."

Rhian looked at him. "The Pen must have switched him for a reason. What if Aladdin *is* Evil . . . but the Pen thinks I can *make* him Good? What if he's a test?"

"To turn a Never into an Ever?" Rafal scowled. "Impossible."

"But we both agree this boy isn't Good and we don't make mistakes when it comes to a soul," Rhian replied. "Yet if I can *turn* him Good . . . if I can make him into an Ever . . ."

"Then what would stop you from doing it with *all* Evil souls?" Rafal mocked, expecting Rhian to laugh.

But his brother didn't. Instead he smiled, as if it was exactly what he'd been thinking too.

Rafal went cold. "What happened to *balance*?"

"It's the Storian's test, isn't it? Take it up with the Pen," Rhian quipped. Then he saw the dark expression in his brother's face. "I'm only joking, Rafal. A soul can't be changed. Either we're wrong and he *is* Good—"

"We're never wrong," said Rafal.

"—or the Pen is wrong, and my attempts to turn him into an Ever will fail," said Rhian.

"And fail miserably," Rafal sniped. He peered at his brother. "But you'll still try?"

"Wouldn't you, if you thought the Storian might be on your side?" Rhian teased, nudging him.

"Perhaps," said Rafal. But he pulled away, as if a challenge had been issued.

Each brother, silently claiming the student for his team.

A student they had yet to meet.

The School Masters reached the theater. Rhian glanced at his Evil twin, seeing he was the pensive one now. "You know, Rafal, ever since we've been teenagers, you've become very moody."

"We've been teenagers for a hundred years," Rafal replied.

"Precisely," said Rhian, before he placed his palms on the wooden doors and pushed them both open.

5.

Like most kids in the Endless Woods, Aladdin had assumed the School for Good would be a feast of swordfighting, pretty girls, and late-night mischief in the dormitories.

What he didn't expect was so many rules.

"Rule number 10," said Professor Mayberry, Dean of Good, an elegant, dark-skinned woman who stood so straight and snapped her consonants so crisply it made Aladdin's buttocks clench. "Good and Evil are both invited to the Snow Ball, the winter dance that takes place on Christmas Eve. All Evers are required to go—"

"And all Nevers are encouraged *not* to," growled a skeletal man next to her, his skin a peculiar shade of gray, his hair more salt than pepper, and his eyebrows thick and very black. This was Professor Humburg, Dean of Evil. "After the first year, you will be divided into three tracks based on your performance. One for Leaders, one for Followers, and one for Mogrifs."

Aladdin yawned and yanked at his bow tie, bored out of his skull and irritated that he'd been harnessed in this cockamamie outfit, complete with ruffles and tails, like he was a circus monkey. (Also, what in the world was a *mogrif*?) He looked around the theater, just as froufrou as his uniform, with ornate wooden pews and rosette windows, and he wondered how the Evil kids could put up with all this puffery. Indeed, the Nevers were seated across the aisle, about fifty of them in the same frilly

uniforms as Good, while on his side, twenty-five Everboys listened obediently to the Deans, as did the twenty-five Evergirls
seated in the rows behind him. One had caught his notice, a
small girl whose feet barely touched the floor, with bright pink
eyeshadow, rosy cheeks, and purple ribbons in her black hair.
Aladdin tried to make eye contact, but her focus was firmly on
Professor Mayberry.

"Rule number 11. The School Masters' study is strictly
off-limits," the Dean of Good declared, "as are all faculty
offices—"

If he wanted rules, he would have stayed in Shazabah, Aladdin grouched silently. By now, he'd have made his three wishes
and have a princess and a palace and everyone here would know
his name. He patted at the lamp in his jacket pocket. He hadn't
a second to himself since he won it from Salim. What good was
having the lamp if he never got a chance to *use* it?

Aladdin glanced over at the Nevers, dressed just like the
Evers, but then he looked closer and saw they were subtly alter-
ing their uniforms, slashing sleeves and cutting holes in the
shirts, while showing off scars and tattoos and the weapons
they'd managed to sneak through.

Rule-breakers, Aladdin thought.

Definitely his people.

He whirled around to the girl with purple ribbons. "Want to see something?"

The girl ignored him, her eyes on the stage.

"Rule number 12," Mayberry was saying. "You are forbidden to leave your dorm rooms after 9:00 p.m.—"

"Look," Aladdin pestered, reaching into his pocket. "It's the magic lamp."

"Sure it is," the girl snipped, not looking at him.

Next to Aladdin, a tall boy with fair skin and red hair chortled. "Good luck. That's Kyma, the Princess of Maidenvale. Every guy's got his eye on her for the Snow Ball, including Hephaestus."

He nodded down the pew at a muscular brown boy, with a shaved head and pure green eyes, who all the other Everboys kept peeking at, seeking his approval, even though Hephaestus seemed unaware of their existence.

"Which means you don't stand a chance," the red-haired boy warned Aladdin.

This was the wrong thing to say, because now that Aladdin had the magic lamp, he could make a wish for anything he wanted, including thrashing Hephaestus in a wrestling match or taking Princess Kyma to the Snow Ball. But it was even more the wrong thing to say, because now that he could win his princess with the lamp, he wanted to win her without it.

He spun back to Kyma. "I swear it's the magic lamp. Straight from the Cave of Wishes."

Kyma sighed. "No, it's not, because everyone including my father has tried to find the Cave of Wishes and it cannot be found. So by all means keep telling lies, but not to me, because lies have a certain smell on the breath and yours is starting to stink."

Aladdin flushed, his teeth gritting. "Guess I'll have to *show* you, then."

He raised a hand to the lamp to rub it—

"You there!" a voice snapped from the stage.

A sea of Evers and Nevers turned to Aladdin.

The boy froze, like a cat trying to blend with its surroundings.

Kyma smirked at him.

"Is there something you'd like to share with us?" Professor Mayberry asked, frowning.

"No," said Aladdin.

"He says he has the magic lamp!" the red-haired boy to his right heckled.

"The lamp from the Cave of Wishes!" hooted another boy to his left, who'd been eavesdropping.

Students on both sides of the aisle jeered and sniggered.

Aladdin could see Hephaestus giving him a pitying look.

"I do have it! And there's a genie inside!" Aladdin defended angrily, holding it up, but the laughter was louder now, a theater full of new students bonded by a fool to mock. Aladdin leapt to his feet, raising his voice. "When I make my first wish, I'll turn all of you into frogs! Then you'll see!"

"Let's hope it won't come to that," a male voice echoed.

Everyone in the theater went still, the Deans included.

Aladdin watched the twin School Masters enter, gliding down the aisle, the Evil brother with spiky white hair and milky-pale skin, the Good brother warm and wild-haired, both of them in matching blue robes. Aladdin had heard rumors of these two immortal teenagers who ruled the school and protected the Storian that wrote the Woods' tales. But now in their presence, he sensed the power behind their light-colored eyes. Eyes that were focused entirely on *him*.

"Let me have it," the Good brother ordered.

Aladdin didn't dare disobey, even if parting with the lamp made him sick. He surrendered his treasure.

The Good School Master inspected it, then glanced at his twin before offering the lamp back to Aladdin. "A fake. No doubt about it."

The Evil School Master studied the lamp over his shoulder,

equally unimpressed . . . But then something in his face changed. A twinkle in the frosty pools of his eyes, as if the ice had cracked.

"I'm not sure I agree, brother," he said, snatching the lamp before Aladdin could retrieve it.

The Good School Master gave the Evil one a confused look, but the Evil brother was already striding down the aisle, handing the lamp to Dean Humburg before whispering quite loudly, "Lock it in your office, where no one can get it."

Dean Humburg shot Aladdin a glare. "Certainly, Master Rafal."

The Good brother seemed baffled by all this, asking his twin: "Can we get on with our Welcoming speeches or shall we investigate other students' keepsakes in case they're the Holy Grail?"

"By all means, give your speech first," Rafal replied. "You know, since the Storian is on *your* side."

Rhian pursed his lips. "With that attitude, maybe it should be."

Both School Masters peered at each other, then looked out at the students.

At *a* student.

But Aladdin didn't notice their stares, the boy consumed with a single thought.

How to get into Dean Humburg's office.

A thought that the Evil School Master seemed to be encouraging, because he grinned right at Aladdin the moment the boy settled on a plan.

6.

Tempting a thief is never a good idea, especially a thief who thinks you've stolen from him.

Since Professor Humburg was Evil's Dean, his office would be on the west side of the manor, which meant Aladdin had to break out of his room, sneak over to Evil's wing, find Humburg's lair, and steal back his lamp without anyone catching him. Even for a cocky optimist like Aladdin, the challenge was steep. Luckily, the Good dormitories were unguarded after the teachers went to bed, trusting in the virtue of their students, so a short while after midnight, Aladdin tiptoed past his sleeping roommates and out into the hallway, towards the stairwell—

He stopped short.

Hephaestus and Kyma were on the steps, halfway down the staircase, playing cards. Hephaestus was in a tight, sleeveless shirt and Kyma in purple pajamas that matched the streaks in her hair. Neither spoke nor made a sound, but from the way they peeked at each other after each move, gloating or grinning, the whole game felt more romantic than if he'd caught them kissing.

Aladdin snorted angrily and the two Evers craned their heads, but Aladdin was already hustling for the rear stairwell, his fists curled. He wanted to storm to Professor Mayberry's room and report them for breaking rules; he wanted to see those arrogant lovebirds *punished*. But since he too had snuck out of his room to do something even worse, he could only swallow his bitterness and stick to his plan. How could she choose that dead-eyed, overinflated dunce instead of him? How could she be so predictable? Aladdin sucked in a breath. Kyma was just like everyone in Shazabah. Everyone who underestimated him and his worth.

No matter.

Soon he'd have his lamp and Princess Kyma would be his.

Didn't matter how he got her love. What mattered is that the world see him as *worthy* of her love. Then he would be like Hephaestus: wanted and valued, not just in the minds of others, but also in his own.

First things first. Humburg's office.

He hurried downstairs, crossing the foyer to the west wing stairwell—

Aladdin stopped cold.

Mayberry.

Sweeping from the dining hall in a velvet dressing gown and spooning a chocolate pudding she'd retrieved for a midnight snack.

She lifted her head, about to see Aladdin—

All of a sudden, the Dean froze, as if petrified to stone, the pudding spoon still in her mouth.

He waited for her to move, but Mayberry just stood there, her gaze fixed past him.

Slowly Aladdin reached out his hand and touched her face, her skin warm, her pulse strong. But she didn't flinch or shift, her body stiff as a statue.

Aladdin hesitated, unsure what just happened.

But like he'd learned when he'd stumbled upon the lamp in a market alley, one mustn't question good fortune.

He ran past her, up the stairs.

By the time he looked down, Professor Mayberry had unfrozen, already tasting her next dose of pudding and ambling on her way.

There is a difference between good fortune and too much good fortune, though.

From the moment he entered the west wing, forces seemed

to be clearing obstacles away, as if he belonged here.

As if Evil was his *true* place.

The dorm halls were too dark at night to navigate, a maze of corridors and stairwells, and yet, whenever Aladdin reached a crossroads, a rat or a cockroach would skitter by and peep— *"This way!"*—pointing him in the right direction.

When a one-eyed teacher turned into his hall, the wall reached out and yanked Aladdin back.

An ogre guard slumped to sleep the moment he spotted the boy.

Then two bats fluttered by, yipping *"Humburg, Humburg, Humburg"* and leading him to a door at the end of a hall, the Dean's name carved into it.

And if all of this wasn't proof enough that Evil was conspiring in his favor . . . the door to Professor Humburg's office mysteriously unlatched for him.

Aladdin slipped inside, assuming he'd have to search for where the Dean locked the lamp. But instead, he heard a rattling from a drawer in the corner desk—a drawer that when he couldn't pick the lock popped open with an exasperated creak as if it had no time for amateurs.

The moment he set eyes on it, the lamp sparkled like a jewel, then went warm in Aladdin's hands, purring softly, like it had willed the boy to find it and now it was home.

So was it the lamp helping me all along? Aladdin reconsidered, watching his reflection in its surface. *Maybe I am actually Good, then. Because why would the lamp help someone Evil?*

A snore came from another room. Humburg's bedchamber.

Aladdin seized his treasure and scampered out.

*Who*s or *what*s or *why*s didn't matter.

The lamp was his once more.

Soon he was back down the stairwell, firmly on the side of Good, and it was here on the balcony outside his room, while his roommates slept, that Aladdin at last had the peace and quiet to thrust his prize into the moonlight and rub it hard, once, twice, thrice—

Red smoke spun out, rising into a shadowy, slithering form, a snake surging high into the night, before shoving its face against Aladdin's.

"Young Masster," it hissed. *"What is your firssst wissshhhh?"*

Aladdin recoiled. He'd always imagined the genie to be more friendly, more cuddly and less . . . scaly.

"Ssssspeak, boy!" the genie spat, eyes glowing red.

Aladdin bucked up. It didn't matter who was granting his wish. It didn't matter if he was Good or Evil. What mattered was the wish itself, made with the purest Good intentions.

He glared into the snake's eyes.

"I wish for Princess Kyma to fall madly in love with me."

7.

A few floors up, in their study, the brothers were having a late dinner.

"Bragging about his lamp? Threatening to turn everyone into frogs? How can anyone think that boy is Good?" Rafal groused, biting into his steak. "The Pen is wrong about him. Which means the Storian can no longer be trusted."

"The Pen that named *us* as School Masters? The Pen that keeps our world *alive*?" Rhian said, sliding a piece of fish off his knife. "Forgive me if I still trust the Storian over you. If it says Aladdin is Good, it must be true. Just wait and see."

"If he *is* Good, then why didn't you see it to begin with?" Rafal challenged him.

"Why didn't *you*?" Rhian slung back.

Rafal exploded. "Why is the Storian interfering in our school! Why *now*? Good has won five tales in a row and suddenly the Pen's giving you my well-earned students, too?" He swatted his plate off the table, crashing it against a bookcase. "Suppose you're right? What if the Pen *is* on your side? What if

it wants to do away with Evil entirely! Then what!"

Rhian sighed. "Calm down. The balance will work itself out, like always. In the meantime, you've wasted a perfectly good dinner. Again." He kneeled down and cleaned up the mess. "Besides, it's only four tales. The Pen isn't done with the tale of Peter Stumpf. He was one of your best students when he was here, wasn't he? Now he's a man-eating werewolf, who might very well have his day."

Rafal walked over to the white stone table as the enchanted steel carved THE END into a book's final page.

"Well, Peter Stumpf just got burned at the stake and a dog's licking the bones, so not sure it's the victory I'm looking for."

Rhian took a sip of wine. "Oh."

Rafal tossed the finished book onto the floor. "Well, if Aladdin shows he's Evil, that will rebalance things. And it'll prove we were right about him all along. That we were doing our *jobs*. The days of trusting the Storian blindly will be over. About time we had faith in our own judgment—in Man instead of Pen."

Rhian said nothing, downing the last of the wine.

"Pity the Little Thief doesn't have his lamp anymore," Rafal added. "His wish would be very enlightening."

Rhian peered at him suspiciously.

"I know what you're thinking," said Rafal. "You're thinking, 'Why does my brother always cause trouble instead of being happy the way things are? Why can't he be more like me?'"

"I'm thinking that without me, you wouldn't know you were Evil and without you, I wouldn't know I was Good," said Rhian.

"True, but all twins know there is one that was created better," Rafal needled. "It is the secret that bonds them."

"I thought the secret was love," Rhian replied. "Especially since it's our love that keeps us young and immortal. Break that bond and we'd grow old and die."

"I can love you and still think I'm better," said Rafal. "Which is why when Aladdin proves himself Evil, I'll enjoy watching you squirm—"

There was a scratching sound behind them.

In the corner, the Storian had opened a new book and begun to write.

"Strange," Rhian observed. "Normally it takes a couple days' rest after it finishes."

They stood and saw the Pen painting a colorful portrait of a boy they both knew.

"Aladdin," said Rafal.

He was holding a magic lamp, a Snake genie unfolding in thick red smoke.

Rhian glowered at Rafal. "'*Pity the Little Thief doesn't have his lamp anymore . . .*'"

"Oops," Rafal said, grinning. "Let's see if he does any better than Peter Stumpf!"

But the Pen didn't write about Aladdin.

Instead, the Pen wrote something else.

Once upon a time, there were twin School Masters, Good and Evil, whose love kept the world balanced. As long as the brothers loved each other, the Pen favored neither Good nor Evil, each side equally powerful in the Endless Woods. But then one day, a student arrived who would change everything between them.

Rhian and Rafal glanced at each other, stunned.

The Storian had never written about the School Masters.

In *any* of its tales.

The Pen and its protectors had always been separate.

Anxiously, the brothers looked down, awaiting the next part of Aladdin's tale.

A tale that, for the first time, seemed to be about *them*.

8.

The next morning, Aladdin woke singing a song of love.

Love with a note of vengeance, because soon, he would arrive at the Supper Hall to not only see a real-life princess throw herself at him in front of the whole school, but also witness her lunkheaded love abandoned and betrayed . . . Was there any greater happiness than watching a wish come true?

The Supper Hall was built in the round, like a theater that gave you a good seat to the action wherever it was playing out. Evers and Nevers were supposed to eat meals together, but Nevers generally stayed up too late and missed breakfast, leaving Good to claim the hall each morning for itself. Behind a curtain, enchanted pots and pans boiled and bubbled, filling plates in rhythmic symphony, cherry pancakes, eggs *à la français*, and honey-dipped bananas, which floated out to tables. Flowers filled the centerpieces and carvings of frolicking cupids rimmed the walls, an endless chase of love.

As Aladdin entered, humming and drinking in sugary scents, he noticed Princess Kyma seated with Hephaestus at a center table, a flock of boys angling for her and a gang of girls cozying up to him, while the pair only had eyes for each other.

Without the slightest hesitation, Aladdin strolled up, swiped a banana off Hephaestus' plate, and bit into it, before perching on the table and swinging himself in Kyma's direction. "Well?" he grinned.

Kyma glared witheringly at him. "Well, what."

Aladdin's mouth flattened. "Don't you have something to say?"

"Only that boys who wave around phony lamps and mess around with other boys' bananas don't deserve my words," Kyma said.

Aladdin's stomach wrenched. "But I thought you'd be . . . you're supposed to be . . ."

A shadow fell over him, muscular and bald-headed, dwarfing him in the center of the hall. The other students backed away, leaving two gladiators to fight.

Now Aladdin knew for sure.

The lamp hadn't worked.

And if the lamp hadn't worked, then Kyma wasn't in love with him. And if Kyma wasn't in love with him, then he'd just stolen Hephaestus' food. Hephaestus who was standing behind him, about to mash him like the banana in Aladdin's fist.

Aladdin spun around—

Hephaestus gazed back.

The boy's big green eyes glistened. His lips were wet and parted. His hands clasped over his heart like he'd been struck with an arrow.

"Hi . . . h-h-hello . . . Aladdin . . . ," Hephaestus stammered, his bluster and confidence gone. "I know we've only just met . . .

but . . . would you go to the . . . Snow Ball with me?"

Aladdin dropped his banana.

Oh no.

Noooooo.

The lamp. That shoddy sham of a lamp.

It didn't make Kyma fall in love with him.

It made *Hephaestus* fall in love with him.

There is a quiet that has no sound, like the black, empty silence at the bottom of the sea. No one in the Supper Hall moved. Even the enchanted pots had frozen in the midst of flipping pancake batter and cracking eggs.

Aladdin gaped at Hephaestus, flailing for words, but all that came out was a raspy hack, like mothballs in his mouth. His hand went to the lamp in his coat pocket, as if the lamp was his heart, a heart that had failed him.

Princess Kyma, too, looked like she'd been slapped, her would-be prince having lost interest in her and now drooling over the one boy she despised. But then she peered closer at Hephaestus, at his starry-eyed blankness, at his whole form slouched in submission. Slowly her eyes went back to Aladdin . . . to his hand on a lamp, glinting inside his coat . . . a phony lamp that had been confiscated . . . a phony lamp he'd insisted could grant wishes . . . and all of a sudden, Princess Kyma caught on to the story. That here, in a magical school, the first act of consequential magic had happened. Magic gone bad.

Her eyes narrowed at Aladdin. "Well? Hephaestus is asking you to the Snow Ball. Aren't you going to give him an answer?"

Aladdin snorted, expecting Kyma to laugh at her own joke. But she didn't laugh. No one laughed.

"Wait, you don't expect me to go with . . . ," Aladdin floundered.

"Hephaestus?" Kyma said icily. She turned to her former object of affection. "Hephaestus, please tell Aladdin why he should go with you to the Snow Ball."

Hephaestus sank to one knee. "Because he is the sun that shines light on the parts of my heart I never knew. He is the first sight of land when I'm adrift at sea. He is the path through a dark, dark wood. I know no love but Aladdin. And when love is true, it must be spoken out loud. Because that's what Goodness is. Honoring our heart. Showing ourselves without fear. It's why I ask you to the Snow Ball, Aladdin, here in front of our school. Because if you say yes, you not only honor me, but all of us humbled by love."

Aladdin rolled his eyes, about to tell this fool off, once and for all—

But then he heard an unexpected sound around him.

Sniffles.

Sighs.

Evers were holding hands over their hearts, wiping tears, catching back emotion, moved by Hephaestus' words. Even Kyma looked stricken.

"Noooo way," Aladdin retorted, turning on Hephaestus. "No way am I taking *you* to the Snow Ball. Over my dead body."

"Well, I won't eat until you say yes," said Hephaestus defiantly. He sat on the floor and bound himself to a chair leg with his tie. "Our love will feed me."

Aladdin waved his hand. "Great. Go live on love. Better your dead body than mine."

The room went quiet again. The air sucked out of it.

Kyma's eyes cut through Aladdin. "This is the *Good* school, remember? Evers believe in true love. To mock it seems like something a Never would do. And given that you interrupted the Welcoming, lied about having a magic lamp, and belittle and shame Hephaestus after he professes his love, as if you don't believe in love at all . . . is it reasonable to think that you cheated and thieved your way in? That you aren't worthy of your place here at all?"

Tension spiked, everyone in the Supper Hall looking at Aladdin differently.

Even the cupids on the walls shamed him with their glares.

Aladdin's cheeks went red.

Unworthy at home.

Unworthy here.

And a real-life princess, his one chance at love, at *respect*, staring him down like he was nothing.

He didn't know what to do . . . his soul was in a panic . . . and before he knew it, he was on his heels, peeking up at Hephaestus, the words sputtering out of his mouth—

"Sh-sh-shall we match outfits for the Ball?"

9.

Rafal burst out laughing, watching the Storian paint the scene taking place in the Supper Hall.

"'*Shall we match outfits for the Ball?*'" he read, practically doubled over. "Your precious little Everboy, in love with a girl, and now taking the boy *she's* in love with to the Ball. And the Snow Ball isn't for months, so imagine the suffering in store for all of them. Bet the Storian didn't see that coming."

"The Storian is telling a tale about *us* for the first time. The Pen that is supposed to write about our students. Aren't you the least bit disturbed?" Rhian berated, arms folded as he leaned against a bookcase. "Oh I forgot. You're too busy meddling in a Ball!"

"Well, because of my meddling, this tale *isn't* about us anymore," Rafal fired back. "The Pen said Aladdin would change everything between us. Well, nothing has changed and it hasn't made a peep about us since. Instead, I've ensured every word of this story will be about a boy you thought you could turn Good, now proved to be very much Evil."

"But why was the Storian writing about us to begin with!" Rhian hounded. "And don't even start. You've proved nothing. You tricked that boy into thinking his lamp was real, lured him into your castle and practically handed it back to him—"

"Only a fatuous idiot would think that lamp was real," Rafal snapped. "It was laced with bad magic, some homemade hex intended to punish the wisher. And given your Everboy is a thief, I'm sure there were plenty of people he fleeced in Shazabah eager to bestow him with a curse."

"Well, whatever you've wrought, I want you to fix it," said his brother.

"And why should I?"

Rhian stared him down. "Because it is your duty to protect the Pen and school, as much as it is mine, and your cheap trick isn't just a blatant attempt to sabotage the Pen, but also a deliberate attack on the well-being of our students. And seeing you've never gone so far as to interfere with Good's affairs before, it makes me wonder if you still have the judgment to be School Master. A twist in the tale that is very much about *us*. So perhaps you've fallen into the story's path, exactly as the Pen planned."

The grin vanished off Rafal's face. He felt a hurt so deep he couldn't speak. Never had his brother questioned his integrity or his commitment to the school. What started as a joke, a harmless bet over the leanings of a boy's soul, had festered into something harsher and more significant. As if a deep, unseen rot had finally shown itself.

He averted his eyes to the window. "Well, it's too late now. I can't fix it. There's only one antidote to bad magic. To turn it good. Meaning the boy has to achieve his original wish on his own."

Rhian bristled. "Let me get this straight. In order for Hephaestus to stop mooning after the boy, Aladdin has to win Kyma's love *fairly*?"

"More than just love. True love's *kiss*."

"A kiss. From a girl who has no interest in him, who suspects he attempted a love spell on her, and who no doubt wants to see the boy punished?"

Rafal was smirking again. "Precisely. You claimed you could turn a soul Good. Well, now it's your turn to prove *you* have the judgment to be a School Master."

Rhian flinched, his eyes meeting his brother's.

Behind them, the Storian wrote Rafal's words beneath a painting of the two twins, facing off.

What it didn't write was the thought going through the Good School Master's head.

Such a mess this had become. All over a silly wager.

Fixing this couldn't be left to students.

If his brother was going to meddle in this tale on behalf of Evil, then he would intervene on behalf of Good.

That was always the best path to solving things, wasn't it?

Balance.

10.

The first week of classes made Aladdin want to ask a stymph to eat him.

He'd hoped that accepting Hephaestus' invitation to the Ball would buy him time to somehow reverse the genie's hex, but once again, his plan was thwarted. For one thing, he couldn't get the genie to come out of the lamp again, no matter how much he rubbed it, the brass trinket now cold and dull, emptied of whatever curse it held before. For another, Hephaestus followed him everywhere like an adoring puppy, showering him with homemade gifts and love poems so horrible that Aladdin couldn't tell if it was part of the genie's curse or if Hephaestus was this daft.

"I think they're sweet," his roommate countered, a pale, willowy boy named Rufius who spent every free moment baking pastel-colored beignets and nougatines.

Aladdin was apoplectic. "A magical watch that chimes '*Hephaestus Loves You!*' every quarter hour? A misshapen clay mug carved with our initials? A box of chocolates with our faces painted on them? Who gives chocolates to a *boy*!"

"The chocolates were my idea," Rufius said quietly. "I helped Hephaestus make them."

Aladdin gaped at him. He wanted to ask how anyone could believe that Hephaestus, the boy who had been in love with Kyma, would suddenly now be in love with him. How anyone wasn't seeing through this very obvious love spell that was ruining his life!

The problem, of course, was that he couldn't confess his crime, not after Kyma called him a cheater and a thief. Admit that he'd cursed the most beloved boy in school and he'd be more detested than he already was. Plus, this was a school where love was celebrated, every type of love, and the more Aladdin questioned it, the more unpopular he became. (Rufius didn't help matters by telling everyone about the chocolates.)

"I wish a boy would give *me* chocolates," Kyma said as she passed Aladdin on the way to history class. "Maybe I should *wish* for a boy to love me." She gave him a long, lingering look as she turned the corner.

Aladdin's heart imploded.

She knew!

Of course she did.

Kyma was as sharp as she was beautiful.

Which meant she knew he'd tried to cheat his way to her heart.

How could he ever win her now?

On top of all this, Aladdin had classes to deal with.

Classes he was failing.

Most classes at the school combined Evers and Nevers, part of the School Masters' way of breeding respect between the two sides. Plus, it gave rise to spirited debate between Good and Evil and healthy competition in the challenges that determined their marks. But regardless of whether Evers or Nevers performed better in a particular test, Aladdin always ended up at the bottom of the pack.

In Physical Training, he left his team behind to capture the flag, breaking a cardinal rule. In a challenge about Chivalry, Hephaestus gave him a lift up a tree and Aladdin kept climbing, eager to be rid of him, rather than help Hephaestus up too. ("That was the test?" he asked incredulously. "Why should I help him up when he's strong enough to climb himself?" The teacher looked at him, stone-faced: "Chivalry.") In Forest Groups, where Evers and Nevers went into the Woods to learn about flora and fauna, he confused a hive of wasps for a hive of fairies and ended up getting his whole group stung.

Now that word "Mogrif" came back to haunt him. Because as it turned out, anyone who ended up at the bottom of the ranks wouldn't just wear the indignity of failing. They'd also be turned into an animal or . . . *plant*. For life.

"*That's* what a Mogrif is?" Aladdin reacted.

"Where do you think princesses get their helpful animals from or giants get their beanstalks?" Rufius said. "They're trained at this school."

"Why would you go to a school where you can be turned into a lemur or pine tree!"

"Or a slug or a stinkweed if you're at your level of bad," Rufius added. "That's the chance you take to come here: win glory or live an eternity in shame. Better do well in the Wish Fish challenge. That's Evers only. And it counts for a lot."

Thankfully, the Wish Fish challenge seemed easy enough.

It took place at the shores of a pond behind school, led by the Animal Communication teacher, a golden, muscular centaur with russet hair named Maxime, who explained that each of the Evers would take a turn dipping their finger into the pond and focusing their mind to summon their deepest wish, before a thousand tiny Wish Fish, white as snow, sprang to the surface and painted their soul's desire. As long as a student produced a wish of Good intentions, they would pass the test.

"Wonder what *your* wish is going to show," Kyma said, next to Aladdin. "More bogus lamps, maybe?"

"Probably," Aladdin sighed.

Kyma scowled at him. "This isn't a joke. If you fail this, that's three fails in a row. You'll be certain to end up a Mogrif."

"Look at Maxime," Aladdin said, nodding at the centaur, tall and powerful in the sunlight. "He's a Mogrif and he's doing fine."

Kyma rolled her eyes. "Not a Mogrif. Maxime is a born centaur and probably graduated top of his class if he's a teacher now. The fly buzzing around his *backside* is a Mogrif."

Aladdin's throat clenched.

Rufius went first, slipping the tip of his forefinger into the pond, and the fish whizzed into action, painting a boy outside a shop—"Patisserie Rufius"—with beautiful breads and pastries and chocolates in the window.

"That's the most Goodness your soul can summon?" Maxime pressed Rufius, arching a brow. "Wishing for your own *bakery*?"

"Where I'd give out free croissants every morning to the poor children of the village," Rufius defended.

"I see no children," Maxime returned.

"They are sleeping," said Rufius.

"Fail," said Maxime. "Next."

Aladdin tensed harder. If sweet, helpful Rufius who made Hephaestus' chocolates failed, how was *he* supposed to pass?

For Kyma's turn, her Wish Fish painted her father dancing with her at her wedding after years of suffering with a bad hip.

"Pure Goodness," Maxime extolled.

Of course, Aladdin thought. Not just beautiful and smart, but virtuous too.

Then came Hephaestus, who wished for his twin brother to take his place at the school instead of him.

"He deserved it more than I did," Hephaestus confessed.

Kyma gazed at him with love-pooled eyes.

"Honestly thought he'd wish for me," Aladdin cracked.

She gave him a lethal look. "Wish Fish find your deepest wish. Not fake ones planted by second-rate hexes."

Aladdin winced. "Why haven't you told on me, then?"

"Because you're more than capable of digging your own grave," she said.

"Aladdin, you're next," called Maxime.

The boy gulped.

Slowly he approached the water, the fish a mass of sparkling shadows under the surface, like diamonds to be mined. Aladdin sensed the Evers huddled behind, itching for him to fail.

Wish for something Good, he exhorted himself. *Wish for something Kyma would wish for. Or Hephaestus. Or anyone here but me . . .*

He dipped his finger in.

Instantly, the fish swirled into motion, painting a rubied seat atop a mountain of gold, the Sultan's throne of Shazabah, Aladdin crowned and wrapped in silks, his fingers ringed with jewels, a mob of thousands bowing at his feet. And if that wasn't bad enough, he was gripping something in his lap . . . a magic lamp . . . the *real* magic lamp . . .

Maxime's eyes narrowed.

Kyma folded her arms.

Aladdin cringed, mouthing: *No, no, no, no—*

Then all of a sudden, the fish dispersed into a ragged mass.

Their scales reverted to white, erasing any remnants of Aladdin's wish, before they launched back into motion, painting a new scene . . .

Aladdin, a bald, wrinkled old man, making breakfast and doting upon his companion in their cozy cottage. A silver-haired, stooped figure, who looked just like . . .

Hephaestus.

Aladdin yanked his hand out of the water. He spun around and saw his whole class gawking at him, Hephaestus included, the boy's eyes glassed with tears at beholding their future together.

"A true Ever's soul," Maxime spoke wistfully, watching the fish still hold on to the scene. "May you and Hephaestus find your Happily Ever After."

Aladdin waved his arms. "Wait a minute. That wish doesn't make sense . . . that can't be my . . ."

Then he saw Kyma.

No longer glowering at him with loathing or disdain.

For the first time, she looked at him like he was a real person. Reassessing him, inside and out.

"What a lovely wish," chimed a familiar voice.

The Evers turned to see the Good School Master strolling by in his sweeping blue robes.

"The fish normally disperse the moment your finger leaves the water, but even they want to hold on to Aladdin's soul," Rhian said, sauntering along. "The best wishes surprise all of us, including the wisher. Carry on, Maxime."

The next Ever was called to the water, but no one paid attention, their eyes still darting between Aladdin and Hephaestus, as if they'd found a new standard for love.

Kyma sidled closer to Aladdin, cracking a quiet joke about how he'd avoided eternity as a newt.

But Aladdin was watching Rhian as he walked away, Rhian who'd appeared like a charm just as Aladdin's wish revised. As Aladdin had this thought, the Good School Master glanced back and smiled at him, the same way the Evil brother had smiled at him at the Welcoming, before things had all gone wrong.

11.

From the window of their study, Rafal watched his brother leave the class of Evers, the Evil School Master's mouth twitching.

What an amateur Rhian was. Thinking he could just swoop in and change the contents of a boy's soul! Couldn't he just admit that the Pen made a mistake? That the boy was Evil as they come? True, Rhian had gotten that wispy, self-righteous girl to reconsider Aladdin, but how long would that last? Soon, the boy would revert to his selfish, thieving ways and Rhian wouldn't be there to save him. Only a matter of time before Aladdin showed himself for Evil, once and for all.

Then Rhian would have to eat his words, all those unjust things he'd said about Rafal being traitorous and reckless and unfit for the post of School Master. Instead, it would be Rhian who was unfit, believing he could turn Nevers into Evers and that the holy Pen was on his side, when it was Rhian's ego and delusion from the start. *How can you serve as School Master when you believe the balance favors you?* The Storian had made a clear mistake with Aladdin, putting the boy in the wrong school. Both he and Rhian knew that. But Rhian trusted the Pen instead of his brother, instead of *himself*, and now they were at war over a boy's soul, the two of them meddling in a fairy tale, when it was their job as School Masters not to meddle in the stories they were supposed to protect.

Rafal gritted his teeth.

Whatever happened from here, it was Rhian's fault. He incited this story. *He* was the villain.

And just like the Pen had been humbling villains in its latest tales, Rhian would be humbled too. Aladdin proved Evil and Rafal's judgment upheld over a Pen's.

That would be the fair ending to their fairy tale, wouldn't it?

The Evil School Master breathed with relief.

No doubt Little Lamp Boy was making an ass of himself at this very moment.

12.

At first, Aladdin was quite sure the School Master had interfered with his Wish Fish. That it had been the Good wizard who redirected his soul's deepest wish from a Sultan's riches to a quaint, quiet love. That it had just been another hex, puppeting Aladdin the same way a rogue genie had puppeted Hephaestus. To teach him a lesson, of course. A sorcerer's way of making him think twice about dabbling in love spells.

But then came Good Deeds, another class just for Evers, led by Dean Mayberry, who presented them with the Frog Kiss Challenge. All the Evers were blindfolded, before Mayberry turned half of them into frogs. These cursed frogs were then dumped in a vat of *real* frogs, at which point the still-human Evers doffed their blindfolds and had to distinguish between student frogs and actual frogs. Each human could choose one frog to kiss and only one: kiss a student back to two-legged life and both of you would pass. Kiss a lowly pond frog and you failed.

Aladdin and Rufius were put in the human group; Kyma and Hephaestus in the frog group.

It was nearly an impossible challenge, given all the frogs looked identical and all they could do was croak and hop, but one by one, they used Good Deeds to make an impression—a frog might polish your boots to earn a kiss or eat a fly that was hovering around your nose or do a little dance for you, like Kyma did for Rufius—and soon all the human Evers had successfully kissed a changeling back to life . . . except for Aladdin, who was too afraid to kiss a frog, in case it turned out to be Hephaestus, because kissing Frog Hephaestus felt too close to kissing Real Hephaestus.

Another fail.

As class ended, he slumped for the door—

"I heard about your wish, Aladdin," Professor Mayberry said.

Aladdin turned, red-faced. "It wasn't my wish. Fish got confused."

"Maybe," Professor Mayberry replied, shuffling papers at her pink desk. "Or maybe it sensed your fear and dug beneath to find your truth."

Aladdin bit down. "Listen. I don't want Hephaestus—"

"Because your definition of love is small and distorted," said the Good Dean, looking up at him. "You see love the way Nevers do, nothing but kisses and flowers and the superficial. Indeed, you probably thought today's challenge was about the kiss itself, which is why you were afraid to give it. But a true Ever knows love is about *connection*. About having a champion, a teammate, a flagbearer who sees the real you under the frog skin. That kind of love is bigger than the romance you seek with a girl. Like the love of family. The love of community. The love of a friend. And is it not impossible that one day, you and Hephaestus become such good friends, brothers in arms, that at the end of your lives, you take care of each other? That you rely on each other for company? Could that be what you were seeing in your wish? The longing for something more lasting than a pretty princess? The longing to be less alone?"

Aladdin looked at her, a calmness coming into his heart.

"Wish Fish are more powerful than you think," Professor Mayberry said. "The honesty of your wish is perhaps the only reason me and the other teachers haven't turned *you* into a frog."

In the days that followed, Aladdin thought about the Dean's words carefully. Truth was, he'd never had a real friend. In

Shazabah, he was so obsessed with finding his fortune and escaping his oppressive house that he'd never bothered to find allies. He'd always assumed he'd go at life alone. Even when it came to love, he thought he'd have to bamboozle a girl into choosing him. The idea of winning someone's heart without tricking them never seemed possible. Did he really think so little of himself? Did he think so little of others?

Maybe that's why he was so embarrassed by Hephaestus loving him, when all the other Evers took it in stride. Because deep down, Aladdin knew he'd cheated to win this love. Would it have been any different if the genie had granted his wish for Kyma? Or would Aladdin have been humiliated by that too, knowing it was a sham from the start? If love is connection, as the Dean said, what's the point if it isn't real?

Deep down, his soul was craving more. A bond, a friendship that was honest and true. The safety of being himself with someone, even a boy he'd tricked.

In which case . . . could those Wish Fish have been *right*?

But that still left the problem of Hephaestus. A boy who had been hijacked by a hex. A boy who Aladdin had treated poorly. How would he feel if *he'd* been cursed like Hephaestus? If he'd been left with no choice who to love?

Aladdin blushed with shame.

Then he shoved it away.

Enough feeling bad about himself.

He still had a month until the Snow Ball.

Time to get to know the boy he was taking to it.

"What are some things Hephaestus likes?" he asked, plopping in front of Kyma at breakfast.

She spat out her blueberry scone. "What?"

"You know, things that make him happy," Aladdin said, eating a few grapes off her plate.

Kyma pulled her ponytail tighter. "Look, if you're going to play another trick on him—"

"I saw him kicking a ball around. And he practices archery sometimes. So I know he's into sports," Aladdin pressed. "Anything else?"

Kyma stared, disarmed by his earnestness. "Uh . . . I honestly don't know him that well. Not like that, I mean . . . I guess he likes cheese sandwiches, because he eats a bunch of them after he swims. And he's pretty good at poker—"

"Thank you!" Aladdin said, hustling away.

Kyma watched him, baffled.

That night, as Kyma started to fall asleep, she heard shuffling in the hall and muffled voices.

She peeked out of her room, following the sounds . . . to see

Hephaestus and Aladdin, halfway down the staircase between floors, in the middle of a poker game. Hephaestus bit into a cheese sandwich off a pile of them.

"These are killer," said Hephaestus, mouth full. "Better than my usual ones."

"Bribed an enchanted pot in the kitchen to make them," said Aladdin, drawing a new card.

"How do you bribe an enchanted pot?"

"You clean the greasy stove it sits on. Figured it must be like sleeping in a wet, stinking bed."

"I heard Nevers sleep in wet beds," said Hephaestus. "Part of learning suffering and all that."

"You want suffering? Try growing up in a house where your parents force you to be a tailor. I don't even *like* clothes. Wouldn't wear them if I didn't have to."

"Because you come from a desert kingdom, where it's boiling hot. I'm from the mountains, where two furs isn't enough."

"Can't you just . . . move?" Aladdin asked.

Hephaestus frowned. "It's where my family is. That's our home."

"Well, if I was you, I'd move my whole family to Bahim Beach."

Hephaestus chuckled. "Sound like my brother."

"I thought you said he was the Good one between you," Aladdin pointed out.

Hephaestus sighed. "He wanted to be an Ever so badly."

"There's a difference between wanting to be Good and being Good," said Aladdin. "That's probably why you're here instead of him."

"You're better than the both of us," Hephaestus said, tossing down a straight flush. "You're willing to go to the Snow Ball with me, even though you want to go with Princess Kyma."

Aladdin snorted. "You only want to go to the Snow Ball with me because you're not in your right mind."

"I'm perfectly clear-brained, thank you."

Aladdin snorted again, shuffling the deck. "Kyma would never go with me."

"Why not?"

"Because she sees who I really am. A selfish prat," said Aladdin. "You see someone worth knowing. The kind of guy I *wish* I was. Big difference."

He looked up at Hephaestus. But this time there was no gooey, spell-struck romance in Hephaestus' eyes. It was as if the curse had vanished and they were there together, two boys seeing each other for the first time, where they'd each seen wrongly before. Aladdin fidgeted, feeling exposed, vulnerable, like he was no longer in the presence of the possessed Hephaestus, but the real one, the two sharing company by choice instead of magic. And yet the feeling didn't scare him. It was welcoming, warm.

"Another game?" Aladdin prompted.

"Happy to beat you all night," Hephaestus puffed.

Cards were dealt once more.

Behind the wall, Kyma smiled and tiptoed back to her room.

Perhaps, she, too, had seen wrongly.

Her eyes choosing Hephaestus, when her heart had closed too soon to another.

She slept with a curious smile on her face . . .

The next morning, a storm awakened the Good students with a black, violent fit of lightning and thunder.

Rain battered their windows, before missives flew on the wind, slamming against every glass, parchment edicts adorned with thorns. An order from the School Master.

The Snow Ball.

It had been moved up.

To *tonight*.

13.

Rhian stormed into the chamber, half-dressed. "You can't just move up the Ball!"

"Too late," Rafal snipped, watching the Storian paint his brother, red-faced and dripping wet. "What's the matter? My Nevers are ready. Are your students so ill-equipped and fragile that they can't meet the challenge of a *dance*?"

The Good School Master unleashed. "Don't be a twit, Rafal. The Snow Ball has always been on the same day every year and the Evers need time for proposals, for rehearsals . . . They've barely begun classes! They hardly know each other yet! And besides, your Nevers don't even go to the Snow Ball. They just pull pranks and act like hooligans and make nuisances of themselves. They shouldn't be invited at all!"

"Well, they are invited because they're part of this school, just like *I* am, much as you hate to admit it," Rafal replied, "and I decided the date needed changing and you were too busy swimming in the pond—"

"I *always* swim at this hour—"

"—and I didn't feel like waiting, so I issued an edict like School Masters do, because I am still School Master, am I not?"

Rhian sucked in a breath. "You're only doing this because Aladdin has made that girl take another look at him and with more time, he'll earn her love and break the spell. Which means you know the Pen's tale ends with Good winning and you looking like a fool, no matter what idiotic moves you make to disrupt it."

"And have you not disrupted it too? Have you not interfered as much as I have?" Rafal taunted, heating up. "Besides, like you said, the Evers *live* for balls. So why delay? I see no reason to wait. Let us all indulge in the spirit of love. That's what you want, isn't it? For Evil to be more like Good. For me to be more like *you.*"

"Enough. This was never about the boy or a ball. This was about you trying to prove you knew better than the Pen and now you're learning your lesson." Rhian glowered at him, yanking on a shirt. "I'm calling it off." He spun for the door—

Sounds echoed beyond it, screams and shouts and a clattering thunder.

The two brothers looked at each other . . . then darted out of the office.

From the stairwell, they watched Evergirls and Everboys dash around the halls, arms heaped with tulle and silk and satin, crashing into each other like headless chickens, their shrieking chorus resounding. "The Ball! The Ball!"

Rafal grinned at his twin. "Like I said . . . Too late."

14.

With several hours to prepare for the Snow Ball instead of weeks and months, there are casualties.

The fashion, for one. There is no time to solicit garments from the usual seamstresses; boys and girls must work with what they have, in many cases a far cry from what Professor Mayberry deems acceptable ("It's a suit!" Rufius insists; "It's pajamas!" Mayberry barks). Pairings suffer, too. Boys do not get their first-choice girls, since the girls panic and accept the hand of any male with a pulse, for fear they might not receive another proposal. The weenier boys capitalize on this panic to snag girls who would ordinarily reject them, which makes the more desirable boys nervous, since their picks are now taken, so in turn, they jump the gun and ask any girl who straggles by. The sum total is no one is happy with their date nor their outfit nor their date's outfit, so the two-by-two parade to the hall, usually a swooning, jaunty affair, set to a floating cricket symphony, now has the mood of a group trip to the dentist.

But then the doors open and the Ball is revealed, a colorful

Toyland, with oversized tin soldiers, dancing teddy bears, and a lit-up Christmas train on tracks, while magical snow falls and turns to glitter on the dance floor, the walls twinkling with frosted blue ice. Word is that the Good School Master decorated it himself, which livens the mood and reminds the Evers they are lucky to be here, a school where heroes are made, and it is their duty as standard-bearers of Good to not only make the most of any occasion, but be grateful for it. Their bond is solidified when the Evil students come storming in for their traditional prank, but it is a weak one—marbles thrown onto the dance floor, quickly swept up by a few enchanted brooms—after which the Nevers slink away, clearly as rushed in their plans as the Evers were.

As for Aladdin and Hephaestus, one might ask why there's been no mention of them, the couple most important to this story, but there is nothing to say yet, because they are late.

"My pants are falling!" Aladdin growled, yanking at his waist and chasing after his date. "Correction. *Your* pants!"

"How could you come to school with no proper clothes?" said Hephaestus as he sprinted ahead in an emerald-green doublet and fitted breeches.

"I was kidnapped! I wasn't supposed to come to this school at all!" Aladdin snapped, fussing with his borrowed red waistcoat. "This is ridiculous. Why are we going to a dumb dance! Let them do their stupid Ball while we have the run of the place!"

"Spoken like a true Never," Hephaestus teased. "Hurry up!"

"Come on, Heph. We'll raid the dining room instead. I can get the pots to make us fish and chips—"

"If we don't get there before the first dance, they'll turn *us* into fish and chips!" Hephaestus assailed, running faster.

Aladdin's eyes widened. "First *dance*?"

Hephaestus veered around the corner, slipping and sliding to the hall as Aladdin caught up, and together, the boys flung the doors open—

Pairs glided past to a ballroom waltz, Evers spinning and whirling in wintry colors, like the blooms of Christmas roses.

It was Aladdin's worst nightmare, made worse by the entranced look in Hephaestus' eye as he watched couples dance. Aladdin seized his arm and dragged him to a banquet table in the corner, teeming with colorful sugar cookies and pitchers of flavored milk.

"Kyma did well for herself," Hephaestus observed, still fixed on the dancing. "Abram is fourth in line to the throne of Foxwood."

Aladdin glanced back and saw Kyma in a mulberry gown with short sleeves and ruched silk, dancing with a ruddy, stout blond boy.

"Fourth in line?" Aladdin mumbled, mouth full of cookie. "Lot of people have to die before he gets anywhere."

Hephaestus glared at him. "At least he's dancing."

"Dancing is for monkeys," Aladdin said grimly, downing banana-flavored milk.

"Then you're calling my brother a monkey, because he used me as his dance partner all those nights he rehearsed for this, thinking he'd be picked for school," Hephaestus fired back. "Oh come on, Aladdin. Let's do one song. Can't say we went to a ball, if we don't dance together."

"That's the spell talking," Aladdin scoffed.

"What spell?"

Aladdin steeled himself and looked Hephaestus in the eye. He couldn't lie anymore. "Okay . . . look. Remember that magic lamp I had at the Welcoming? Well, um . . ." He took a deep breath. "I stole it back from Dean Humburg, summoned the genie, and wished for Kyma to fall in love with me, only the genie was cursed and made you fall in love with me instead of her. So all your feelings for me? They aren't real." He quailed into the corner, expecting punishment.

Hephaestus peered at him curiously. Then he shrugged. "A likely story."

"It's the truth, you fool!"

"So is I how I feel."

Aladdin moaned. "Heph. You don't even know me."

"I know that you chew your lip when you're trying to bluff me in poker," said Hephaestus. "I know you always leave a little piece of cheese sandwich, even when you eat another one. I know you walk on your tiptoes too much, so that when you run, it looks funny. I know you like your bananas too ripe, your tea too dark, and your girls very short, because if Kyma's not around, you give Farina looks, and she's the size of an elf. I also know you don't like my laugh, because you wince if I crack up. And I know you like to dance, because you did a little shimmy in the common room when me and the boys messed around with the kettledrums. So yeah, I don't know you, do I?"

Aladdin blinked at him, his lips rimmed with sugar. He raised his finger. "My run is *not* funny."

"I can't tell whether it makes you look more like a ballerina or a robber trying to sneak out of a bank."

"If I like girls who are too short, then what about you? You were after Kyma first!"

"And now I only have eyes for you," Hephaestus replied.

Aladdin slumped, his cheeks blushing. "These good things you see in me . . . When the curse is lifted, you won't want anything to do with me, let alone be my friend. All of this," he said, motioning between the two of them, "will be gone."

Hephaestus thought about this a long while. "Well, if you

did put a love spell on me, you're probably right. First thing I'd do is punch you in your very handsome face. So for your sake, better hope the spell lasts forever."

All Aladdin could do was smile.

The crickets began a spirited rondo and before Aladdin knew it, he could feel his toes tapping and shoulders swaying without his consent. Hephaestus eyed him intently.

Aladdin groaned. "Oh for god's sake. Fine. Fine! But only because you rehearsed—"

Hephaestus grabbed his arm and swept him onto the dance floor, Aladdin following his lead, spinning out and twirling back in, missing every other step.

"I have no clue what I'm doing!" Aladdin yelled.

"You're dancing!" Hephaestus laughed.

"You're right. I don't like your laugh!" Aladdin said.

Which made Hephaestus laugh even more.

And soon, too, was Aladdin, trying in vain to match the other pairs springing through the hall. Faster and faster the crickets played, Hephaestus smooth and strong, Aladdin a doddering oaf, and yet the more he failed, the brighter he beamed, safe in the grip of his best friend, and only when it reached its end too soon, speed and thrills evaporating in a trill of flutes, he and his date sweat-faced and aglow, did he realize that all the other couples had stopped to watch them.

Silence thickened, like the glittery snow under their feet. All the Evers were gazing at Aladdin. And for the first time, there was no suspicion, no superiority, only heartfelt admiration, as if he hadn't just proven himself Good, but Good's worthy leader.

Kyma sifted out of the crowd, leaving Abram behind.

She stepped up to Aladdin and held out her hand.

"May I have the next dance?" she asked.

Aladdin smiled and glanced at Hephaestus.

His date squeezed his arm chummily, then moved aside.

The crickets played a slow, mystical waltz, Aladdin clasping Kyma's waist and leading her as best he could, the other pairs orbiting around them. Kyma didn't seem to mind his lack of rhythm or his tromping on her toes, her dark eyes locked with his.

"You impress me, Aladdin of Shazabah," Kyma said.

"Because I'm dancing with you while wearing your boyfriend's pants?" Aladdin said.

"Because you're willing to admit you're wrong."

"Couldn't let Hephaestus die on his hunger strike."

"Tell me something that surprised you about him. Something I don't know."

"His closet is organized by color."

"That is . . . surprising. Tell me something else."

"He has his own basket of soap that he uses instead of the school stuff. He says he has a sensitive nose and likes his soap better."

"What does it smell like?"

"The school stuff."

Kyma laughed. "If you'd been yourself when we met instead of trying to show off with your stupid lamp, things would have been much more straightforward."

"All it took was for your true love to fall in love with me," said Aladdin.

Kyma peeked back to make sure Hephaestus wasn't near. "He's not my true love," she said. "And it's more than that. You've made the best of an impossible situation. And you're open to where a story takes you, unlike other boys here. Hephaestus was acting like my boyfriend before we even got to know each other. Like it was set in stone that we'd be together. And Abram is already talking marriage after one dance, because the Princess of Maidenvale with the Prince of Foxwood would make a good alliance for our kingdoms. Good has a habit of presuming how things *should* be. Which is why Evil beats us half the time. We're too busy anticipating our Ever Afters to find the happy endings along the way."

Aladdin smiled. "If I'd known I'd end this story with

Hephaestus as a best friend and you on my arm, I'd have asked that phony genie for more wishes."

"Did you get your wish in the end?" Kyma asked.

"Can't tell you that," said Aladdin. "It's a secret."

Kyma's eyes sparkled. "Well, I better make sure of it, then."

She stood on her tiptoes and put her lips to his—

CRACK! Lightning ripped through the hall, the snow suddenly flurrying, assembling into a strange, shadowy mask that sneered at the young couple. Then it roared a frosty blast of wind like dragonfire, slamming all Evers to the ground.

By the time Aladdin recovered, scraping to his knees in a daze, he saw the Christmas train sizzling with lightning and hurtling off its tracks, headed straight for . . .

Kyma.

But she was still on the floor, too shaken to see what was coming.

Aladdin jolted to his feet, sprinting madly across the ballroom, before his princess spun to see him flying at her, throwing her out of the way—

The train bashed into Aladdin, launching him against a wall, accelerating, faster, faster, cornering him, about to crush him to pieces . . .

A golden glow surged into the hall and lassoed the train like a rope, ripping it away from the boy and hurling the rogue vehicle high into the air. Haloed in gold, the train suspended over the gobsmacked Evers, wrangled into submission . . . then dropped with brutal force back onto its track, the Christmas Express resuming its merry, gentle ride, before its music sputtered out and it keeled onto its side, like a child that's had too much fun.

Everyone dashed to Aladdin, the boy bleeding and bruised against the wall. Kyma shoved through the crowd, pushing people away—

"Aladdin!" she cried.

He pried open his eyes at the sight of her, managing a weak, pained grin.

Kyma slouched with relief. "You okay?"

"Besides being hit by a train?" Aladdin said.

"Besides that."

"I could do with another kiss."

"Train didn't seem to like it."

"It can run me over as much as it wants if it means kissing you again."

"All right, smooth talker. Let's get you on your feet."

Little by little, she and the other Evers helped him up, Aladdin able to stand on his own two legs, his adoring eyes fixed on his princess.

"Wait," he said. "Where's Hephaestus?"

Slowly, they all turned.

Hephaestus stood in the middle of the dance floor, his brown, chiseled face spotlit in arctic light.

"Aladdin," he said. "Why are you in my *clothes*?"

He stared at Kyma next to Aladdin.

"And why are you with my *date*?"

"What do you mean? You're *my* date—" Aladdin started.

But then he saw Hephaestus' eyes.

Hard. Angry.

His best friend gone.

"Oh no," Aladdin croaked. "The spell. It's—"

He never finished his sentence.

Hephaestus' punch sent him back to the ground.

15.

In the School Masters' chamber, a golden glow spilled in and touched down to the floor, turning back into its maker.

Rhian called out. "Trying to kill my students after they beat you at your game? That's a new low, even for you. This claim on the boy's soul. It's corrupted your own."

His brother didn't answer.

The room was quiet. Even the Storian had stopped its work.

Rhian grew angrier. He stormed towards their bedchamber. "Pushing the limits of Evil only makes Good stronger. Any move you make to undermine my school weakens yours. That's not the pact we made when we took our place as School Masters. Our bond is bigger than bitterness and rivalry and the quest for anything more than balance. Because there is no endgame but balance, Rafal. Balance preserved by our school. By our love as brothers. To crave more than that is to invite our doom—"

He threw open the door.

No one was inside. Smoke snaked from blown-out candles.

Behind him, the Storian was scratching again.

Rhian approached the Pen, watching it paint a picture of . . . him.

The Good School Master gazed into his own eyes as the Pen inked two final lines, finishing its tale.

For a hundred years, two brothers had ruled as one.
But now one would rule for two.

Rhian looked around the empty room.

"Rafal?" he whispered.

But there was only a gust through the window and the sting of icy chill.

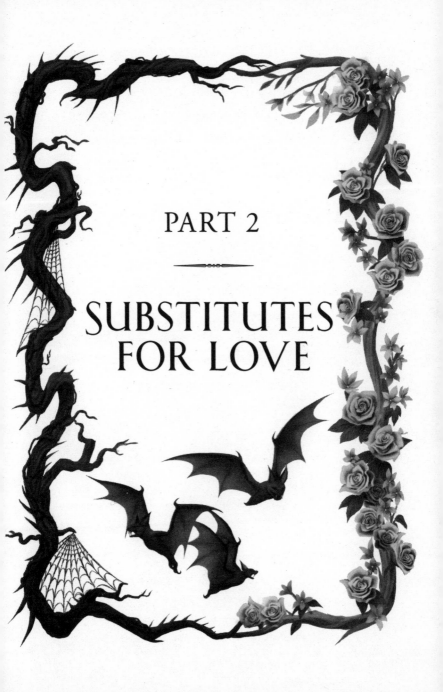

PART 2

SUBSTITUTES FOR LOVE

1.

"Higher!" Rhian called from the ground.

The wolves looked like they might drop the bricks on his head. They peered down from the scaffolding and grumbled as they lifted the mounds of glass on pulleys, so high they seemed to vanish into the sun. The wolves craned their necks over the edge, glaring at Rhian.

"Still higher!" said the Good School Master.

He hurried away before they could react.

When he first hired the wolves to help build the new school, he'd pitched it as a small upgrade—a way of refurbishing the school while his brother was away. But with each passing day and no sign of Rafal's return, Rhian found himself escalating plans for the castle, making it bigger and grander, pushing the wolves to work harder, faster, as if the feat of building a new school had turned into an act of revenge against his twin. Now the construction site was so large that it dwarfed the old school in its shadow, the students still attending classes there and bustling through halls, flashing wary glances out the window at the new castle in progress.

Rhian headed back into the old manor, passing Aladdin and Kyma on the stairs, who interrupted their snogging to give the Good School Master a respectful nod before the lovebirds joined a pack of Evers on their way to class. Six months after the Snow Ball and the little thief and princess were still going strong, a welcome reminder that the Storian picked its love stories well. Meanwhile, a pack of Nevers flashed Rhian skeptical glares, the same ones he'd been getting from Evil students for six months, as if *he* was the reason their Evil School Master was missing.

Rhian ascended to his and Rafal's old office. He closed the door and leaned against it, letting out a long sigh.

Truth be told Rhian was as unsettled by his brother's absence as the Nevers were.

At first, Rhian had let Rafal be, leaving him to sulk after the Snow Ball, like a child having a tantrum, assuming he would return once the Aladdin business blew over and his bruised ego healed. They'd fought before, of course, with each huffing off to lick his wounds, but the duties of leading the school and protecting the Storian brought them back within a day or two. They loved each other and that bond of love trumped everything. It was why the Pen had chosen them as School Masters in the first place—their loyalty to each other over a side, no matter what came between them.

But weeks passed, then a month, and Rhian had started to sense this was no usual spat. He'd told the faculty and students that Rafal had gone on a soul-finding expedition, hunting exceptional young Nevers for a future class, given Good's winning streak and the need to counteract it. It sounded like a plausible explanation. But Rhian knew the truth. In Aladdin's tale, the Storian had embarrassed his twin for all to read, picking a side between two brothers where it had never before.

Rafal could handle many things.

But not humiliation.

Pride was his weak spot.

And now a thorn in the rose of their love.

Which meant Rhian would have to swallow his own pride to win him back.

So he'd written to kingdom leaders, Ever and Never, asking if they'd heard word of Rafal's arrival to their realms, but there was no news to be had. Then he'd hired a fairy brigade from Gillikin to search the forests and hills north of the school to no avail. He'd even visited a witch in the Murmuring Mountains who had an all-seeing crystal ball, but Rafal remained elusive, as if he'd evaporated into thin air.

Rhian had waited for the hammer to drop: some prideful demand or ransom or revenge plot that Rafal would inflict on his brother or the Pen . . .

But it never came.

So Rhian grew angry. *What a spoiled, surly brat*, he'd thought. Deserts his brother, abandons his students, leaves Evil in a lurch, with Good to pick up the pieces . . . Rhian's heart grew stormy, his other half once so predictable, so much a part of him, now feeling like a stranger. He couldn't sleep, woken by spells of fear, his chest tight and heart rattling . . .

But maybe it's better this way, Rhian tried to convince himself as more weeks passed. Rafal would come back eventually. Otherwise, the Storian would have punished them—robbed them of their immortality or summoned a new School Master to take their place. The love between them was still intact. The balance unbroken. In the meantime, Rhian would manage both schools without the usual fights and provocations. Perhaps he'd even foster a new sense of peace. He wouldn't *interfere* with

Evil, of course, but under his watch the Nevers could become better versions of themselves. *Enlightened Evil,* Rhian mused. And wouldn't that force his Evers to raise their level? Two sides empowering each other, both under his domain.

Respect. Progress. Balance.

In the hands of one School Master, rather than two.

Rhian smiled at this thought as he looked out the office window at the new castle in progress, a castle he told himself he was building for only good reasons . . . a fresh start . . . a step into the future . . .

But slowly the Good School Master's smile tempered, the tightness in his chest returning.

All the thoughts in the world cannot extinguish a feeling.

The feeling that without his Evil brother, he was incomplete.

That without Rafal, he himself was out of balance.

2.

At that moment, a pale and thin lad named James Hook was seated in class at a school called Blackpool, far far away.

The subject of today's lesson was Dueling, and Hook took exception with the outcome.

"That's bad form! You can't call him the winner," he insisted, wiping a shallow wound on his arm. He could feel the rest of the students peering over his shoulder, hoping to get a glimpse of his strange, blue-colored blood, a trademark of the Hook family. "He already surrendered when I pinned him with my sword." James glared at the grinning boy behind him, who resembled an underfed ferret. "There are rules to Good and Evil. He can't stab me after it's over and claim victory, like some lawless hooligan."

"Who ye callin' hooligan!" Ferret Boy yipped, waving his blunt training sword. "This ain't some school for Good and Evil! We be pirates, ye puffed-up twit! There ain't no laws!"

"There should be," Hook mumbled, tossing his wavy black hair. "Like speaking in intelligible sentences, taking a bath once a week, and having more than four visible teeth."

All the boys in class peeked around at each other, unwashed, dentally challenged, and fully incapable of polished thoughts.

"Then there ain't be a soul in this place but ye!" a bald boy barked.

"Exactly," said Hook.

"Boo! Boo!" the boys cried.

"James does have a point," said a voice from the front of the room.

The headmaster of Blackpool—or the Pirate Captain, as the lads called him—put his feet up on the desk and faced the class of twenty young men. He tilted up the brim of his wide black hat, revealing a dark, handsome boy about eighteen years of age, with rumpled brown locks, steely green eyes, and muscles that strained the sleeves of his shirt.

"Blackpool produces the best pirates in the Woods, rebels of land and sea that fight the age-old powers that hoard wealth and opportunity for themselves," spoke the Pirate Captain. "But we can't ignore the rules of Good and Evil entirely. Because if we operate without *any* rules, we'll be painted as pests and bottom-feeders, no better than the Night Crawlers who drink the blood of young sailors who cross their path. There is a fine line between challenging power and savagery."

"Yer sayin' I shouldn'ta stabbed him then?" Ferret Boy demanded.

"I'm saying that James is right to expect more of you," replied the Pirate Captain. "But then again, if this was a real duel, he'd be *dead*."

Ferret Boy leaned to his friend. "Did I win or did I not win? Captain be talkin' in riddles again."

James locked eyes with the Pirate Captain and quickly looked away. The Captain made him nervous, which was strange because no one made James Hook nervous. He was well-educated and from a rich family, which together made

James think of himself as noble and Good and on the side of right in all things, certainly more than the ruffians at this school. That's why the boys hated him here, James decided. Because they were jealous of his bravado and breeding and wit, like Evil was of Good, like villains were of heroes. And yet, the Pirate Captain was witty and smart and well-bred too . . . and the boys *loved* him. The thought gave Hook pause. There were rumors the Captain wasn't young at all and lived on an elixir of blood and gold that stopped him from aging. But James wasn't convinced. No . . . that wasn't it. It was just that some boys in the world were meant to be captains, while the rest were meant to be peons. The problem in this school was that the peons thought they were captains.

As class ended, the Pirate Captain walked with James.

"Your family's ship, the *Jolly Roger*, has a long history," the Captain said, boys nodding at him respectfully while shooting James dirty looks. "Every Hook has been trained at Blackpool, where they have recruited a loyal crew to sail to Neverland after graduation and fight the Pan. And every Blackpool headmaster dreams of teaching the Hook that beats him. Myself included. I assume you wish to *be* that Hook."

"Yes, sir," James replied. "No one in my family has managed to kill the Pan and take Neverland. My father died at the hands of a *boy*. And now a new Pan has risen, more Evil and arrogant than before. It's why, with all due respect, you should push the lads away from cheap skullduggery and towards good form and discipline, so I have the best crew to take on Pan—"

"What makes you think they want to be on your crew at all?" the Captain asked.

James stared at him.

"Given they find you prissy, arrogant, and self-obsessed, I'm quite sure they'd serve any captain *but* you, which makes me wonder if you have a future as a pirate," said Blackpool's leader, arriving at his office. "Or if you belong at another school entirely."

"Like the School for Good?" James scoffed. "No thank you. I have bigger ambitions than that dull place—"

The Captain pushed the door open and James' voice trailed off.

Someone was sitting at the Pirate Captain's desk.

A boy with milk-white skin, sleek-spiked hair, and a gold-and-blue suit.

He squinted at Hook, then smiled at the Pirate Captain.

"I see why no one likes him," said Rafal.

3.

Meanwhile, at the School for Evil, Rhian had a rogue fortune-teller on his hands.

The dust had finally settled amongst the Evers after the magic lamp affair, with Hephaestus grudgingly accepting Kyma and Aladdin together and only because Hephaestus had moved on to twin sisters from Runyon Mills. But now the Nevers were in tumult because a girl named Marialena claimed to be a seer.

"Who's next?" spoke the short, frumpy girl with wet dark hair, oversized glasses, and moony brown eyes, seated cross-legged on a couch in the old common room, one of the last places students could congregate, since the other rooms had been dismantled in advance of the move to the new castle. "Who wants to have their fortune told?"

"Me! Me! My turn, Marialena! Will the Storian ever tell my tale?" a tattooed boy demanded, packed into the crowd of Evil students.

"Pay the fee, please," Marialena said, pointing at the basket.

The boy waddled up and put a silver coin in. "So? Will I be famous?"

Marialena touched her thumb and middle fingers together and closed her eyes. Then she opened them. "No, you'll die before you're eighteen. Next!"

The boy blinked. "How do I die?"

"The fee only covers one question," said Marialena.

"Marialena, will I kill a prince like my mum did?" shouted a bony, bald girl, tossing a coin in the basket.

"You'll languish a poor scullery maid until you succumb to malaria," Marialena replied.

"And me? What do you see for me?" another boy called, waving his silver piece.

"You'll be murdered by someone in this room," Marialena decreed.

"Who!" the boy said, shocked.

"You'll have to pay again," said Marialena.

The boy dropped more silver in. "Well?"

Marialena closed her eyes. Opened them. "Could be anyone. I sense the stain of guilt in all their souls."

The boy shook his fists at the room. "If any of you losers kills me, I'll kill you first!"

"Go ahead and try!" a girl ripped.

"Why don't we kill you now and save the trouble later!" another Never yelled.

Then the chant that Evil waited for every Friday night: *"Fight! Fight! Fight!"*

Someone threw a coin, then a shoe, then a couch, and the entire room erupted in a brawl that smashed two of the walls and left eight Nevers in the infirmary. Which is how Marialena ended up in the School Masters' office, defending her powers of foresight.

"Dean Humburg says this business was started by you claiming to be a seer," Rhian intoned, seated at his desk.

"My whole family are seers," said Marialena, glancing around the room, as teams of wolves hauled away bookcases filled with the Storian's fairy tales. "Why are we moving to a new castle?"

"Because I ordered it," Rhian clipped, smoothing his blue robes. "Now as to your behavior—"

"I don't think your brother will be happy you've built a new school without his permission," the girl offered.

Rhian peered at her, his tone sarcastic: "Is that what you see with your mighty powers?"

"No, just a hunch."

"I've dealt with a lot of poor behavior in my time, but pretending to see the future is new, I have to say. May I remind you that by divine law, *real* seers aren't allowed to answer questions about people's fates," said Rhian. "If you were real, you'd age ten years every time you answered one as a penalty."

"If I told the *truth*," Marialena said.

The Good School Master sat back. "Ah. So you claim to have the one-in-a-million gift of sight, but rather than use it to good purpose, I'm supposed to believe you lie about your class-mates' futures for . . . pocket change?"

"Why do you think I'm in the Evil school and not yours?" Marialena quipped.

Rhian glared at her. "They're *both* my schools now."

Marialena met his eyes, unintimidated.

Rhian exhaled. "Look, we're here to address your lies . . ." He turned sharply to the wolves, who were about to move the Storian. "No! Not that—"

The Pen glowed red and aimed at a wolf's eye, before the wolves backed away, paws up. Once at a safe distance, the Sto-rian resumed its work.

"Sure you don't need another School Master to help you? A substitute for your brother?" Marialena asked Rhian, with a grin. "Seems like it's all getting to you."

Rhian bottled his rising anger. The girl had just insulted him three times in one go: implying he needed help, insinu-ating he was overemotional, and suggesting his twin could be replaced. When Evers were sent to him for discipline, it was usually for dueling over a girl's hand or kissing in the bathroom after curfew, and a couple days of dish duty or toilet cleaning solved the problem. Now he wondered if he was ill-equipped to manage the Nevers, because his first instinct was to throw the girl out the window.

Perhaps he was more like Rafal than he thought.

"See the Storian over there?" he said, forcing a measured tone. "Let me tell you about the new tale it's writing. The story of an arrogant young pirate named Hook out at Blackpool, who like you, doesn't think much of his classmates' intelligence. And judging from how unsympathetic the two of you are, I suspect Evil's losing streak will continue both on and off the page."

"The worse Evil does, the more anxious Nevers are about their futures, which means more money for me," said the girl, standing up. "May I go?"

"Sit down. I haven't figured out how to punish you," said Rhian.

"Feel free to call me back when you do," Marialena breezed as she walked away. "I really think you should consider replacing your brother. From what I can see, he's already on his way to replacing you."

Rhian stood up, teeth clenched. "More lies—"

Marialena turned from the door. "Careful calling a seer a

liar. My family has more power than you think."

Rhian stared at her coldly. "This family you speak of. What's their name."

"The Saders," the girl answered.

"Never heard of them," Rhian retorted.

Marialena smiled calmly. "You will."

Then she brushed between the wolves and was gone.

4.

"Who are you?" Hook asked, eyeing the boy with the frost-white hair at the Pirate Captain's desk.

"This is Rafal, headmaster of the School for Evil," the Pirate Captain replied. "He has a proposal to discuss with you in private."

Hook turned to the Pirate Captain, but Blackpool's master was already tipping his hat at Rafal with a cheeky grin and striding out of the office without so much as a look at James. The door snapped shut.

Rafal scanned Hook up and down. "I hear the new Pan is tall and solidly built for a boy of twelve. Not sure you'll match up well."

"He's cocky, vain, impetuous, and the loyalty to him

amongst the Lost Boys is softer than he thinks," said James. "Think I'll do just fine."

"I'm sure all your elders said that too and now they're dead," Rafal replied. "Each Pan gets a hundred years on earth, frozen in the prime of youth, while each Hook dies by the age of twenty, humiliated by a child. Your headmaster longs for a Hook to break that curse and take Neverland for pirates. It would be the Pirate Captain's crowning glory . . . But I don't think that Hook is you."

James searched for a retort, but instead lingered there stiffly.

Rafal stood and walked over to him. "Hold out your hand."

James did—

Rafal's finger glowed and he slashed it like a knife across Hook's palm, drawing a ribbon of rich, blue blood.

"What the . . . !" Hook cried, but the School Master was sniffing at the blood like a curious dog before he healed the boy's gashed palm with his glowing finger and dropped the boy's hand.

"I have a job for you," Rafal declared.

James was gaping at his healed skin, before he registered what the stranger said.

"What? What job?" James asked, but the Evil School Master had already turned his back and opened the window to warm salt air. Gold-pearl skies evanesced into mist over the steep bluffs leading down to the sea. "Follow me," Rafal ordered, climbing out the window.

Hook obeyed, not just because he was curious about this job, but also because the Pirate Captain left him with this strange wizard for a reason and Hook had already given Blackpool's leader reason to doubt him. James slipped out the window and followed the Evil School Master onto the rocks, the wind whipping the tails of Rafal's crisp suit and the starchy button-up that Hook favored, which Blackpool boys mocked, given their penchant for grimy, open shirts that showed most of their chests. Down by the sea was Blackpool's training vessel, the *Buccaneer*, a rickety old ship that could barely sail, a class of boys running through rigging drills while a grizzled instructor abused them for slow times.

"You're at the School for Evil," Hook called out. "Shouldn't I be talking to your brother? The Good one?"

Rafal spun and looked at James like he had two heads. "What in the world makes you say that?"

"Because the whole Hook family is on the side of Good," said James. "We're the heroes of Neverland. It's the Pan that's Evil. A selfish, immoral, creepy little imp. If you're looking for a villain, he's the one you want."

Rafal studied him. "You remind me of my brother. So self-righteous and sure of his own morality. Only you're not as handsome and even more delusional."

He hiked ahead.

Hook tramped after him. "So you're saying I'm Evil?"

"You and your family are obsessed with killing a child. Doesn't sound very Good, does it?"

"Then why didn't you take any of us for your school?"

"The Pirate Captain and I have a deal not to poach each other's students," Rafal explained, the wind doing little to his spiked hair. "But rarely do our lists overlap. Students who make exceptional villains and those who will succeed as pirates have different qualities. Villains are lone wolves, obsessed with their own selfish motives. Pirates, on the other hand, crave family and community, outside the usual structures and norms. Despite your Evil soul, you are most certainly a pirate. A captain in search of his crew. So when I came to your school's master, asking to borrow you for my mission, he was surprised. But also relieved, given how little your classmates want to be *on* your crew. It seems he wants me to take you off his hands."

James bristled. "I'm his best student here."

"Because that's what everyone wants in a pirate. Good *marks*," Rafal jabbed, looking back. His eyes glittered, inspecting the boy. "You really do remind me of my brother. Thinking that everyone loves and wants you."

"And yet you're the one here who wants me for a job," Hook said coldly.

"You know, when I read that your blood was blue, I didn't quite believe it," Rafal mused, gliding up the bluffs. Before Hook could ask the question, Rafal explained: "It was in your file. As School Masters, we have files on every young soul in the Woods. Yours didn't stand out much. Like I said, you're more fit for a pirate than a Never at my school. But blue blood . . . that's something you remember."

"So you came all this way out to see a freak," James flung at Rafal's back. "Maybe I should come out to your school. Then I can see *two* freaks who wear the same face. And after those mean things you said about your brother, I wonder what he'd say about *you*."

Rafal stopped on the rocks, shoulders tense, fists curled. For a moment, James thought the Evil School Master might kill him.

"Sorry," James said quickly, "I didn't mean it. Maybe I am Evil like you say—"

"My brother is a *cheater*," Rafal seethed.

He turned and looked at James, then kept walking. "The

Storian has turned against me, favoring Good, and Rhian seems to have no problem with it. In story after story, Good wins and he just grows more and more smug. So I left him, determined to find out why the Pen that is supposed to keep our world balanced has now chosen to break that balance. I went to mystics, oracles, prophets, but all insisted that there is no disturbance between Good and Evil. That the Pen is uncorrupted. I even went to the Night Crawlers, those scavenging bloodsuckers, asking if they'd found anything in the sea to suggest things were amiss . . . but there was no treasure to offer that was worth their help. It was only when I saw a stray newspaper along the way that my luck began to change. It told the story of a family of seers named the Saders, accused of fraudulently selling prophecies and jailed in an underwater prison called Monrovia, deep in the northern sea. But at trial, the family proved their powers of sight were real. Didn't end up saving them—it's illegal for seers to sell fortunes—but it appears the Saders can indeed see the future. Which means if I can meet these Saders, they can answer my *questions* about what they see."

"What does this have to do with me?" Hook asked, yawning.

Rafal glanced back. "You who seeks to rule Neverland . . . who yearns to beat Pan where no one has done it before . . . Wouldn't you like to ask the seers *how* to do it? Or if it's even *possible*? Otherwise you're wasting your time here at pirate school, where no one likes you. This is your one chance to learn what your future holds and control your fate. To be the first Hook that people remember."

Hook's mouth twitched. He hustled faster after the School Master. "Is there a way to get to this underwater prison?"

"That's precisely why I'm here, talking to you. It requires a crew that can sail a ship downwards, into the depths of the Savage Sea," said Rafal.

James snorted. "Well, I don't have a crew, let alone one that can do that."

"I do," Rafal said, stopping on the cliff. "I just need a captain. And aren't you the *best* captain in your class?"

Hook looked at the young School Master. Then he saw what was behind him.

A large ship called the *Inagrotten*, anchored on the coast, every inch of it shiny, polished black, like a hunk of pure onyx with diaphanous black sails, that in the sunlight made the ship shimmer like a mirage. On deck were a fleet of black-clad men with pale, pink skin, their faces shaded by floppy black hats and long black veils, shielding them from the sun.

"Night Crawlers?" said Hook. "You said you had no treasure to offer them."

"That's where you come in," said Rafal, suddenly at his side.

James' heart chilled. "What did you offer?"

"What do you think?" Rafal's whisper was like a kiss. "Your *blood*."

5.

Rhian chose an all-glass castle for the school's new home.

Light and airy, glistening with radiance. A fresh, sparkling start to his reign.

On the eve of the move, Rhian fantasized about how his brother would react when he laid eyes upon it. How his Evil twin would see the smiles on everyone's faces in their brand-new school and know he wasn't missed one bit . . .

Well.

Turns out a glass castle is better in theory than in practice.

The new castle was hot, too hot, the sun beating down on the glass and tormenting the kids inside like bugs in a green-house. The Good students didn't like that any teacher walking the grounds could spy on them, given how much Evers sneaked into each other's rooms after curfew. The Nevers didn't like the views of sun and nature; they didn't like seeing their reflections in the glass; they didn't like the new cream-colored furniture and plush white rugs; and most of all, they didn't like that there was no Evil School Master around to complain to.

Soon, the Deans of Good and Evil visited Rhian in his new office.

"It isn't very often that you come and see me *together*," the Good School Master mumbled, not looking up from his work.

"Dean Humburg and I are in agreement," Professor Mayberry huffed, fanning herself and dabbing at the sweat on her forehead. "The Nevers feel like you are favoring Good. The Evers are melting in the insufferable heat. The food in the kitchens is going bad. And the Good and Evil faculty are upset they weren't consulted on the decision."

"Present company included," grouched Humburg.

"Everyone will get used to it," Rhian said impatiently, not looking up.

"If they agree to go back inside," said Humburg.

Rhian raised his eyes. His Deans nodded out the window.

On the lawn, the Everboys had stripped to their underpants and the Evergirls to their petticoats, sunbathing and having a beach picnic of charcuterie, cheese, and chilled cider. On the other side of the grass, Evil had erected a dusty tent city, the Nevers willfully homeless, with giant signs tethered outside: "NO HABITATION WITHOUT REPRESENTATION."

"What does that mean?" Rhian asked, flummoxed.

"It means we have a full-scale revolt on our hands," said Humburg. "A revolt we wouldn't be having if your brother was still here."

"Are you blaming me for his absence?" Rhian retorted.

"I am blaming you for the fact no one likes your vainglorious home improvement project, when we had a perfectly good school before, the proof of which is there are no *students* inside this one at the moment," Humburg shot back.

"Then perhaps we should find a new Evil Dean who supports his School Master in his decisions rather than attacks him for them," Rhian flared.

"Or a new School Master who believes Evil voices deserve to be heard just as much as Good ones," said Humburg.

"This bickering isn't helping," Mayberry snapped. "Rhian is perfectly capable of running the school by himself—"

"See?" Rhian puffed at Humburg.

"That said," Mayberry tempered, "since Rafal left, things have begun to slip through the cracks. While you've been focused on building your new castle, an endeavor that didn't seem like the *best* use of your time, the Nevers' performance has been sinking, their morale has disintegrated, and they feel like both the Storian and their School Master favor their rivals.

The Evers think the same—that they're invincible—which has turned them bored and restless and now they're out there with the Nevers, asking for things to go back to the way they used to be when your brother was here. Even if I wish for Good to win in all things, I must confess that without Rafal, the school does seem woefully out of balance."

"Praise Mayberry," Humburg harrumphed.

"You're both dismissed," Rhian said quietly.

"Rhian—" Mayberry started.

"*GO!*" he barked and by the time he looked up, they were gone.

Sitting alone in his office, Rhian thought about his relationship with his Evil twin. The way that whenever Rafal lashed out with particular vengeance, it was because Rhian had said something truthful. Something his brother couldn't accept.

He'd attacked Mayberry the same way.

Because she was right. *Both* she and Humburg were right. Rafal's absence had left him disturbed, unsettled, and prone to rash decisions. Since Rafal left, he hadn't taken the time to learn the Nevers' names or meet with them or even acknowledge he was their School Master, just as much as Good's. Instead, he'd left the Evil students to fend for themselves. No wonder they distrusted him! And now, so too did the Evers, because when

Evil loses its way, so does Good. Even in his most dysfunctional moments with Rafal, they'd never faced anything like this: Evers ditching classes . . . Nevers homeless in tents . . . an open rebellion against the school. A dark hollowness spread in Rhian's chest. This new castle. This whole project. He'd done it for the wrong reasons. Because he was mad at Rafal. Because he *missed* Rafal. It had been a way of distracting himself. A substitute for love. Only now he wasn't just alone. He was failing.

Something had to be done.

But what?

There was no getting Rafal back here, at least not at the moment. Yet, if he could replace him somehow, just temporarily, with an Evil figurehead who might help Rhian run the school and give the impression of balance . . .

Only one name came to mind.

Vulcan of Netherwood.

Rafal had interviewed him for the Dean of Evil position before he'd hired Humburg instead. Rhian had caught a quick glimpse of the man and been intrigued by the tall, strapping stranger, not grim and decrepit like Humburg or most Evil professors, but stylish and handsome and alluring. He'd remembered that Vulcan had smelled good, nothing like Rafal's usual candidates, and he'd even given the Good School Master a wink before Rafal had whisked him off to his interview. Why Rafal hired Humburg instead, Rhian didn't know, given he and his brother had 100% control over their own Deans. But bringing Vulcan in for a short while might prove to the Nevers that Rhian wanted them to feel just as supported and significant as the Evers. Add in that Vulcan's arrival might keep Humburg more humble and on his toes . . . and the fact that Rhian *needed* the help, with two schools to manage and a new castle in disarray . . . The more he thought about it, the more he basked in warm hope. This is what he craved all along. To not feel so lonely. To have a friend at his side.

A new substitute for his brother's love.

This one in the name of balance.

So it was on a muggy, rain-soaked morning that Vulcan of Netherwood arrived to the castle, teachers watching him approach from the windows, Evers and Nevers watching from Evil's protest tents, which provided both sides cover from the rain. Everyone but Rhian saw him coming, the Good School Master preoccupied with the Storian, which had stopped writing after the young James Hook had met a mysterious stranger on the bluffs outside Blackpool, a stranger the Pen wouldn't name. The pair had boarded a ship, filled with bloodsucking Night Crawlers . . . before the Storian went dormant for days, having no more tale to tell. Rhian tapped the Pen firmly, making sure it was still alive—

"Ah, so Good is cheating!" said a rough and heavy voice.

Rhian turned to see a young man in the doorway, golden-skinned and powerfully framed, with a long black beard, a tattoo of a black bat under his left eye, and his eyelashes lined with kohl. His red-and-black doublet was open to the chest, another large tattoo peeking out from beneath, symbols which Rhian couldn't read. He stared at the Good School Master so intently that Rhian's voice got tangled in his throat.

"No . . . uh, I was . . . it's stopped writi—"

"I'm teasing," said Vulcan, sweeping in and sitting on Rhian's desk. "Thank you for invitation. I was flattered to receive your note. Your brother is coward who has left and you need Evil School Master. This is why you call Vulcan."

"Wait . . . no . . . not School Master . . . ," Rhian disputed, wrangling his words. "I just need a bit of help until Rafal is back—"

"As your equal. As School Master. That is why I'm here. And from looks of it, you need equal partner. Pen not writing . . . students not in class . . . ridiculous glass castle . . . ," said Vulcan. "We will be good team. I like you. You like me. Problem with twins is that they are family so they cannot be friends. Also a little creepy.

You and I? We don't have such problems."

Another smoldering stare.

Rhian's face felt hot. "Look, can we discuss this all later? A lying student has been claiming to be a seer and I've called her here a second time to figure out punishment—"

"Kill her," said Vulcan.

Rhian blinked at him.

"Teasing again," Vulcan repeated. "You have handsome face. More than your brother."

"More teasing," Rhian groaned.

"No, that was the truth," said Vulcan.

He winked at Rhian.

Rhian girded his loins.

That's when he saw Marialena watching them from the hallway.

"Oooh, your brother is going to be *maaaaad*," she said.

6.

Once a day, right after supper, young James Hook had to dip his feet in a bucket of leeches, which sucked out his strange colored blood, leaving the bucket water blue and the young pirate weak.

This is not what James had agreed to.

"You said a few drops of blood a day to get us to the Saders," he groaned, hunched on deck against a pole. "Instead, you're giving those vampire creeps every ounce in my veins."

"The Night Crawlers are the only ones who know how to find the prison where the Saders are kept," Rafal reminded him, standing on the prow, beneath an endless sweep of stars. "Eight-day journey. Eight days of blood. That was the deal we made. *You're* the one who assumed a 'few drops.' It's a small price to pay to get the answers we need. The answers *you* need."

"Easier for you to say. It's not your blood!" James fought, hunched on the floor against a pole. "First few days I put up with it. I thought it was worth the pain to ask the Saders how to beat Pan. But I can't even sit up straight anymore. Why couldn't they take your blood? You're a *wizard*. That wasn't good enough for them?"

"You tell me. Apparently, they've been hunting Hook blood for a long time," said Rafal. "What is it that makes your blood blue? What's special in it that the Night Crawlers want?"

"Legend claims that a Hook once had a child with the Queen of the Mermaids and ever since then, the bloodline has been tainted," James muttered. "All a bunch of nonsense."

Rafal tapped his chin thoughtfully. "I wouldn't be so sure . . ."

James was too drained to press the point. "Look, you said you needed a captain. Me. *Captain* James Hook. Not a hostage to feed to vampires. Do you do things like this to your brother? Make a deal, then cheat? No wonder the Storian likes him better. Don't need the Saders to explain that!"

Rafal chuckled. "Now you *really* remind me of my twin. Do you have siblings, James?"

"A sister," James said, resting his head against the pole. "Elsa wants to be one of Pan's Lost Boys. Like how is that possible? She thinks he's the hero and I'm the villain for wanting to kill him. When I ask her *why* she likes him, she says it's because he's cute and sweet and just wants to be loved. As if that's some kind of answer. There's nothing cute and sweet about that devil and he doesn't have a loving bone in his body. Especially not for girls. Only plays with boys, Pan does. And still she pines after him."

"Your sister and my brother have that in common: pining after the wrong boys," Rafal murmured. "There was an alluring young man from Netherwood that I wanted as my Dean of Evil, but Rhian seemed so taken with him I went with an old grump instead. The last thing I need is my brother mooning over my Dean. It is the problem with souls like his and your sister's—when confronted with their opposite, a soul radiant with darkness, a soul confident in their evil, they can get confused. Instead of seeing this Evil as the enemy, they can get beguiled . . . manipulated . . . seduced by everything they are not. Before they know it, they're swept away."

"My sister's head is just screwed on backwards."

"No, it's more than that," Rafal said intensely. "Your sister and my brother think their souls so pure that they can't be attracted to darkness. But we all have two sides. Even the best of us. I confess that I do the Good thing on occasion. So why is Good so afraid to admit they can be Evil? To deny one's impulses only makes these impulses stronger. Take our siblings. Elsa sides with a lawless, diabolical Pan; Rhian is mesmerized by an aspiring Evil Dean . . . Is it a crush? Have they fallen in love with them? Or is it that they want to *be* them? That's why you remind me of my brother. Your obsession with good form. With rules. With justice. When what you really want is to be like *me*."

But Hook had stopped listening, his eyes on the doors to the interior as the Night Crawlers flooded out onto deck. There were twelve of them, hats and veils gone, their faces so chalky and pale against their black clothes that they looked like little moons in the night.

"They're back for me," James croaked.

But instead, they pulled on the ropes in crisp choreography, adjusting the ship's sails. Hook had no idea what they were up to. Conditions on the sea were dead calm. But then a moment later, the wind picked up, catching the angled sails, and the ship continued on its course. The Night Crawlers herded together like zombies and without a word, they went back inside.

"How did they know the wind was coming?" Hook said.

"Why don't you ask them?" Rafal cracked.

James sighed. The Night Crawlers never spoke, never changed expression, except when they wanted Hook's blood. Then their eyes quivered, their tongues hung out, and they all made a strange humming sound, like a chorus of bees, as if the blood of others was their one connection to life. Hook's blood had special value to them. Enough that they would chauffeur this mission to a prison at the bottom of the sea. Was it the rich blue color? Or something else? Something they could taste in it that Hook would never know? Whatever the answers, James knew one thing for sure. He couldn't survive being their blood slave much longer.

"Tomorrow is the eighth day, which means tomorrow we go under," Rafal soothed, as if reading his mind. "You'll be okay."

"Oh please. What do you care," James growled. "For all I know, you'll kill me the second we get to the prison."

Rafal's lips twisted.

James bolted straight. "You're going to *kill* me?"

"Mmm, I was planning on it," Rafal admitted. "I only needed you for your blood. Once the Night Crawlers dive us to the prison, I can find my way back. It doesn't seem like the Pirate Captain wants you returned anyway. It'd be more convenient for us both if you disappeared."

Hook couldn't look paler, given the blood loss, but somehow he bleached a new shade of white. "All that tripe about me asking the Saders about how to beat Pan—"

"You're the one who trusted an Evil School Master," Rafal shrugged. "Even your sister would know not to do that."

James couldn't speak.

"You do remind me of my brother, though," Rafal added. "And much as I find my brother whiny, self-righteous, and weak-boned, qualities you both share . . . there is something endearing about having him around . . ." He looked out at the sea, leaving the boy to decipher the Evil School Master's plans for him.

All James could think was: *Keep talking. Keep reminding him of his brother.*

"Why is the ship called the *Inagrotten*?" James asked.

Rafal paused, as if weighing whether to keep engaging with this boy he planned to kill.

"All Night Crawler ships have the name," he said finally.

"'Inagrotten' is their word for paradise—a land of infinite night that awaits them on the other side. People think the Night Crawlers are scavengers, but they're explorers. Only instead of sailing east and west, they sail *downwards*, searching for the promised land. In the meantime, by living on the blood of young men, they pump their hearts with enough force to survive deep, long dives. It's why they covet your blood if it might be part-mermaid. Imagine the powers it would give them to live beneath the sea . . ."

"Well, I don't drink men's blood and as far as I can tell, neither do you," James pointed out. "So how do *we* survive the dive?"

Rafal laughed. "I'm immortal, you fool. Wizard blood fills my veins. I need the Night Crawlers to find the prison, but the dive poses no threat to me. As for you . . . well . . ."

James stared at the Evil School Master, stricken, but Rafal was gliding past, into the galley, without looking back.

Hook slept like he was dead. He was so weak that he hardly remembered the final leeching or what he did to pass the morning, other than contemplate his death the moment the ship would dive underwater. Meanwhile, the Night Crawlers and Rafal gathered over a map in another room, Rafal speaking in low tones, the Crawlers returning stone silence. How did the bloodsuckers communicate? Rafal had negotiated this trip with them. He'd made the deal for Hook's blood. Clearly, they understood him and he understood them. Did his sorcerer powers extend to reading minds?

Hook fell asleep again.

When Rafal woke him, the sun had set and the Evil School Master pulled him out to deck, where the Night Crawlers had dispersed on the sails like a high-wire circus troupe, some manning ropes, some dangling from rigging, some perched on masts.

"It's time," said Rafal.

The panic of what was about to happen burned through James' throat; he resisted the School Master's grip. "You can't kill me . . . My family . . . They'll have your head—"

"You really are like Rhian," said Rafal, thrusting him against a pole. "The two of you. So trusting. So open to those who could hurt you. How can you live with a heart that big?" James stared at him, lost for words, as the School Master lashed him to the post with a thick coil of rope. "Don't let it come undone."

"I don't want to die!" Hook cried, but the Evil School Master was already cinching a rope around his own waist.

"Ready!" Rafal called to the Crawlers, their faces white in the dark like masks.

The Night Crawlers grabbed onto the ropes and rigging,

spawning a low hum, the same ominous buzz that came when they craved Hook's blood . . .

"No!" Hook gasped.

All at once, they leapt from the ropes, collapsing the sails and rigs, toppling the masts to one side and tipping the *Inagrotten* into the sea. Saltwater inhaled the ship and stormed into Hook's nose and lungs, the young boy too panicked and weak to expel it, his body drowned from the inside out. Flailing against the pole, he swallowed the sea, his mind fogging, blacking, his swollen limbs limp, but still, he clung to his rope, choking his last breaths . . .

Then he felt chilled hands on his neck and through the slits of his eyes, he glimpsed Rafal entangled with him, the School Master suspended from the rope around his own waist. He gently lifted James' chin, put his mouth to his, and breathed frosty air into him, so cold it burned through like dragon heat. Suddenly James could breathe again and breathe underwater, his heart kickstarting with a strange new rhythm, slow and languorous, his senses hardened and dull. There was a deadness inside now. An evaporation of compassion. What was left was cold-eyed selfishness. Any fear or doubts about being here were gone. He'd come for the answers to kill Pan and rule Neverland. And he wasn't leaving without them.

In the dark, he saw the icy light of Rafal's eyes pinned on

him, a curious expression on his face, as if instead of killing the boy, he'd done the opposite and given him new life.

"What did you do to me?" James asked, words cutting cleanly through water.

"Breathed some of me into you," Rafal said. "It's temporary, don't worry." Then he grinned. "Unless you like it."

There they stood, locked in a gaze, endless, eternal, and Hook wondered if Rafal was seeing him anymore or whether he was seeing himself, the two boys frozen like a mirror and reflection, time and space disappearing into the dark hollow of sea—

Golden glow awakened them.

The two boys looked down.

Far below, a giant gold cube shimmered, fortified by a thousand long iron spikes, each guaranteed to kill.

Rafal smiled.

They'd reached the prison.

7.

There were many problems with Vulcan's new presence at the school, but the most pressing was that everyone was in love with him.

Students, faculty, Ever and Never . . . They all had starry-eyed crushes on the young, tattooed man with the black beard, who strutted around the castle in half-buttoned doublets of suede and leather and made it a point to go for an ice-cold dip in the pond at the crack of dawn, a spectacle which roused half the school to their windows to watch.

"Do you know what the tattoo on his chest says?" Rhian heard a Nevergirl whisper to an Evergirl on the way to class. "*Memento Mori.* 'Remember you will die.'"

"Why can't *our* School Master have tattoos?" the Evergirl lamented. "And why does he wear those old *robes*?"

With Rafal, Rhian never had to worry. His brother had no interest in the students' opinions of him. But with Vulcan parading around, cool, calm, and chic, Rhian could sense both Evers and Nevers looking to the new arrival as if *he* was the School Master—especially since Vulcan gave himself the title over Rhian's objections.

"School Master Vulcan. Nice to meet you," he'd say as students passed, Good and Evil. "School Master Vulcan. Hello, you have nice smile . . . School Master Vulcan. I see you play rugby on lawn. Legs like bull! . . . School Master Vulcan. You look like my cousin Miroslava . . ."

At first, Rhian put up with all this, not just because he knew

Rafal would return and order would be restored, but because he, too, was drawn to Vulcan, just like the students. There was something about Vulcan's presence that made Rhian stand taller, his senses more alert. With Rafal gone, he'd forgotten what it felt like to be around strong Evil energy. Now the blood churned faster through Rhian's veins.

"Shall we have dinner tonight?" Rhian asked on the third morning, finding Vulcan on a balcony, sipping black coffee. "I know you've spent two days observing the classes and students, getting your handle on the school—"

"You asking Vulcan on date?" Vulcan said, grinning.

Rhian stiffened. "No. My brother and I . . . we did dinner most nights. So I just thought it appropriate . . ."

"Where I come from, having dinner with someone not your brother is a date," Vulcan replied. "Besides, your brother was School Master and you say I am not School Master. So you are giving . . . how do you say . . . *mixed* signals."

Rhian exhaled. "Look, I only brought you to help me until my brother comes back—"

"But that is cheating. Putting a stooge in Evil to do your bidding, like I am itty-bitty henchman. No. Evil needs own leader. That is point of having two School Masters. That is why you call me. Because without Evil School Master, you and your

Good students become lazy and spoiled, like cats that are too fat. This is why you like Vulcan. This is why you ask Vulcan on date. Because you need someone to kick you and remind you that you are not boss of everything." Vulcan raised a boot and kicked the Good School Master in the rump. "See? You feel better!" He winked at Rhian and swaggered off.

What could Rhian do but laugh?

The school was certainly doing better with Vulcan there. The Nevers had given up their tents and protests and returned to the glass castle, which brought the Evers back too. Humburg and Mayberry resumed daily duties, the complaints about Rhian and his new school receding. Indeed, with the castle at peace, Rhian found himself thinking less and less of his brother and more of the strutting, stylish new stranger who seemed—dare he say it—like an *improvement*? There was a fresh energy in the School Masters' office now, a tension between Good and Evil that seemed hot and kinetic and alive. A new kind of balance.

"I'm glad you agreed to dinner," Rhian smiled, at a candlelit table on a roof.

"Last time I had dinner like this, it was with girl who was in love with me," said Vulcan, heaping his plate with strawberry salad and salt-baked fish. "Like you."

Rhian spat out his food—

"Teasing," said Vulcan. "Storian still not writing?"

Rhian shook his head and took a sip of wine. "Whatever Hook and that stranger are up to . . . the Pen isn't telling us yet. Hook made a poor decision going off with him, I suspect. There is a reason we teach Evers not to talk to strangers."

"And yet you let one into your castle," Vulcan said, raising a brow.

"I'm keeping a close eye on him," Rhian parried back.

"Why do you and your brother not have crest for the school?" Vulcan asked. "Like a symbol everyone in Woods will know and respect?"

"We talked about it," said Rhian. "We could never agree on one. He wanted something dark and intimidating. I wanted it noble and inspiring. A school crest can't be both things."

Vulcan put down his fork. "Problem with you and your brother is you don't have trust. School Masters must trust each other to do what is right for their school. School comes first. Not ego. Not pride. You trust me, no? To do what is right?"

"I'm learning to," Rhian said sincerely.

"Good boy," said Vulcan.

Rhian went to sleep that night thankful for the way fate had unfolded, as if the Storian's tale about his rift with his brother had paved the way for a new chapter in his life.

At least that's how Rhian felt until Vulcan began to make changes.

It started on the twelfth day.

Vulcan roped off a wing of dorm rooms for the Nevers and set fire to them, leaving behind black, scorched facades, which the Evil students cheered. Next Vulcan turned his attentions to the Never uniforms, rejecting the idea that Good and Evil should dress the same, and instead clothed his Evil students in black leather bottoms and an array of sleek black shirts, blouses, and jackets, encouraging them to add their own Evil flair, whether a skullbones pin, a snakeskin belt, or a crown of death-head moths. But it wasn't just aesthetics that Vulcan overhauled. With Evil's marks lagging and their constant losses to Good in school-wide challenges, he added a new "Doom Room"—a chamber jammed with sweet-smelling flowers and fairies playing happy music. Vulcan sent out a proclamation: "Any Evil student who fails a challenge will spend the night in the Doom Room." Never ranks went up immediately. Soon they were outperforming the Evers, even in tests that Good usually won, like chivalry, horse riding, and grooming.

Every time Rhian tried to talk to him about all this, Vulcan suddenly had an appointment to attend or shielded himself with students, days shuffling by, until Rhian finally cornered him in their office while Vulcan had his coffee. "You have no right to make changes to the school without my permission," the Good School Master berated.

Vulcan peered at him. "Didn't you say you trust me? As School Master? As your *equal*?"

"I trust you only to take my brother's place until he's back," Rhian said. "And when he returns and sees—"

"—that Evil is excelling where it was disaster before? Then what? He will feel embarrassed for his own incompetence. That a substitute has done so much better," Vulcan taunted, eyeing the dormant Storian, still lifeless on the table next to the half-finished book about Hook. "I am not complete with changes, by the way. I think we should burn this office too. It was your idea, an ugly den hidden away? Maybe that's why the Storian won't write. It's offended by its home." He tossed the dregs of his coffee out the window and handed Rhian the mug. "Also who's to say your brother will come back *at all*?" he said, parading away.

Rhian stood there alone, holding the dirty cup.

This Vulcan problem had to be solved.

Quickly.

He tried to rally his Good troops to beat back Evil's challenge, but with the Nevers' new dorm rooms, new uniforms, and rising marks, Evil tramped around the school as if they owned it and repeatedly defaced the school sign to read: "THE SCHOOL FOR EVIL AND GOOD." Instead of mounting a response, the Evers seemed startled and stultified, as if they'd gotten so used to winning and being the kings of this school that they'd forgotten how to fight. *Fat cats,* Vulcan had called them and now it was all that Rhian saw in their spooked, spoiled faces. (Marialena took advantage of their disarray by loudly predicting death for all the Evers within a month, which one Never hastened to fulfill by poisoning their pancakes—a gambit that failed only because an enchanted pot caught the rogue and bashed him in the head.)

Rhian ordered Vulcan to punish the lying seer, but the new Evil School Master refused.

"And why not?" said Rhian, locking the office so no one else would hear. "She's a liar! She almost *killed* my entire school! How does that not deserve punishment?"

"The problem until now is Evil was *not* trying to kill your school," Vulcan drawled, sitting in Rhian's chair, his feet on the Good School Master's desk. "You put them in same uniforms, in same classes, in same halls. You made the Nevers soft. That is the imbalance. And that is why I am here. To correct it. Also, I think there should be two castles. One for Good. One for Evil. Better balance, yes? You do your school. I do mine."

Rhian bit down. "*No*. One castle for *one* school. That is how it's always been. One home for the Storian. And the way things are going, maybe there should be one School Master too."

"Is that a threat?" Vulcan said dryly. "If not for me, students would still be outside in dirty camp, protesting *you*. Go ahead. Try to get rid of me. They will stop you."

Rhian balked. All this time, he assumed he could dispose of Vulcan the same way he'd brought him in. Rhian was a sorcerer, after all. He could make the man disappear.

Only he'd forgotten about the students.

Students who wouldn't let their new School Master go without revolt.

Vulcan's fingers ran over the bat inked beneath his eye. "But what if there *was* a second castle, like I said? And Storian was kept in whichever school won the test?"

Rhian broke from his fog. "What test?"

"A test between schools . . . ," said Vulcan, thinking out loud. "You and I . . . we each pick our top student. Then we send them into arena. A forest or a cave or a place we control. You put your obstacles and I put mine and whoever survives the night wins. Yes . . . a trial in the Woods . . . when students are ready and skills are strong . . . Then we pick our best . . ." He stood up, walking towards Rhian. "If Evil wins, there will be second castle. Just for Evil. That's where Storian will live. This way the students have pride . . . purpose . . . They are never soft again."

Rhian's cheeks simmered. Here he was, hunting to find a way to evict this impostor and Vulcan was acting like he'd be here forever. The School for Good and Evil already had pride. It already had purpose. He stepped forward, about to scorn this presumptuous, peacocking idiot . . . But then the words stalled in his throat. His fury cooled, giving way to a new feeling.

Opportunity.

"Those are your terms? Well, here are mine," said Rhian. "If Good wins, you give up the title of School Master and leave at once. You return to your kingdom and go to the King of Netherwood and tell him that in exchange for me sparing your life, you and the whole Netherwood army will search the Woods for Rafal. And we don't hold this test when the students are 'ready.' We hold it *tomorrow*."

Vulcan rocked back on his heels, surprised. He sighed forlornly and gave a small shake of the head. "Ooh la la. To think, we once had a beautiful date with strawberry salad. And now you want me gone, just like your brother . . . So much for school before ego."

The words hit Rhian like a blow. He thrust out his hand,

teeth clenched. "Do we have a deal?"

Vulcan smiled, a trace of pity in it. Then his eyes hardened and he crushed Rhian with his grip.

"Deal."

Behind them, the Storian jumped off the table, jolting out of sleep.

It had something new to write.

8.

One look at the thousand long, lethal spikes protecting the prison and the Night Crawlers had enough.

They'd only agreed to dive Rafal here. The rest was none of their concern.

Once they drew close, they released the School Master and his pirate ward into the sea and sailed the *Inagrotten* back up, while Rafal and Hook swam down. Rafal's sorcerer powers meant he could breathe underwater and so too could James, now that the School Master had seeded his magic in the boy's lungs, and together, they kicked their way around the golden cube, searching for a spot to land, like two mermaids circling a rock.

James knew he should be afraid—he was at the bottom

of the sea with a nefarious stranger, relying on powers not his own—but whatever Rafal had breathed into him had left the boy fearless and hard. Suddenly, he didn't care about his safety or getting back to Blackpool. He cared about one thing and one thing only: killing Pan and taking Neverland. Which meant finding the Saders to ask them how.

As Hook canvassed the cube for an opening, a fleeting thought crossed his mind. Until five minutes ago, he'd been different. More Good. Less Evil. That piece of Rafal's soul had turned him cold and unyielding. Like a reflection of the School Master himself. But if this is how Rafal felt . . . so free from warmth and compassion . . . so empty of anything but villainous purpose . . . what was stopping him from destroying everything in his path? From killing his Good brother and taking over the Woods?

The Storian, of course.

The Pen that had turned against him.

And now Rafal had come to the Saders to learn the Storian's secrets . . .

What if they gave him the key to controlling the Pen?

What would happen to the Good School Master?

What would happen to the Woods?

James felt these questions bubble and churn inside of him, as if he wasn't the one asking them . . . as if they had come straight from inside Rafal's soul . . .

"Do you see a door?" the Evil School Master called, his voice cutting through water.

"No. There's too many spikes," James answered quickly. "We can't even get close."

"Look," said Rafal, holding up a glowing fingertip. He lit up the side of the cube, revealing the outline of a latch.

Hook swam closer.

A spike rocketed off the side of the cube, straight for Hook's head—

Rafal kicked him in the chest, bashing him away just in time.

Then came another spike and another and another, the entire cube deploying protective spears at the intruders.

Rafal dodged them, nimble and unthreatened, so the spikes turned to James, grazing his arm, his thigh, his ear as the boy twisted wildly, his blood streaking through the sea.

"HELLL—" Hook shrieked, but Rafal was already there, gripping him and thrusting out a finger, casting a shield of icy glow, the spikes ricocheting off with thunderous noise. *BOOM! BOOM! BOOM! BOOM!* All the while, James huddled in the Evil School Master's arms, but instead of cold emptiness, now there was warmth. Unexpected. Out of place. A warmth Hook hadn't felt since his father was alive. The warmth of *love*. And now James knew that this too was part of Rafal's soul . . . that what held him back from killing his twin *wasn't* the Pen, but the bond he craved with his better half . . . and it was this that had made Rafal spare Hook instead of killing him . . . as if James had become the substitute for his brother's love . . .

BOOM! BOOM! BOOM!

Then . . . nothing.

Rafal looked up into quiet waters, the golden cube shiny and smooth, all the spikes gone.

He dropped his hand, the shield dissolving.

Rafal let Hook out of his arms, into the sea.

A sound behind them.

The sound of metal.

One spike left, ejecting from the blind side.

It went for Hook's throat.

Rafal screamed—

Hook stabbed out his finger and a wall of glow erupted, blasting the spear away.

The boy panted into silence . . . then saw Rafal gaping at him.

"It's your magic!" Hook yelled, panic releasing to anger. "Isn't that what it was supposed to do!"

Rafal blinked back. *"No."*

Behind them, the latch in the cube opened and lowered, revealing a brown-skinned woman in the doorway, surrounded by twenty guards, armed with harpoons.

"Hello, Rafal," the woman said. "Welcome to Monrovia Prison."

She wore a slim pantsuit of gold lamé and a glowing blue necklace in the shape of an orb. Her hair was a beehive of braids, her lips painted gold, and she had golden rhinestones around her eyes. All her guards wore the same glowing blue necklace that she did.

She flashed a patronizing smile. "Your presence is unauthorized, so I suggest you find your way back to the surface before the situation escalates."

"I love when the situation escalates. My kind of fun," said Rafal. His eyes flickered. "You look familiar . . ."

"Quintana of Drupathi. I was a student at your school," the woman replied. "You told me I was arrogant and self-righteous and wouldn't amount to much."

"I was right, wasn't I? You run a prison. A prison controlled by kingdom leaders, so you are little more than an *employee*," said Rafal. "Hardly the stuff Evil legend is made of."

Quintana scowled. "And yet here you are, trying to *enter* my prison. Wonder what it takes to kill a wizard. Would be fun to try."

Rafal didn't react. "We're here to see the Saders."

"I know. They told me a week ago you'd be coming with a young failed pirate whose peculiar blood convinced the Night Crawlers to sail you." Quintana gave Hook a glance, then looked back at Rafal. "But as you well know, trespassers aren't allowed."

"When's the last time someone successfully broke in?" Rafal wondered.

"Under my watch? Never."

"That will change today," Rafal said.

"Then there is no question of whether I'm going to kill you," said Quintana. "Only the question of how fast."

"Indeed," said Rafal.

He aimed a finger at her, but nothing came out.

Quintana smoothed her sleeves. "They also said what spell you'd use, so we created a shield against it in advance. You know . . . *my* kind of fun." Her eyes met the School Master's.

"Fire," she said.

Her guards shot their harpoons, barbed spears scudding at Rafal—

A blast of light erupted, smashing the spears and harpoons

away and swallowing Quintana and the guards in a giant water bubble.

Rafal stared in astonishment, as if he was dreaming . . . then slowly turned to Hook, who had his finger outstretched, glimmering with glow.

Hook eyed Quintana. "I'm assuming this part they *didn't* see? The part where the *failed* pirate wins?"

But all he heard were Quintana's muffled shouts, as the bubble floated away with her and her guards inside.

Hook saw Rafal frowning at him.

"What?" said James.

"Definitely taking my magic away from you when we're done," said Rafal, grabbing the boy by the arm and swimming him into the cube.

James was thankful that Rafal couldn't feel his palms sweating in the sea. Both times that Hook had wielded magic, he'd done it without thinking, a new, raw force inside of him that unleashed without his conscious control. On the one hand, it saved his life and Rafal's. On the other . . . he didn't like the alien feeling of not knowing his own body anymore or what he was capable of or what he was going to do. But anytime he got too deep into thought or close to fear, that dead emptiness returned, refocusing him on the mission, as if his soul had a new compass.

The inside of Monrovia Prison was the opposite of what he expected. The cube was pristine on the inside, a stacking of aquarium jail cells, lit by phosphorescent gold water ferns and undersea vines. No guards were in sight and Hook suspected he'd taken care of all or most with his spell outside. As for the cells, each was its own tank, a prisoner trapped within, wearing white robes and glowing blue necklaces, the same necklaces he'd seen on Quintana and the guards, which Hook suspected must keep the magic that let them breathe underwater. He scanned the rise of cell tanks, up, up, up. There were at least a hundred of them.

"How do we find the Saders?" he asked Rafal.

"Seers are hard to jail, since they know everything that's coming," the Evil School Master replied. "Look for the cell that's the most secure."

"There," said Hook, pointing.

From the ceiling, steel chains descended like the strands of a chandelier, suspending a separate tank.

"First you're rescuing me and now you're seeing things faster than I can," Rafal murmured.

"Maybe I should take your brother's place," Hook said impishly. "Imagine that. Me at the School for Good."

Rafal didn't respond.

As they drew closer to the tank, James saw it didn't hold one

inmate, but a family of them, all fair-haired and slim in the prison's white robes—a mother, a father, a grandmother, and two teenage sons. The mother watched them approach, no sign of surprise in her hazel-green eyes, her long blond locks undulating around her turned-up nose and wide-set eyes like little snakes.

"Hello, Rafal," she said, her voice crystal clear through water. "I'm Adela Sader."

"Mother of young Marialena Sader, I assume?" Rafal replied.

"Thank you for taking her to the School for Evil. Otherwise she might have ended up in here with us," Adela said. "Despite the fact her powers of sight are . . ."

"Nonexistent," the older son snickered, and the younger one laughed.

The father swatted them both. "She works harder at her powers than you two. Maybe she's not a natural, but her sight will come along."

"Tell that to all the people she swindles. Been selling fake prophecies for years," one of the boys mumbled.

The father ignored him and addressed Rafal's companion. "You must be James Hook."

"The failed pirate you didn't see coming," Hook jabbed.

"Oh, we saw you coming," said the older boy, smiling crooked teeth.

"We lied to the guards," the younger boy chimed in, "otherwise how else could we get rid of them?"

Hook saw this was news to Rafal too, the School Master's wintery eyes pinned on the two boys. "Why would you lie for us?" Rafal asked.

The whole family looked at each other.

"Because you're going to free us, of course," said Adela. Then she paused. "Well, I shouldn't say *you're*, because that implies the both of you. *One* of you will free us."

Rafal's brow furrowed. "And the other one?"

"Well that's the thing," Adela sighed. "One of you kills the other."

9.

"One of you kills the other."

The Storian's words haunted Rhian as he leaned over a glass balcony, drinking a goblet of wine. A full moon presided overhead, the dark Woods stretched before him.

Earlier that day, the Pen had resumed the tale of James Hook, bringing him and his mysterious new friend to a prison at the bottom of the sea. There, they'd visited a family of seers, called the Saders, in search of answers—only to be told that one of them would die at the hands of the other.

It was the type of twist the enchanted Pen loved, the perfect cliffhanger before it paused for the rest of the story to unfold. Normally Rhian invested little in these twists and turns . . . but there was something strange about this story that left the Good School Master unsettled.

Why wouldn't the Storian name the stranger who took Hook from Blackpool? The Pen had revealed what Hook planned to ask the seers—how to kill Pan—but why wouldn't it reveal the question the *stranger* intended to ask? And those Saders . . . Wasn't that the family Marialena said she was from?

But there were bigger problems to worry about.

Under Rhian and Rafal, the School for Good and Evil had been one school. Under Vulcan, it was turning into two. In the past day alone, Vulcan had made even more changes: Nevers would eat all meals alone in a new Evil Supper Hall; Evil's joint classes with Good were replaced with Evil-only sessions; and he made a fang-toothed bat the official crest of the School for Evil, plastering it everywhere, on walls, uniforms, books, as if he alone had the right to brand the school.

Rhian's fingers tightened around his cup.

He kept thinking of that boy Hook. A thoughtful, well-meaning soul whose fate had been hijacked by a stranger with his own agenda.

Rhian knew something about that. Whatever was happening deep in the Savage Sea was mirroring the tale of the Good School Master, a hostage to his own stranger.

If Vulcan and his Evil students won the Trial, there would be a second castle. The Pen kidnapped within its walls. The ancient balance between Good and Evil, between School Masters . . . shattered.

Rhian gritted his teeth. The terms of the Trial favored Vulcan, but he didn't care. Right now, all that mattered was getting rid of the louse. The students and faculty had fallen for Vulcan the same way Rhian once had, and now it was too late to eject him without a mutiny. Rhian's only hope was for Good to win the Trial and send the bearded invader back from where he came.

He sucked down the last of his wine.

Why hadn't he appreciated Rafal when he had him? Why hadn't he made him feel loved instead of wary? *Evil attacks, Good defends.* Wasn't that the first rule of fairy tales? And he'd been the one feeding his Evil twin's paranoia that the Storian had turned against him. What started as a joke had turned into a careless attack. Now he was paying the price. In Vulcan, he thought he'd found a substitute for his brother's love. Someone who would balance him out. Instead, he'd trusted an enemy. Just like Hook.

Strange, isn't it? Rhian thought. That the Storian's last tale was about himself . . . and this new one, too, seemed to reflect his fortunes so precisely.

Rhian smiled wryly. He was being a narcissist. Exactly what Rafal always accused him of. Thinking everything was about him. The tale of James Hook had nothing to do with what was happening here at school.

And yet . . . something was needling at him . . . something inching towards the surface—

The sound of hoots and whistles below snapped him from his thoughts.

Rhian tensed. At lunch, he and the Evil School Master had announced the Trial to the students, laying out the stakes. If Evil won, they'd get their own school and bragging rights to the Storian kept within. If Good won, Vulcan would return to Netherwood and lead a search for Rafal.

Naturally, the Nevers were more excited. The Evers didn't know what to think. Evil could win a new school and they could win . . . what?

In the meantime, Vulcan rallied his Nevers together to vote for their combatant—the meeting that Rhian was now hearing below. Judging from the cheers, they must have agreed on who Evil would be sending into the forest the following night.

Rhian, on the other hand, told the Evers that *he* would dictate who would go into the Woods to represent Good. With so much at stake, he couldn't leave the choice up to students. Especially since he knew the Nevers would vote Timon as their flagbearer—a musclebound one-eyed, half-ogre boy who could crush anything in his path.

Rhian hadn't the faintest clue who to put against him, and he sensed the Evers' stares as they passed him in the hall, not only doubting their chances in this Trial but also him, their leader, for agreeing to it.

The next morning, Rhian and Vulcan met to rope off the arena.

A two-mile section of the Woods had been chosen for the Trial, with each School Master responsible for filling it with obstacles of their choice. At sunset the two contestants, Good and Evil, would enter the arena and whoever survived until dawn would be declared the winner.

"If Evil loses, I expect you to leave the school without a peep," Rhian said, fortifying the last bit of enchanted shield around the playing field. "And take your stupid bats with you."

"Scared little boy. Acting so childish when I am only trying to make school better," Vulcan replied. He probed the invisible boundary with his fingers and absorbed the sizzling shock without a flinch. "Good and Evil should be equal. Two strong leaders. But you are weak and threatened by strength. If I win, *you* should leave. Go back to Mommy's house and drink her milk."

"Your mother should have named you Vulture," Rhian retorted.

Vulcan burst out laughing. "Is that Good version of insult? Look at you. Like ugly little duckling who thinks it's swan."

Rhian narrowed his eyes. "And if it's a *tie*, if both your fighter and mine survive until dawn, then you *still* have to leave."

"Because you say so, Duckling?" Vulcan threw back. "No. If both survive, then they fight each other. Eventually one will die."

"This is a school, you idiot. We don't kill our students and if you were a real School Master, you'd know that. They need a way to surrender."

"In my kingdom, if you surrender, we kill you anyway."

"Pity you never surrendered, then," said Rhian, red-hot.

Vulcan chewed on a stick. "Okay, Duckling. Since you are throwing tantrum. Give your fighter teeny-tiny flag and if they are coward and drop it, then okay, surrender. But mine doesn't need. I don't teach my students to be chicken."

"No, you teach yours to be barbaric and brainless like you," said Rhian. "That's why Timon is your choice."

"Ah, so bitter and petty, as if *you* should be Evil School Master!" Vulcan replied. "Is that why you drove your brother out? Is that why you don't like me? Because you want my job?"

Vulcan walked away, leaving Rhian speechless.

Night came fast.

By the time he'd conjured his obstacles in the arena (killer rabbits, changeling fairies, collapsing trees), then changed into an embellished tunic to rival whatever Vulcan planned to wear, the sun had whittled to a brass coin and the students from both schools had begun herding towards the Woods.

Rhian lagged behind. He still hadn't settled on a choice for Good's fighter and he needed time to think. As he walked towards the Woods, he could hear the grunts and growls from the forest, the creatures of night rousing out of slumber. Rhian suddenly wondered whether it was wise holding the Trial in open woods where anything could happen. There was a reason they forbid students of the school from going into the Woods after dark and now they were flinging two of their own into the forest . . . It was far too early for a test like this!

Rhian had demanded the Trial happen tonight the same way Rafal had moved up the Snow Ball, recklessly and impetuously, with little thought for the students he was supposed to protect.

Vulcan's words stung him with their echo—*"as if you should be Evil School Master!"*

It wasn't true, of course.

Rhian had always been the better soul.

But without Rafal there, he'd lost his compass. His balance. And now he didn't know who he was anymore.

Which was surely why he was struggling to pick Good's fighter.

Should he choose someone valiant and pure of heart, like Hephaestus, even if he lacked the guile and cleverness to outwit Timon? That's what the old Rhian would have done. Bet on Goodness and believe the better man would win. But the new Rhian wondered if he should pick a wilier child . . . who could scheme and fox his way through whatever Vulcan had planned . . . the kind of student Rafal would have picked . . .

At the forest edge, the Nevers buzzed with excitement, wrapped in blankets for an all-night vigil to support their fighter and armed with banners and signs:

EVERS STINK! NEVERS RULE!
FIGHT FOR EVIL!
BRING HOME THE PEN!
A NEW CASTLE IS OURS!

The Evers, meanwhile, looked glum and nervous, throwing darting glances at giant Timon, with his bloodshot eye and bulging arms.

Vulcan approached Rhian, flaunting a velvet doublet, the color of blood. "So tell us. Who does Good choose?"

Rhian's thoughts were still on his brother.

Who would Rafal pick if he were me?

His eyes fixed on Timon, his palms sweating.

Not Hephaestus.

He'd pick someone who'd play dirty.

Someone who'd do anything to win.

Even cheat.

Rhian's mind drifted away from Hephaestus.

To a soul his brother branded Evil.

Rafal had been so sure . . .

What if Rafal was right and the Pen was wrong somehow?

Who better to fight an Evil brute than someone who might well be Evil . . . or close to it at least . . .

His throat bobbed.

But should I do what Rafal would do?

Isn't the point of being Good to not do what Rafal would do?

But if I do what I would do, then . . .

"Well?" Vulcan demanded—

Rhian blurted out a name.

Before he'd even made the choice.

The name his Evil twin would have told him to say.

The Evers slowly parted, revealing a boy who was busy kissing Kyma, lost in first love, and hadn't the faintest clue he was part of this story.

Then he saw both schools ogling him.

"Me?" Aladdin choked. "You're choosing *me?*"

But Rhian had turned to Vulcan. "Let's begin. Aladdin against Timon. Whoever survives until sunset—"

"We don't pick Timon," said Vulcan.

Rhian startled. "What?"

All the Nevers were grinning.

"We pick Marialena," Vulcan replied.

Rhian snorted, as if it were a joke. "Why would you pick a lying seer to fight a Trial?"

"Because if I told the *truth* about what I see, your brother wouldn't have picked me for the School for Evil." Marialena stepped forward, armored in a dark cloak. "If I told the truth about my visions, I'd be in Monrovia Prison right now with the rest of my family." She peered at Rhian through her glasses. "My family, who your brother is *visiting* at this very moment."

Rhian fluttered his hand at her. "What nonsense. More lies from—"

Monrovia Prison.

The prison in Hook's story.

The undersea jail where the Saders were kept.

He looked back at Marialena.

She was staring at him, her eyes clear brown pools.

Not a trace of deceit in them.

And suddenly, Rhian understood.

She was telling the truth.

She'd been telling him the truth all along.

Marialena *was* a seer.

She could see into the future, just like her family.

But unlike her family, Marialena *lied* about all the things she saw.

Because by lying, she hadn't been arrested with her family when the time came. Instead, by deliberately hiding her true powers, by sinfully selling lies, she'd caught the eye of an Evil

School Master and secured her ticket to this school, long before the Saders got sentenced to jail. Marialena had foreseen all this. Her family being jailed . . . her joining them in their cell . . . unless she hid her powers behind lies and took that extra step into Evil. Lie about the things she saw, catch Rafal's attention, and she'd end up free, at a legendary school, instead of at the bottom of the sea.

But now Rhian's heart went colder, that unsettled feeling returning that came whenever he'd thought about Hook's tale.

Because if Marialena was a real seer, she wasn't just telling the truth about her powers. She was telling the truth about the other part too.

The part about her family.

" . . . *who your brother is visiting at this very moment.*"

Which meant that mysterious stranger with Hook . . . the one who'd gone to the Saders for answers . . . the one fated to either kill James Hook or die himself . . .

That wasn't a stranger.

It was *Rafal.*

Rhian looked up at Marialena with wide eyes.

The seer about to fight for Evil in this Trial.

The seer who could see everything before it happened.

Rafal's future. Rhian's future. The future of this school.

And from the way she smiled at him, the Good School Master was very, very scared.

10.

It took a moment for Adela Sader's words to sink in.

The prophecy that one of them would kill the other.

This, after Hook and Rafal had *saved* each other to get here.

The boys glanced at one another, Hook's face edgy and anxious, Rafal's utterly blank, before the School Master peered at Adela in her aquarium cell.

"I'm not sure what future you're seeing," said Rafal, his voice slicing through the sea, "but I'm immortal and cannot be killed, so there is no question of Hook killing me. As for me killing Hook . . . if it hasn't happened by now . . ."

He gave Hook a grin. Treading water next to him, James let his edginess slide away. He had a window into Rafal's soul, now that the School Master's magic was inside him. He could sense the feelings Rafal had grown for him, protective, warm, as if the boy had filled his brother's place. Which meant James knew for certain: the School Master would never hurt him.

"Yeah, total bunk," Hook dismissed. "There'll be no killing."

Adela shrugged, her outlines blurry in the tank's blue light. "I'm telling you what I see."

"What we all see," said her husband, the two kids and grandmother nodding along.

The grandmother raised a bony finger. "First you free us. Then the murder."

"That's not what happens," the older son argued. "He kills him first. Then we're released."

"Mmm, I see what Grandma does," the younger son piped in—

"Regardless of details," Adela cut in, pivoting to Rafal, "what we do agree is that you free us. So might we get on with it? There's a lock on top of the cell. Once you break it, you'll pull the latch and we'll swim out."

"We never agreed to free you, no matter what your sight tells you," Rafal reminded. "If you'd like us to entertain the idea, James and I have questions first."

"Many questions," Hook added, despite his legs tiring from cycling through water. Because now that James had the chance to see his future, he wanted to know everything. Not just how to kill Pan, but how to kill the next Pan and the next and all the Pans that followed—

"One question each," Adela countered. "Seers can't answer

questions without aging ten years and that is a steep enough price. Answer one question and you free my sons. Then the other will be answered and you'll free the rest of us. Do we have a deal?"

Rafal mulled this over. Then he turned to Hook. "James, you go first—"

"*You* first," said the whole Sader family at the same time.

All of them locked on Rafal.

Rafal hesitated. "All right." He stood taller. "How can I make the Storian favor *me* instead of my brother?"

The Sader family traded looks.

But it was the father who answered, his smooth, rosy face suddenly hard, his voice laced with a deep echo as if it came from somewhere beyond the sea.

"The Pen senses a restless soul, Rafal," he said. "Questioning whether a brother's love is enough. For many years, you kept each other in balance. But now one soul wants more. To grow beyond a brother's reflection. To test the peace you've been entrusted to protect. But the Pen is warning: this is a fool's game. That is why Evil suffers. Because as long as one side strays, the Storian reflects this imbalance. Only when love restores peace, when love overrides a restless soul, will the Pen let both sides win equally again. That is the Pen's way.

That is the Pen's balance."

Father Sader finished his words. Then slowly, the wrinkles in his face hardened; the gray in his hair overtook the blond; the muscles in his arms and chest softened. "Ten years of life," he sighed softly. "The price of truth."

Rafal said nothing.

Hook could see him lost in his thoughts. Then, inside James, the School Master's magic turned colder, pulling Hook's spirit deeper into darkness. That flame of love Hook had found in Rafal's soul—the longing for his brother, the yearning for his other half—had given way to something else.

Doubt.

Rafal's eyes stayed on Father Sader. "Things have changed between Rhian and I. That is true. I strayed. He didn't. But I can fix it, right? I'll love him. I'll stand by his side like I did before."

The Saders said nothing.

"Answer me," Rafal ordered. "Will I fix it? Will my love be enough?"

"One question each," Adela Sader said, nodding between Rafal and Hook. "That is what we agreed."

"Then I'll use James' question too," Rafal snapped.

James whirled to him in shock. "No way—I get mine, just like yo—"

Rafal shot him with a spell, sealing his mouth. He stared icily at Hook as if the boy was a stranger. As if now that he and his brother's love was on the line, his warmth for James had evaporated.

Rafal turned back to the Saders. "Answer my question."

But the two sons were pressed against the glass, flushed with anger. "You cost my dad ten years. No more answers until you free us," said the elder.

"You promised," insisted the younger.

Rafal ignored them and James' garbled shouts and instead, addressed Adela. "Will my love be enough?"

Mother Sader gave him a stony-eyed stare. "You heard the boys. We had a deal."

"ANSWER THE QUESTION!" Rafal roared. "WILL IT BE ENOUGH!"

"No," said Adela, unflinching. "It will never be enough. Betrayal. War. Death. That is what awaits you and your cursed souls."

"Liar," Rafal spat.

But slowly, Adela's hair lightened with strands of white. Her eyes dulled. Her skin sagged, sunspots rising at her temples.

Ten years had found her.

Which meant she'd told the truth.

Rafal stiffened, her words resounding.

"Betrayal. War. Death."

But it wasn't just Rafal to whom this prophecy mattered.

James' chest seized, his blood heating up.

Two questions had been asked and answered.

Hook's chance was gone.

He unleashed a cry of rage, the magic inside him swelling and busting through Rafal's spell. "YOU DIRTY CHEAT!" he screamed at the School Master.

Rafal barely looked at him. "Let's free them. I have to get back to school."

He swam to the top of the tank, using a glowing finger to burn the lock. There was something in the way the Evil School Master did this, in the way that he'd spoken, that froze James' anger. The sadness in Rafal's face. How chastened he was. And now James understood: the Saders' prophecy had scared him. Whatever bitterness he'd built towards his twin, he'd already put it aside, determined to fix what was broken and avoid the prediction of their fate. Rafal snapped the lock, about to open the cell—

Hook's face gnarled.

Rafal may have gone soft. But James hadn't. The School Master's magic was still inside the young pirate, the pirate who'd come here for answers to kill Pan and who wasn't leaving until he got them—

Hook bashed into Rafal headfirst, knocking him off the tank.

"No one is free until I get my turn," James gritted, glowering at the Saders through glass—

Rafal rammed into him, hurling him away.

Instantly, the Sader boys grabbed the latch and opened the tank, sliding out on a wave of water and dragging old grandma behind them, while their mother and father kicked to follow.

Seeing his hope for answers escaping, James chased after them, but Rafal shot him with a spell, ricocheting young Hook against the tank. Without thinking, James stabbed a glowing finger at Rafal, deploying Rafal's own magic against him, a spear of light noosing around the School Master's throat and choking him before Rafal managed to pry free. But Hook was already on him, trapping Rafal in a headlock, suffocating him, fueled by a strength and fury neither could control. Indeed, Rafal could no longer subdue Hook, not with Rafal's own magic heavy inside him, and as he tried to ward off the boy, he saw the features of James' face twisting, magically morphing into *Rafal*'s, as if Hook had lost touch with his own soul, subsumed entirely by the School Master's. Suddenly, Rafal could feel something weaken inside of him . . . his own magic fraying . . . and he realized his immortal soul was being drained by the boy who shared a piece of it, a furious, rage-filled, now *powerful* boy . . . Losing air, Rafal thrashed at his strangler, who was wearing his own face, his own Evil twin.

"Stop, Hook . . . you're killing me . . . ," he wheezed. "Their prophecy . . . you're making it *true* . . ."

Hook's grip on Rafal wavered . . . the boy's real soul re-awakening for a moment . . . long enough for Rafal to snatch him by the neck and smash him against the nearest tank. Hook bellowed with vengeance, Rafal's spirit powering him once more, and they clashed in waterlogged fight, all the prisoners of Monrovia watching wide-eyed from the safety of their cells. For hours they fought, punching and kicking and wounding each other, their magic dwindling, then regaining strength, Rafal and Hook, Hook and Rafal, Rafal and Rafal, the two boys spewing ribbons of blood, until finally they faltered, souls empty, magic failing, their powers to breathe underwater fading to a cold, painful drowning at the bottom of the sea. They fell away from each other, spinning into the deep, the Sader warning of a murder come true, only for *two* instead of one—

But now there were shadows, spindly and black, like streaking jellyfish, grasping for Hook, pulling the boy upwards, leaving Rafal to sink to his death.

Air filled the boy's lungs as he broke the surface, into chilled night air, before he was dragged onto a shining black ship, the bloodstained lad coughing and hacking out salt water, until he pried open his eyes and glimpsed his rescuers.

Night Crawlers, veiled in black, humming for his blood.

One drew a knife and cut his arm open, thirsting for Hook's precious blue nectar to spill . . .

Thick redness bubbled out.

Hook smiled up at them, his face slowly turning back into Rafal's.

The Night Crawlers screeched in anger, diving for him like vultures, but the Evil sorcerer was rising into air, the sea sloughing off him, giving way to flight.

As he soared into darkness, like a bat stretching its wings, Rafal inhaled the night, tears welling before he could stop them. A sting of grief, harsh and unfamiliar. Mourning for the pirate with whom he'd shared his soul. Hook. *Captain* Hook. The boy he'd tried to love. The boy he'd destroyed instead.

Rafal smeared at his eyes.

Love turned to poison.

Good intentions turned Evil.

Betrayal. War. Death.

You and your cursed souls.

There and then, high above earth, the Evil School Master made a vow to himself.

That this could not happen again.

That this story would not repeat with his brother.

That a second prophecy must never come true.

11.

Through the familiar gates, the Evil School Master came. He'd swallowed his pride in slinking back to his twin. He'd shaken loose all the resentments of the past and hid them in the corners of his mind. It was time to start over. To be a good School Master. A good brother. With the Storian between them, he and Rhian would revere a new balance. An enduring love. One almost drowned deep in the sea. Rafal forged a smile. In his brother's arms, he would find redemption . . .

Then he realized there was no school.

Just an empty, ripped-up field at the edge of a forest, tall shadows zigzagging across.

Slowly Rafal turned and lifted his eyes to a glass cathedral looming over him, glittering in sun.

For a moment, he wondered if he'd accidentally drifted to Gillikin, where they built such hideous, impractical things . . .

But then, through the glass, he witnessed familiar Good students chained and gagged like prisoners, lined up in halls, while Evil students in black leather, carrying rods and clubs and whips, barked orders and gave them whacks, like menacing jail guards.

What? Rafal thought.

He blinked away the illusion, thinking perhaps he'd spent too much time underwater . . . only to see the Evers still there, bound and frightened, prisoners to the Nevers within their own castle. A *new* castle.

Stymphs flew overhead, diving west.

Rafal blanched.

Two new castles.

Because the dark-furred birds descended on a second school, next to the first, jagged and black, with four twisting spires, a new home for Evil, each tower crowned with the sculpting of a bat. One of these towers was taller than the rest, with a large open window and the glimpse of a silver pen inside, suspended in air as it wrote in a book . . .

Rafal shook his head.

The Storian?

In an Evil tower?

A silhouette obscured the Pen, the figure of a bearded man, with dark, smoldering eyes, glowering down at the School Master.

Tension spiked inside Rafal, the stab of animal threat.

Something terrible had happened since he'd gone.

Something unforgivable.

"Psssst!"

It came from behind.

Rafal swiveled and through the forest, he caught a flash of movement.

The Evil School Master made his way into the thicket, weaving between trees, the gold of the sun winnowing to ghostly light.

That's when he saw him.

A figure, lurking in shadows.

Shame-faced, plaintive.

Without a shirt, his eye blackened, his body battered.

Hunched beneath a bush, an exile from his school.

From *their* school.

Rhian held up his hands, like he was surrendering, like he didn't know where to start.

His Evil twin glared down at him.

All thoughts of peace and love evaporated.

"So," said Rafal.

His eyes brimmed with fire.

"So!"

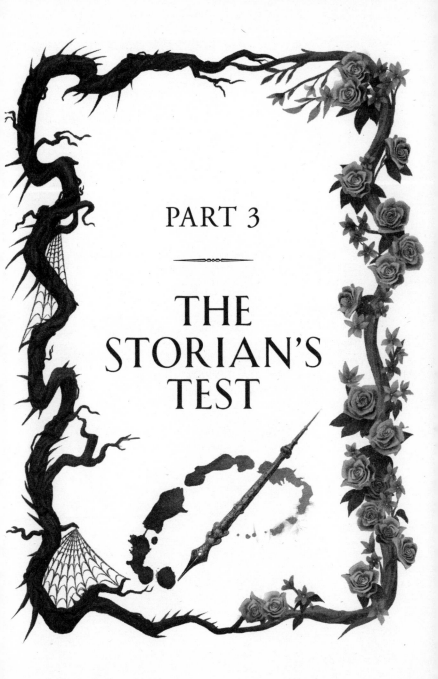

PART 3

THE STORIAN'S TEST

1.

"It started with Aladdin," Rhian sighed.

"Doesn't it always?" Rafal replied.

———⋯———

How am I even in here, Aladdin thought as he entered the dark forest.

The Evers assumed the Good School Master would pick Hephaestus to represent their side, so Aladdin had slacked off like everyone else.

Why would Rhian choose him? Everyone in the Good school knew he was mediocre in class, morally dubious, and terrible at fighting. The School Master must have totally lost his mind to send him into the Trial. In fact, ever since his brother left,

Rhian had been acting funny—first that glass castle, then inviting a cocky weirdo to lead Evil, then agreeing to this contest with no upside for Good, and now selecting him as if somehow *he* could clean up a School Master's mess. The worst part was all the Evers were counting on him to win, because Good always won against Evil, even though Aladdin barely knew the rules of this blasted thing. Survive until sunrise, right? Wasn't that the point? He touched the surrender flag in his back pocket. All he had to do was *not* let this flag touch the ground until dawn. That didn't sound too hard. The Trial arena was big. He just needed to find some cave or ditch to hide in and he'd be back in Kyma's arms in no tim—

Treeeep.

Aladdin whirled around.

What was that?

It was a strange sound, high and grating, at once a whine and warning.

He squinted into the dark, seeing nothing but the outlines of trees.

Treeeep.

Treeeep.

Aladdin took a step back.

All around him, pairs of eyes lit up, small and beady, with red pupils.

Oh no.

Aladdin ran—

A ball of white fur launched on his face, shrieking and snapping sharp teeth.

Treeeep!

Treeeep!

Treeeep!

Aladdin grabbed whatever it was by the throat and held it up, catching just enough moonlight to see big ears . . . a pink nose . . .

A *rabbit*?

It lunged for his neck, fangs out, thrashing in Aladdin's hands and screeching for blood.

Killer rabbit.

He flung it to the ground, but now there were more coming, murderous white puffs, leaping onto his legs, clawing and biting—

Then he remembered.

They'd learned about killer rabbits!

Mayberry had put emphasis on it, as if she knew they would be part of the Trial.

There was an antidote, she'd said. A way to defuse them.

What was it?

Pull its leg?

Pat its head?

Slap its butt?

Yes!

That sounded right.

One jumped onto his neck—

Aladdin grabbed it by the hind legs and smacked its behind.

All the rabbits suddenly went quiet, gaping at him.

With vengeance, they sprung, bashing him to the ground and attacking triple force—*TREEP TREEP TREEP TREEP*—

He couldn't breathe, blood drawn from every inch of him, the rabbits biting harder, faster, sure to kill him . . .

A hand reached into the fray and tickled their noses.

One by one, the rabbits pulled off him.

Tickle. Tickle. Tickle.

Aladdin pried open his eyes to see Marialena standing over him, surrounded by doting bunnies.

He jumped to his feet, bloodied, bruised. "What are you—"

She smiled and held up a flag.

His flag.

Aladdin reached for his back pocket.

Nothing there.

"You cheater!" he cried.

Marialena mouthed his words as he said them.

"Exactly like I saw it all in my head," she boasted. "Oh,

watch out for that last rabbit. The one I didn't tickle."

Aladdin stared at her. Then he looked down and saw a rabbit blinking red eyes. It launched up and bit his behind.

Aladdin yowled—

"Saw that too," Marialena said.

She dropped his flag and watched the boy disappear.

Drenched in morning sun, Rhian hung his head. "Three minutes from when he went in to when it was over," he lamented. "Maximum damage always happens in the shortest amount of time."

Rafal glared back from the shadows, unsympathetic. "I'm surprised he lasted that long at all. Why in the world would you pick that peabrain?"

Rhian shook his head. "I thought it's who *you* would pick!"

"You really are lost," Rafal said quietly. "Keep going."

Rhian sighed and continued his tale.

With the flag dropped, Good's fighter had surrendered from the arena and reappeared outside the forest, clutching his bottom and dancing in pain.

Which meant Rhian had lost the wager on which he'd bet everything.

The Nevers would have a new castle, the two sides split

apart. The Storian would live inside Evil, the balance tipped. Evil's School Master, a man not named Rafal, would no longer be a temporary nuisance but Rhian's permanent equal.

"Vulcan stays! Vulcan stays!" the Evil students roared.

And a few Evers had applauded as if this is what they were hoping for all along.

But soon they reconsidered. Within hours, Vulcan had begun erecting the new castle across from Good's, importing the army from Netherwood to build it.

"The army that was supposed to go looking for *me*, if you won?" Rafal interrupted, raising an eyebrow.

"That army," Rhian said miserably, continuing his tale.

To speed construction, Vulcan's workers needed magic. Luckily, they had Dean Humburg, who now that Vulcan had earned his place as Evil School Master, had accepted his authority the way he once had Rafal's. With Humburg shooting spells left and right, lofting steel and laying bricks, the new School for Evil was built in three days. On the fourth day, Vulcan swaggered into the School for Good, scaled the glass staircase in full view of startled Evers, and snatched the Storian from Rhian's office, marching it back to Evil and giving the Pen a new home in its tallest tower.

Suddenly, the Evers saw their appreciation for Vulcan was

misplaced. This wasn't the chic, hot-blooded rule buster they'd come to love, but an enemy who had just declared war on their side. All at once, the Evers stormed Evil's school, demanding the Storian back without the semblance of a plan—the kind of harebrained attack usually instigated by the Nevers. Indeed, the first rule of fairy tales is Evil attacks, Good defends, and now it was Good doing the attacking. So Evil responded by defending itself swiftly, ruthlessly, the way Good usually did—only this time it was the Nevers taking the Evers prisoner, teachers and Dean Mayberry included, before running Rhian out of his own castle while Vulcan pelted the Good School Master with dung bombs from a window, shouting that if Rhian ever came back, he'd be beaten to a pulp.

"Which is how I'm here, with nowhere to go," the exiled brother finished, slumped against the tree, before peering up at Rafal. "It isn't my fault, you see."

Rafal glowered back. "You bring a stranger to our school in my place. A stranger I *rejected* as Dean, now made *School Master*. You bet the future of our school to this reject. You send a love-drunk imbecile into the bet against a young seer smart enough to outwit her own family. And it isn't your fault? Our students are at war, our school torn asunder, and the Storian has been kidnapped by a man who looks like a drunk pirate! Why didn't you fight back with magic? You're a sorcerer! You have *wizard* blood! And you're chased out by dung bombs and threats?"

"Because he played by the rules," said Rhian miserably. "He earned his new castle and the right to keep the Storian in it. Those were the terms of the wager. When my students attacked, he and Evil defended themselves, just as Good would have done. Evil has done nothing wrong, except claim what was owed to them and quash a rebellion by sore losers. If I were to fight back with magic, that would be against the rules of Good. Rules I teach my students to hold sacred. Fighting back would make me *Evil*."

"I'm going to cut out his heart and mount his head in our office," Rafal seethed.

"Which is why you are you and I am me."

"Well, without me, you've made a royal mess of things."

"Which is why you should have never left in the first place, Rafal. There is a reason there are two of us. I need you."

"Flattery."

"I'm stating a fact. A fact you realized on your own or you wouldn't have come back."

"I did just fine alone."

"The Storian told otherwise."

Rafal squinted at his twin. "The Storian told *my* tale?"

"The second tale in a row about you. But this one ended

with you on your way back to me and to balance," said Rhian. "A victory for us both."

And yet it felt nothing like a victory, Rafal thought, shoving away memories of James, sinking in the sea. But he'd done what he had to do. To get back to his brother. To fix what was broken. To make sure Adela Sader's prophecy about him and Rhian never came true.

He sat next to his twin, the two side by side against the tree, like forest vagabonds. The air was still and crisp. Sparrows trilled overhead. A perfectly ordinary morning.

"What do we do now?" Rhian prompted.

"*I'm* supposed to solve this problem?"

"Like I said, I can't fight back. Not without crossing lines to Evil. The Storian would surely punish Good for it."

"So you need me to do your dirty work," said Rafal. "Evil takes revenge on behalf of Good."

"I see it more as you fighting to reclaim your position."

"A position that was mine to begin with and you gave away."

"Whatever the circumstances, we can't let that snake have our school."

"On that we agree," said Rafal, before pausing. "Why did you bring him here in the first place?"

Rhian didn't answer.

"It's because he's handsome, isn't it?" Rafal said. "Betraying your own blood because of a *crush*."

"That's not it," his brother muttered . . . but his cheeks were flushed and he was looking down. "There's more to it than that—"

"Yes, his strength and conviction and drive to bend the world to his will. All the things Evil has and that you lack. No wonder you thrust him the keys to the kingdom. You can't tell whether you want to marry him or switch souls with him," Rafal stung. "Also, what's with the bats?"

"I've been telling you for a while we needed a crest," Rhian scolded, sitting straighter. "And now he's beat us to the punch."

"Bats are passive, shy, trusting, and gentle, everything you *don't* want in a Never," Rafal moaned. "What an insufferable fraud. I'll take great pleasure in his demise. That said, he does have that seer working for him. Which means he'll know every one of our moves before we make it."

"It isn't a fair fight, then," said Rhian. "Look what happened to Aladdin. There's no way to beat him."

"Of course there is."

Rhian cocked his head. "Mmmm?"

"Two School Masters against one," said Rafal, grinning. "Now *that* isn't a fair fight."

2.

Vulcan peered at the Storian, frozen in air, above the empty black desk.

Three days and it had yet to start a new story.

He flicked at it.

"It won't be writing anytime soon," a voice spoke.

Vulcan turned to see Marialena enter his new office and sit down on a black leather chair near the window. She wasn't wearing Evil's black uniform anymore, but instead a draping green caftan and matching headscarf that made her look like a child playing dress-up. She fogged and wiped her glasses clean. Then she glanced around the Evil School Master's chamber, twice the size of the old one, that had less the warm, scattered feel of a library and more the cold metal tones of a dungeon. A large taxidermied bat, fangs bared, glared down from the wall. The bookcases of fairy tales had been dispensed with, the volumes of old stories crammed into black leather chests, stacked in corners. A tall mirror leaned like a ladder, across from a floor-to-ceiling portrait of Vulcan, barechested and clutching a baby tiger. Curios abounded: black crystals, a burnished skull, a periscope, more stuffed bats, dead roses . . . but they all seemed too new and perfectly placed, as if Vulcan's chamber was more a museum than an office.

Marialena turned back to the School Master.

"The Storian won't start a tale until it knows it can finish it," she explained. "And given there are two School Masters who think they should be the Pen's guardians instead of you, the Pen prefers to wait until things are more . . . settled."

Vulcan rested against the stack of chests, his sleeveless black doublet patterned with bats. "This is because Rafal is back. He looks like skinny snowman. So white and stiff. I saw him from window and was tempted to drop stone on his head. But he is no threat. Nevers don't want him. They want me. And I will keep Evers prisoner until they call me Master too. They will learn. Pen will learn too. The schools are mine now."

"And what is it you plan to *do* with the schools?" Marialena asked pointedly.

Vulcan stared at her. Then he grunted and waved away the question. "You know that this Rafal didn't take me for school? When I was the right age, everyone in Netherwood says, 'It will be Vulcan.' But no. So you ask what I will do? Teach Evers that Good is not their master. Vulcan is. Teach Nevers that Evil is not their master. Vulcan is. That's why Rafal didn't take me when I was child. Because I am more than ordinary student. I am Lord of School. Lord of Pen. It will write soon.

You will see. It will write for *me*."

He eyed Marialena, waiting for the seer to agree with this version of his story.

"Do you know why I helped you?" Marialena asked.

"Because you are Evil like me and want our side to win," Vulcan stated.

"No. Evil is only a means to an end," said Marialena. "I don't care whether Evil or Good wins. I care about *protecting* myself. That is why I lied to be picked for this school instead of going to prison with my family. That is why I helped you win the Trial. Because of what I *see*. And in the future, I see a vision of a single School Master. I don't know who it is or where he comes from or what he looks like. The vision is foggy. But it will be one School Master who rules this school instead of two and he will rule for hundreds of years. The one true School Master who redeems my family and takes them under his wing. Because of him, the Saders will no longer be regarded as criminals. Instead, they will be glorified as the greatest seers in the Woods."

"And you think this true School Master is me," said Vulcan.

"I *did* think it was you," Marialena replied curtly. "But I'm not sure you have centuries of leadership in your future if your only plan is to rub our faces in how great you are. You might not be the one I see after all. Especially now that I can sense what's about to happen."

Vulcan screwed her with a look. "What's that?"

"I can't answer questions truthfully without aging ten years," Marialena replied. "I can only offer advice as a friend. There are two outcomes possible. My sight does not favor one over the other. In one scenario, you reason with Rhian and Rafal. You invite them here and get them in your good graces. This ends with the school at peace and all three of you alive. In another scenario, you go to war with them. This leads to bad things happening. And not just to you."

"Oh shame. Bad things will happen to them too," Vulcan tutted mockingly.

"Not to them." Marialena's eyes pierced through her glasses. "To *me*."

Vulcan's gaze narrowed, his lips curling into a scowl. "I won the game. I'm School Master now. And now you think I bring two crybaby chickens up for tea and play nice? Sorry, little girl. I take my chances. Lord Vulcan does not negotiate—"

BANG! BANG! BANG!

Booming eruptions shook the castle, followed by screams.

Marialena gave Vulcan a look. "The chickens have arrived."

The School Master stood there, paralyzed. Then he sprinted out of the room.

Vulcan dashed down the polished black staircase of his

private tower, a gilded bat carved into every step. He began to smell smoke. By the time he reached the foyer, he couldn't see, his throat and eyes clogged, his hands clawing at blinding billows.

A fireball streaked past him.

He whirled to see a shadowy figure, veiled by smoke, singing a shanty and shooting rays of fire from a glowing fingertip, blasting holes in the lacquered black walls. Gangs of first-year Nevers slung hexes at the intruder, but each time, he'd nimbly pirouette and launch a triple-strength spell back, demolishing a wall above them, sending students ducking for cover. All along, he twirled and sang:

> *"I asked the queen . . .*
> *What is more pathetic than a Vulcan?*
> *She said: Nothing I've seen!*
>
> *I asked the seer . . .*
> *What is more useless than a Vulcan?*
> *He said: Nothing! It's clear!*
>
> *I asked the prince . . .*
> *What is more stupid than a Vulcan?*
> *He said: Nothing! I'm convinced!"*

The figure turned and saw Vulcan in the flesh. "Speaking of the devil." Then he stepped through falling ashes, revealing himself in firelight. "It's gauche, your school. None of the grit of *true* Evil. Looks good on the surface, but doesn't hold up," said Rafal, shielded by fire. "Case in point: a few more shots and your tower will fall, with the Pen still in it. If the Storian recognized you as School Master, it would have made you take the oath. To protect it. To respect it. But it didn't, am I right? Well, I'll make *you* an oath. In a matter of minutes, I promise the Pen will return to the *real* School Master." He hurled another flameball past Vulcan, eviscerating the wall behind him.

"You have mouth of yak and brain of fish," Vulcan seethed, trying to charge at him, but there were too many flames in the way. "This tower is pure rock. It will never fall—"

Rafal shot another blast over Vulcan's head. Exploding bricks slammed into Vulcan, burying him. The new School Master let out a savage roar and launched out of the rubble, storming through fire and tackling Rafal. He gripped the Evil twin by the throat and bared his teeth at him, Vulcan's face singed and sweating.

"Your head will hang on my door," he growled.

"Funny. I was just saying I'll do the same to yours," Rafal quipped. "Maybe we *should* be friends."

Vulcan squeezed his throat harder—

"But now that I think about it, we can't be friends . . ." Rafal cut in, losing air. "Because I take my job seriously . . . like protecting the Storian . . . which you've left upstairs . . . completely unsupervised . . . where anyone and their *brother* can steal it . . ."

Vulcan stopped choking him.

Rafal patted his cheek. "A promise is a promise."

Instantly Rafal transformed into a black sparrow, flying through smoke for the door—

A meaty hand slapped the bird to the ground.

Dazed, Rafal's sparrow peeked up to see dirty, hulking Timon put his boot on the bird's neck, his one bloodshot eye glaring down.

"Vulcan is *Lord*," he snarled.

3.

Upstairs at this very moment, Rafal's promise was being kept.

A white owl slipped through the window and touched the ground, reverting back into Rhian. He took one look at the School Master's new office, wincing at the gloomy black furniture, dark crystals, and dead bat over the mantel, sharp fangs gleaming. Then he saw all the storybooks, hundreds of years of original tales, stuffed into dingy treasure chests like pirate booty, and Rhian clutched his heart. Slowly his eyes went to Vulcan's half-naked portrait on the wall. Rhian's cheeks flushed. He raised a glowing finger and revised the School Master's face into a circus clown's, then turned the tiger in his arms into a skunk.

Vandalism was a hallmark of villainy, but for once, it made Rhian feel Good.

How dare Rafal accuse him of wanting to be that ape!

Of wanting to be someone Evil!

Bah!

But clowning his enemy wasn't why he'd come.

He'd come for the Pen.

Rhian took one look at the Storian, dangling dormant over the empty desk, and snatched it into his hands—

"I debated whether to let you have it," said a voice.

Rhian turned to Marialena at the door, wrapped in a ludicrous caftan and headscarf, flanked by twenty Netherwood guards, armed with steel hand cannons.

"If it isn't Madame Medusa, come to tell my fortune," said Rhian, gripping the Pen.

"You're just mad I keep beating you at your own game," Marialena snipped. "Truth is I should be nicer to you. Maybe you're meant to be the Pen's protector. Maybe you're the one true School Master, who will bring glory to me and my family, and

I should just let fate play its course. But then I remember . . ." She looked in Rhian's eyes. "I just don't *like* you."

The guards shot their cannons, launching thick black netting, which tangled Rhian up.

"Don't bother trying to hex your way out of it. It's batwing, which nothing can break through except another bat," Marialena said. "Vulcan's on his way up. And from what I can see, he's *full* of ideas of what to do with you."

She flounced out, leaving the guards there.

Rhian writhed against the net, the Storian clasped in his fingers, but the net only grew heavier, forcing him into submission. He had to get out of here before Vulcan arrived or who knows what he'd have to endure. Rhian thrashed harder, turning his back to the guards—

All of a sudden, the Storian went boiling hot in his grip. He released it in shock, the Pen dropping to the ground. He reached to grab it, but then saw it had come to life, drawing on the stone floor in soft white lines. The guards hadn't noticed, since Rhian's back was turned, but the School Master pretended to struggle, grunting and moaning, while the Storian painted a picture for him . . . a picture of Rhian and the Pen working together to get out of the very situation they were in now . . . like magical instructions . . . a map of action . . .

Rhian peered closer.

At first he couldn't understand.

Then he did.

Nothing can break through except another bat.

The Good School Master grinned.

Indeed.

"Hey! What are you doin—" a guard started.

Rhian snatched the Pen and spun around, a ray of light shooting out of the Storian's tip, straight at the black crystals on Vulcan's desk. Blinding glow refracted into the guards' eyes, and they shouted in surprise, hands up to defend their faces. Rhian aimed the Storian at the giant bat over the mantel and with another blast of light, severed it from its hooks. The bat fell, fangs out, and slashed right through the net, just like Marialena promised.

"Enjoy the view!" Rhian called at the reeling guards. Then he held the Storian firmly and leapt out the window, morphing back into a white owl, which plummeted straight for the Woods.

In the forest, he waited for Rafal.

They'd made the plan to meet here and plot their next move—once Rafal had escaped Vulcan and once Rhian had the Pen.

So far, all had been going to plan, thanks to the Storian's help.

Rhian gazed at the Pen and the strange string of symbols carved into it, as if he was truly seeing it for the first time.

The Storian had rescued him.

It had taken his side.

Again.

First with Aladdin—favoring him over Rafal.

And now a second time—choosing him over Vulcan.

What does that mean?

Is the Pen protecting Good over Evil?

Rhian smiled at the thought . . .

Then his smile vanished.

Goodness meant doing the right thing, not the selfish thing.

Balance was the lifeblood of the Woods.

Good and Evil winning in equal measure, lessons learned on both sides, that fed the souls of the Woods and pushed their world forward.

And they, as twin School Masters, were responsible for this balance.

If the Pen was favoring Good, that meant the balance had broken.

It was his duty to find out why.

Rhian waited anxiously for Rafal.

He could smell smoke drifting on the breeze from the Evil castle.

All part of Rafal's plan.

A diversion, well-executed.

Which meant his Evil twin should be here any minute.

But minutes passed.

Then hours.

Rafal never came.

Rhian's heart fluttered.

Is he safe?

Should I go back and look for him?

Slowly his eyes went back to the Pen. Despite being unsettled by its help . . . he peered at it hopefully, as if it might help him again.

What now? he asked.

The Pen answered like an old friend.

It squirmed from his hands, floated into air, and painted something in white mist . . .

An arrow.

Pointing ahead into the forest.

Rafal? he thought.

Quickly, Rhian followed the arrow, through longleaf bushes and wildflower vines, his boots trampling twigs and sliding over rocks . . . until he heard two boys' voices ahead.

"You can't kill Rafal," snapped the first. "Not until we rescue my girlfriend."

"Your girlfriend is none of my concern," groused the second.

Rhian peered between vines . . .

"*Aladdin?*" he blurted.

The young thief spun round, bruised and battered, his shirt ripped, his eyes on the Good School Master.

But that wasn't the only surprise, Rhian saw now.

The bigger shock was the boy Aladdin was talking to.

The one who wanted to kill Rafal.

He recognized him from the Storian's last tale.

It was James Hook.

4.

When someone who wants you dead doesn't kill you when they have the chance . . . it's not a good sign.

This is what Rafal thought, his teeny black sparrow trapped somewhere in the new School for Evil. After Timon slapped his beak and plucked a few feathers and started to *eat* the bird alive, Vulcan had interceded and put the sparrow in a cage, covering it with a heavy black sheet, so Rafal couldn't sense what was in store for him. He'd tried mogrifying into an ant or a worm to sneak his way out, but the spell did nothing, as if the cage or cloak thwarted magic. Probably one of Humburg's hexes, he thought, remembering how Rhian told him that Evil's Dean was working for the new School Master. Surely Humburg was just playing along with Vulcan's games, so he could free Rafal when he had the chance. Oh, how he and Humburg would enjoy punishing that swaggering, swollen-headed ass . . . Rafal's feathers ruffled, teenage hormones revving inside his little bird form, that boiling mix of rage and ego he always struggled to control, the curse of immortal youth. No matter how much wisdom or experience he accrued throughout centuries, his young body betrayed him. Too much emotion. Too much life. Rhian was the only one who could balance him, who could calm him down . . .

But where *was* Rhian?

Had he escaped with the Pen? Or was he caught too, having the same worried thoughts for his brother—

The sheet suddenly whisked off and the little sparrow blinked at a giant face glaring through cage bars.

The eyes were jaundiced and bloodshot, the skin so pruny and wrinkled that for a moment Rafal wondered if he was looking at a real head or a shrunken one.

Dean Humburg poked the bird through the bars. "You're alive."

Rafal smacked him with his wing. "I'm immortal, you idiot! Now hurry and help me out of here!"

Humburg unlocked the cage and snatched the sparrow into his fist, Rafal sighing with relief—until Humburg dumped the bird in a bag of white fabric. Before Rafal could react, a green spell shot into the bag, Humburg's signature color, reverting Rafal from bird to man, and he sprung up into his tall, lean body . . . only to find himself bound and swallowed by the white cloth. It was a *straitjacket*, holding him in place, and when he stuck his head through, he saw a velvet curtain, the color of blood, and Dean Humburg standing in front of it, admiring his work in trapping his once-superior.

Rafal narrowed his eyes. "So much for *loyalty*."

"The job of a Dean is to be loyal to a School Master and you are not School Master anymore," Humburg pointed out. "I'd prefer to have a job rather than wait around aimlessly for your return. Wouldn't you have done the same?"

"No," said Rafal, "which is why I'm School Master and you are a peon and when I return to my position, you will beg me on your knees to take you back and I will deal with you in the way you deserve."

"I'm afraid you won't have your position back anytime soon," said Humburg.

He opened the curtain.

Rafal looked out and saw he was onstage in a dark, macabre theater, glazed black arches and pews separated by aisles of bloodred velvet. The Nevers were gathered on one side of the audience, dressed in glamorous black outfits, their expressions stony and cold. On the other side of the theater were the Evers, sleepless and ragged, their hands bound with rope or chain.

"What is this?" said Rafal.

"A trial," said a voice.

Vulcan came through the door, his black robe gleaming with gold-sewn bats. "You think you are School Master. I think I am School Master. So we let students choose. Whoever they pick stays. And the other . . . they *go*."

"Go?" Rafal scoffed, straining against his straitjacket. "I'd like to see you make me try—"

But now he saw who was entering the theater behind Vulcan.

A familiar brown-skinned woman glided down the aisle in a slim pantsuit of gold lamé and a glowing blue necklace in the shape of an orb. She had a beehive of braids, her lips were painted gold, and she had rhinestones around her eyes.

Twenty guards marched in behind her.

"Whoever the students do not recognize as School Master is an impostor and will serve the remainder of their life in Monrovia Prison," Quintana said, glaring at Rafal. "No matter how long or indefinite that life span may *be*."

Rafal glanced between Vulcan and Quintana and bared his teeth. "The *Storian* chooses the School Master. The Pen decides, not the students—"

"The Pen is gone," said Vulcan.

"Gone?" Rafal repeated, thrown.

"Stolen by your brother and no longer on school grounds," said Quintana, "which is why the wards of Monrovia have been summoned. The theft of the Storian is an unforgivable crime."

Rafal tensed. *Rhian had the Pen?* That meant he'd completed his mission and gone to the Woods to find his twin. But he'd know by now that Rafal was in trouble. Where was he, then? Why hadn't he come?

Vulcan snapped him out of his thoughts—"Call the first witness."

A gangly, freckled girl walked up. Rafal recognized her as a Never named Brinsha. He'd had high hopes for her, but she'd proven lifeless and mediocre.

Quintana asked, "Who is School Master?"

Brinsha: "Vulcan."

Next came an Everboy named Madigan with a black eye, his fists cuffed together.

"Who is School Master?" Quintana questioned.

"Vulcan," Madigan croaked.

Rafal watched as they went down the line, Ever and Never, Vulcan leering at him with a smile, which grew wider and wider each time his name was spoken. Rafal's blood boiled under his skin. Silently, he repeated each student's name, Brinsha, Madigan, Gemma, Fodor, Abram, Nagila, name after name after name that he and his twin had given the privilege of acceptance, the honor of being here, and names who now betrayed him, blooming a single, obsessive thought in the darkest pit of his soul.

All of you will pay.

5.

"You're supposed to be *dead*," the Good School Master said, the Storian pointed like a sword at the young Hook. "That's what I read in your story. So unless you have a very good reason why you're *un*dead and threatening to kill my brother, I'll fix your ending the way it was."

"Go ahead and kill me. I'm not scared anymore," Hook spat. "If you read my story, you know your brother lied and cheated and left me at the bottom of the sea. What he didn't know is that the youngest Sader son still had his prisoner's necklace, which let him breathe underwater and swim down and rescue me. When I asked him why, he said I didn't deserve to die. Not after what Rafal did to me. His family had flagged down a passing ship and we all sailed to the seashore before parting ways. Then I made my way here and met . . . him."

Rhian followed his eyes to Aladdin, bloodied and bruised.

"This is all your fault," the Shazabah boy accused the School Master. "I had a girlfriend, people liked me, the Storian made me famous . . . my kind of Ever After . . . until *you* brought that new guy in and the whole place went to hell. Vulcan ties all us Evers up, the Nevers harass us into submission, and either we swear our loyalty to him as the new School Master of *both* schools or die. Naturally, my girlfriend Kyma refuses, because she's stubborn like that, and they lock her in an Evil tower somewhere. So I fight back, demanding to know where they put her, and they nearly clobber me to death, before I jump out a window and escape. Then I run into pirate boy here and ask him to help me find my girlfriend and instead, he asks me for help killing your brother."

"You are welcome to try killing my *immortal* brother if you can find where he is," Rhian barbed at James. "He was supposed to be here a long time ago—"

"Well, my girlfriend *isn't* immortal," Aladdin protested, "so we need to find her first—"

Voices rose behind them.

The boys turned to see the bushes part and a clear, silvery ball bounce into the clearing, with a figure crammed inside, fists chained to ankles, a gag in his mouth.

"*Rafal?*" said Rhian from across the field.

His brother was shouting wildly into his gag—

Twenty guards marched through the bushes behind him, swords and shields out, along with a regal woman in a black pantsuit.

"Deserves to be kicked all the way back to Monrovia," she gloated, punting Rafal's ball again.

It hit Rhian in the face.

"Ow!"

Quintana stared at him across the clearing.

Then at James Hook next to him.

"*You*," Quintana seethed.

Hook spun to Rhian. "Do something!"

Rhian pointed the Storian at Quintana and the guards, expecting it to help.

It didn't.

Twenty guards came at them with swords and spears—

Instantly, Rhian rolled the ball with Rafal in the other direction.

Hook and Aladdin flanked him on either side, the three of them tumbling Rafal through the forest, the Evil School Master flailing around like a fish in a barrel.

"Faster!" Rhian exhorted.

"Noooooooo!" Rafal gurgled inside.

Quintana and the guards chased them, the boys pushing Rafal over logs and rocks, through huckleberry and spice bushes, Rhian hurling hexes back at the guards, which they deflected with their shields. Hook and Aladdin tried to puncture Rafal's bubble with twigs and sticks, Rhian tried with spells and the Storian, but like the guards' shields, it was impervious to magic. All the while, the Evil School Master bellowed and cursed into his gag, at once furious, incredulous, and motion sick. But there was no end in sight, guards gaining ground as the boys shuttled Rafal through a fernfield, then booted his ball over a stream, before catching it on the other side, the chase resuming down the hill. For miles they ran, neither side tiring, until the forest thinned, giving way to rocky slope.

Soon, they smelled salt air, and a thick mist rolled in, the sign that the seashore was coming. As fog flooded off water they couldn't yet see, they swiveled to Quintana and the guards closing in, 150 feet, 100 feet, 50 feet . . .

"What do we do!" Aladdin gasped.

The guards charged, blades out—

BOOM!

A cannonball flew into the guards, blasting the frontline into the distance.

Quintana and her remaining men gaped at each other.

"*Retreat!*" Quintana cried, and they went scampering into the trees.

Gobsmacked, Rhian and the boys turned back towards the sea.

A ship broke through the fog, skull-and-bones flag flying, the cannon still smoking, boys in pirate hats hanging from the mast and hooting with delight.

From the prow, a young man leapt down, dark and muscular. He raised his wide-brimmed hat, revealing tussled brown hair, dewy green eyes, and a cheeky smile.

"Hello, boys," said the Pirate Captain of Blackpool.

Rhian stared, his breath caught, a hot flush in his cheeks.

Then he saw his brother glowering at him through the bubble.

The hot flush went cold.

6.

"My boys heard the Storian's tale. They weren't happy about Rafal leaving Hook to die, even if they can't stand the lad," the Pirate Captain spoke, pushing open a window in his cramped, musty captain's quarters aboard the *Buccaneer*. "Pirates are loyal, even to the runt in the family. So we decide to take the old ship out and confront Rafal about killing one of our own. Then lo and behold, we find Hook alive and Rafal in trouble!"

He turned to Rafal, who was still inside his bubble, slightly green and shaky from his tumble through the forest. They'd perched the ball on top of a messy table, strewn with maps and captain's logs, the seats around the table occupied by Rhian, Aladdin, and Hook.

"We're thankful for your help, Pirate Captain," Rhian said, the Storian tucked behind his ear. "The magic binding Rafal seems impenetrable. But pirates have broken through Monrovia's enchantments before. You must know how to free him."

"Indeed," the Pirate Captain said.

Rhian sat taller. "So help us. Let's join forces to take back our school."

"*Your* school, not ours. And quite sure James wants your

brother *dead*," the Pirate Captain replied, taking a seat at the head of the table. "Given I sent Hook off with him, it's only fair James decides what's to be done with Rafal."

"Kill him," Hook demanded, scowling at the Evil School Master. "Eye for an eye."

Rhian barked back: "You're still *alive!*"

"True," said the Pirate Captain, "and killing an immortal sorcerer sounds more work than it's worth. So how about we make a deal?"

"A deal . . . ," Rhian said warily.

"We'll help you free your brother and take back your school, after which James and my students will sail back to Blackpool." Hook opened his mouth to protest but the Captain held up his hand, his eyes on the Good School Master. "And in return for your brother's freedom and our peaceful departure, you give us the smallest of gifts."

Rhian leaned forward. "What gift?"

"*That*," said the Pirate Captain.

He pointed at the Storian in Rhian's hair.

The room went quiet, maps blowing in the wind.

Rafal burst out laughing, so hard he rolled his ball off the table. (Aladdin hurried to help him.)

Rhian goggled at the Captain. "The Pen? Turned over to *you?*"

The Pirate Captain looked utterly sincere. "And why not? I'm a School Master, am I not? And why wouldn't the stories of Blackpool graduates be any less worthy than those of the School for Good and Evil?"

Rhian stared at him, befuddled. "You are *pirates*. You are exiles and pests in other people's stories."

"And isn't that what you and your brother are now? Exiled *pests*?" the Pirate Captain pointed out. "That's why the Pen isn't writing a new tale, right? Because it has no *home*? Because it doesn't feel *safe*?"

Rhian felt the Pen burn hot behind his ear. Whether because it was agreeing with the Captain or disputing him, Rhian wasn't sure. But given the Pen had helped Rhian twice before, he told himself it was the latter. "The Storian chose me," the Good School Master gritted. "It chose me *and* my brother. We took the oath, not you. So no. You can't have the Pen that rules our *world*."

Rafal harrumphed inside the bubble, echoing his twin.

"Very well, then," the Captain said, standing. "I'll usher you out. Good luck recapturing your school."

Rhian stood angrily. "You can't be serious about this—"

"Perfectly serious," the Captain reasoned. "At Blackpool, the Storian would be well-protected. A new center of power in the Woods. Finally, pirates will get the respect we deserve. And in return, you win your school and brother back."

Rhian fired back: "Over my dead bod—"

"*I'll* give it to you," said a voice.

They turned to see Aladdin, his eyes on the Captain. "On the condition that you help me rescue my girlfriend from the Evil school."

Aladdin held up the Storian. "Do we have a deal?"

Rhian blanched. He reached behind his ear, only to find soft curls of hair.

"Learned from Seer Girl when she stole my flag," Aladdin said. "Sorry, School Master. But Kyma's my princess."

Flabbergasted, Rafal pounded on his bubble wall—

"You have a deal," said the Captain.

Before Rhian could make a move, Aladdin tossed the Captain the Pen.

The Captain slid it in his jacket.

Instantly, Rhian raised a glowing finger at the Captain's head—

"Careful," the pirate warned. "Do something stupid and you'll never get your brother free."

Slowly Rhian lowered his finger.

Rafal let out a thundering howl.

Soon after, the Pirate Captain led the group to the galley, Hook, Aladdin, and Rhian rolling Rafal's ball behind them.

The Blackpool boy who served as chef aboard the *Buccaneer* stood at attention, hands full of shrimp, his face flecked with curry powder. "Yessir?"

"Bring me the electric eel we keep in the kitchen tank," the Captain ordered.

"Yessir," said the boy, hustling away.

The Captain addressed Rhian. "Monrovia Prison is built so deep undersea that it's powered by bioluminescence—an electric charge that creatures at such depth possess. What we perceive as magic is nature's electricity," he said, accepting a white bucket from the chef. "To break this magic, then, all you need to do is cancel out the charge. Which is why every pirate ship in the Woods keeps one of *these*."

He reached into the bucket, yanked out an electric eel, and held the creature against the surface of Rafal's ball. All at once, the eel and the bubble sizzled with a blinding neon flash, a shockwave reverberating through both, before the Captain dropped the eel in the bucket and handed it back to the chef. Then he took a kitchen knife and popped Rafal's bubble with a firm, sharp blow.

The Evil School Master dropped to the ground.

Rafal sparked his fingerglow, slashed it through his chains, and tore out his gag. Then he stabbed his lit finger at everyone in the room, magically slamming them against the wall, the chef boy included.

"I'M IN CHARGE NOW," Rafal boomed.

From his finger, he conjured a whip made of ice and lashed it at the Pirate Captain, thieving the Storian from inside his jacket and reclaiming it into his hands—

Suddenly the Pen went hot, burning the Evil School Master's flesh and forcing him to drop it with a gasp.

Aladdin swiped the Storian off the floor, tossed it to the Pirate Captain, who handled it with ease, the steel gone cold, and slid it back into his jacket.

"Mmm, Pen seems to think *I'm* in charge," the Captain corrected.

The Evil School Master glanced down at his scorched palm. Slowly he met Rhian's eyes, both twins unnerved. Rhian, that the Storian had sided with someone that wasn't him. Rafal, that it had sided with anyone at all.

"Now, would you like me to help you take back your school or would you prefer to continue being *pests*?" the Captain asked.

Both brothers looked at each other, no more moves to make, the fight draining out of them—

A black boot flew across the room and smacked Rafal in the head.

Everyone turned to Hook.

"Just fell off my foot," James murmured.

Lunch was served outside, bowls of bone broth with curry powder and a shrimp cassoulet. Morning fog had broken to a muggy afternoon, the *Buccaneer* anchored offshore, near the forest that led towards the School for Good and Evil.

All the boys sat around the rim of the deck, elbows to knees, eating quietly as the Pirate Captain paced the floorboards, a tabby cat nipping at his heels.

"We are no longer in a classroom, lads. Your first true mission as pirates is about to begin. The goal is clear: take back the schools from Vulcan of Netherwood and restore these men to rule." He nodded at Rhian and Rafal, both seated on barrels in front of him. "At stake is the right to host the Storian within Blackpool's walls. To finally shed the labels given to us—vandals, hooligans, ingrates—and earn some good old-fashioned respect. Look, I know I'll never find the Hook that beats the Pan. Each Hook only gets worse—" He threw a look at James, who glared back stiffly. "But if we can't have the Pan, at least we'll have the Pen!" He peeled back his jacket and the Storian floated out from inside and hovered over his open palm. The Blackpool boys let out an "*oooh*," ogling the legendary instrument. Even the Captain's cat blinked twice. "The power to command the

Woods' attention is in our hands. But only if we have the courage and prowess to fight and *win*," the Captain said. "So listen carefully."

He turned to the twins. "What are we up against?"

"Besides traitors to our own school?" Rhian glared at Aladdin, seated close.

Aladdin reddened. "And here I thought a Good School Master would reward a student who stood up for love."

Rhian fumbled to respond—

"Told you he'd be better in my school," Rafal needled his brother.

Rhian swung back to the Captain. "Want to know what we're up against? Two schools, fifty students each. Nevers will fight for Vulcan out of loyalty and Evers will fight for him out of fear."

"A hundred? Ain't only twelve of us!" one of the boys blurted.

"Aye!" the other boys chorused.

"Since when are pirates cowed by *numbers*?" a familiar voice piped and they all turned to James Hook under the mast. "That's the point of pirates: to take down forces bigger than us by being nimble and quick as thieves! It's why I came to Blackpool. To find a crew who can help me beat the Pan. A Pan who has all of Neverland on his side. But doesn't matter how many Lost Boys and mermaids and island warriors he's got fighting for him. The right kind of crew, bold, ruthless, *fearless*, can take him down. Are *you* that crew? Are you the ones who can kill Peter Pan? Well, you need to prove yourself to me, just like I need to prove myself to you. I know the Pirate Captain thinks I can't do it. And I know you lot doubt me too and think I'm not up to snuff. But the Storian's told my tale. The Pen chose me. The Pen we're fighting for now. Can the Pirate Captain say that?" The Captain raised his brows, but James gained steam. "I've already proved myself. I've shown I'll do anything—Good, Evil, and everything in between—to be a better Hook than my father or his father before him. The Hook that makes Blackpool proud. I've survived blood-drinking Night Crawlers, murderous sorcerers, and death at the bottom of the sea to be here and fight with you. To lead you. As *your* captain. Let's take back this school. Let's claim the Pen for ourselves. And hell, twelve Blackpool pirates are worth more than a thousand namby-pamby Evers and Nevers, I say!"

"*Huzzah!*" the boys cried, jumping to their feet, spilling broth and bowls. "*Captain Hook! Captain Hook! Captain Hook!*"

"That's the half of it, James," Rafal snarled. "Vulcan has a seer working for him. A girl who can see everything before it happens."

The chanting died down.

"Blimey, that don't sound good," a ferret-looking boy spoke out. "How we gunna beat a gal like that?"

Hook leapt onto the mast, swinging from the rig. "Only future she'll see is us running rampant over her school!"

"*Huzzah!*" the boys roared. "Hook! Hook! Hook!"

"And Vulcan has sixty Netherwood soldiers and a fleet of giant wolves," Rhian added, "plus those Monrovia guards, armed with lethal weapons and magic."

The Blackpool boys went mum. They looked at Hook.

"Maybe we should sail back home," Hook wisped.

The Pirate Captain laughed. "Oh, James."

He caressed the Storian dancing over his palm.

"Difference between you and a real captain is the worse the odds of a game are, the more I can't wait to play."

7.

Marialena dressed in her room for the feast.

It was to be a night of celebration, the official start to Vulcan's reign as School Master now that Rhian and Rafal had been evicted and Evers and Nevers had both sworn allegiance to Vulcan. She'd been in the theater when the students took their oath to the new School Master, sealing Rafal's fate. Hidden in shadows, she'd watched the Monrovia guards lock him in a balltrap, her heart skittering. Had she made the right choice aligning with Vulcan over the brothers? Had she picked the one true School Master? The one she'd foreseen who would do right by her family?

Marialena had tried to silence her doubts.

All her loyalty was with Vulcan now.

Not just because he'd outwitted the twins.

But because it was too late to change course.

Vulcan was School Master and Rhian and Rafal were gone.

In her room, she put up her hair and cinched her elaborate petticoat. She slipped her best dress over it, a boxy black gown with a stylish veil that her brothers said made her look like a witch bride, but it suited her mood. Between Vulcan, Rhian, and Rafal, she'd had her fill of entitled boys. But it was all worth it. In time, she'd be reunited with her family, and the new School Master would give the Saders the respect and power they deserved.

If she'd seen right, that is.

If she'd *chosen* right.

Doubt creeped back into her.

She sat on the edge of her bed in the ornate dorm room, with a black silk canopy, black leather couches, and lustrous black wallpaper patterned with gold bats. She closed her eyes, struggling to concentrate. But nothing came. This had never happened before. She could always see *something*. But since Rafal had been wheeled out by those Monrovia guards, her mind had gone blank. As if she had no powers at all. Is this what other people felt like? Living without knowing what was coming? Prisoners to infinite possibilities, so vulnerable and exposed? If so, she felt pity for all their souls.

She closed her eyes and listened harder for answers that didn't come.

Instead, she heard a rustling from her closet.

Slowly, she rose and went to it.

Marialena unlocked the door.

Inside, a girl was bound and gagged, thrashing with muffled shouts amidst racks of clothes.

Marialena smiled at Princess Kyma. "What's that? I can't hear you."

Kyma spat out her gag. "You think he won't find me? Aladdin is relentless."

"Depending on a boy to save you. Groundbreaking," said Marialena.

"A boy who *loves* me," Kyma shot back. "And you know how the stories go. Love always wins."

"Not as long as I have you," Marialena replied calmly. "The more a boy loves you, the more you're worth as a hostage. Don't need my powers to see that."

Kyma exploded: "You jealous, bitter little—"

Marialena pulled Kyma's gag tighter, silencing the princess.

"Don't think you two will last, by the way," she cooed.

Then she relocked the closet, drew down her veil, and made her way to the feast.

8.

"They got away?" Vulcan asked in his office, pulling on a glittering silver-and-black cape in front of a mirror.

"With the Storian," Quintana admitted, surrounded by Monrovia guards. "Pirates arrived on Blackpool's ship to rescue them. Must be long gone by now."

"I see," said Vulcan. He picked the periscope off his desk and stepped to the window, peering through and over the forest. "The *Buccaneer* is still docked at shore. Doesn't look gone at all. Hmm. You and your guards so effective! It's a wonder you have prisoners left in your jail."

Quintana stiffened. "We'll regather and attack—"

"I have a rule," said Vulcan. "Never trust a *fool* twice."

He gave Quintana a stare, then returned to the mirror.

The Monrovia warden blushed. "But the Storian—"

"—will be on its way back soon enough," Vulcan finished.

"You didn't do your job, so now I'll have to do mine. Seems like our feast tonight will have *guests*."

Under his feet rose the echoes of a fiery drumbeat.

Down below, in the courtyard of an Evil tower, a boy named Asrael swallowed a skewer of fire and spewed it back out his nose, officially commencing the feast.

A hundred Evers and Nevers had gathered in the open-air plaza, aglow with red and gold candles, students jostling for food from the buffet line before taking their seats at the banquet tables, the red linens stitched with gold-leaf bats. After the Evers had sworn loyalty and been released from their binds, Vulcan had gone out of his way to make the Good students feel welcome, insisting he'd be a School Master for all, though the fact he'd held the feast at the Evil castle reminded the Evers where his true loyalties lay. Two Everboys waited in line, salivating at the scent of mint-leaf salad, hen-egg risotto, veal tagine, za'atar-spiced scallops, capsicum potatoes, saffron rice, and an array of pistachio-milk pastilles and chocolate honey cakes.

"Heard he melted down an enchanted pot to scare the other pots into cooking the feast," said Rufius.

"And I heard Master Rhian got the Storian back," Hephaestus whispered. "That he stole it before he escaped!"

Rufius straightened. "If that's true, then Vulcan *isn't* School

Master. Not officially. And if he isn't School Master . . . we *have* to fight! We have to take back our school!"

"We're outnumbered and surrounded," Hephaestus said, his eyes roving to the dozens of wolves and Netherwood guards around the perimeter. More were standing on top of the walls that hemmed in the courtyard, carrying swords and crossbows. "Even Dean Mayberry's given up," he added, watching Good's professor at a banquet table, sullenly eating cake after cake. Her index finger on her right hand had been capped with a silver thimble, presumably to lock her magic and prevent her from considering resistance. "Even if all us Evers banded together, we'd get crushed," said Hephaestus. "Unless . . . we somehow get Nevers on our side—"

"Out of our way, losers," Timon growled, shoving them to the ground and cutting in front with eight other Nevers.

"We're in line!" Rufius protested, but the Evil gang cackled.

"What you gonna do? Appeal to our sense of *fairness*?" a spindly Nevergirl heckled. "Good means nothing in this place anymore. This is *our* school now. Might as well get used to it—"

A hand gripped her by the throat. She whirled around.

"By that logic, you better get used to this too," said Vulcan calmly, gazing into her eyes as he squeezed. "Because both schools are *mine*. Yes?"

The entire courtyard had gone silent, watching the School Master who had just entered, strangling one of his own.

"Y-y-yes, Master," the girl sputtered.

He released her, then motioned Hephaestus and Rufius to the front of the line. "In my school, Evers and Nevers are respected equally . . ."

The two boys shuffled forward, before Vulcan finished his sentence.

". . . as long as they respect *me* equally."

Hephaestus spun, glaring into Vulcan's eyes.

"Anything to say, Everboy?" the School Master offered. "Anything on behalf of *all* your Evers?"

Hephaestus bared his teeth, his face crimson, his chest vibrating with fury. He could see his fellow Evers watching him, petrified. Wolves and guards fingered their weapons, ready for a rebellion. A rebellion that would punish every Good student for the words Hephaestus wanted to say.

But that is the difference between Good and Evil.

Good puts others above themselves.

"No, Lord Vulcan," said Hephaestus.

Vulcan smirked. "Good boy." He swept away, his cape shimmering behind him. He raised his arms, addressing the crowd.

"Lord Vulcan welcomes you to my *new* School for Evil and Goo—"

The gates to the courtyard blew open and a swarm of bats flew in, black as death, flapping their wings furiously and shrieking at fever pitch, sending Evers and Nevers diving for cover and Vulcan shrinking into his cape, before the bats suddenly swirled into formation and slashed out of the courtyard, into the night.

Candle flames crackled.

Flies burnt up with spits and snaps.

Slowly everyone lifted their heads.

Left behind in the bats' path was a figure in black.

A girl in a boxy gown, hair in a topknot, her face obscured by a veil.

Guards instantly aimed their arrows.

"Let me guess," Vulcan said, leering. "You come in *peace*."

"Don't you recognize me?" said the girl, in a quiet voice.

Vulcan hesitated. He stepped forward and glimpsed the girl's oversized glasses, glinting through her lace.

"Marialena?"

He moved closer—

"Stay back!" she ordered. "Even the slightest movement will cloud my sight. On my way here, I heard noises from a bathroom. So I went inside and saw *pirates* coming through the window. They'd scaled the tower and found their way in . . ." Her voice quickened. "They gagged me, bound me, *blindfolded* me. Somehow I hadn't seen them coming. I'd lost touch with my own powers. But the blindfold changed everything. Suddenly, in the darkness, I could see clearer than ever! I saw how to escape, how to run here and warn you that they're on the hunt. Rhian. Rafal. Blackpool pirates. They're coming to punish us all. But I can't see anymore. I can't see how to save us. Not with all this light. Even this veil is not enough." She jumped on top of a table and blew out the candles. "Help me bring darkness!" She blew out more candles through her veil. "Darkness so I can see!"

No one moved for a second, but then she grazed by Hephaestus, blowing out more candles, and for a second the girl's eyes met his through her veil.

Hephaestus jolted, then whirled to the crowd. "Help her! Help her bring darkness!" He sprang into action, dousing every candle in sight, and gave Rufius a boot to the behind, spurring him to action too. "Darkness so she can see!"

"Darkness so she can see!" the Evers chorused, blowing out candles, obeying Hephaestus, their leader, and soon the Nevers followed, not wanting to seem delinquent in helping their prized seer, who'd won the Trial and made all of this possible.

Vulcan stood mystified for a moment, watching everyone

snuffing out the light, wolves and guards too, and before he could even register what was happening, the veiled girl blew the last candle and the courtyard went black, not a sliver of glow to be found.

Crickets sang in the dark.

Then a torch roared to life, a raging flame in the middle of the plaza.

The girl wielding it.

"I'm trying to be Good," she sighed. "That's where the Storian says I belong. So let me be honest. All that stuff about darkness and sight? That was a lie."

She pulled down her veil and shook out her hair, revealing . . . Aladdin.

"But all that stuff about pirates breaking in and finding Marialena in the bathroom? *That* was true."

He pointed his torch ahead—

At the courtyard gates, the Pirate Captain held Marialena in her petticoat, the young seer bound and gagged without her glasses.

Around the courtyard, torches sparked, Blackpool boys jumping wolves and guards from behind and cuffing them all to a long metal chain.

Hook snapped the end of the chain on Quintana, before

pulling an electric eel from a bucket and brandishing it to the sky. *"LET IT BEGIN!"*

He slammed the eel against the chain—

Sizzling shock surged through the metal, electrifying all the guards and knocking them out, their bodies collapsing off the wall.

Pirates swiped their swords and crossbows and leapt into the courtyard, unleashing a blizzard of arrows.

Vulcan swelled with rage. *"KILL THEM!"* he bellowed, charging into the fray, bashing Blackpool boys away with his fists. Hook came at the School Master with twin swords, but Vulcan kicked him in the stomach and smashed Hook's face into a table, gashing his forehead and spraying his blood. He grabbed Hook's neck again, twisting hard, about to snap it—

A force threw him against a wall.

Two forces.

"Rejected you as a student. Rejected you as a Dean. Yet here you are," said Rafal.

"About to be rejected as School Master too," said Rhian.

"The skinny dumb-dumbs," Vulcan sneered, his face specked with James' blood. "If you don't want to end up on bottom of my shoe . . . I suggest you return the Pen to me. You have no more power here. Students are on my side."

"Nevers are on your side. This is true," Rafal admitted to Rhian.

Rhian shrugged. "Let's ask the Evers, shall we?"

Hephaestus and a mob of Good students flanked the twins, cornering Vulcan.

"That would be a *no*," said Hephaestus.

The Evers tackled Vulcan, so swift and ruthless that all Vulcan could muster was a single bat-like screech.

"One problem solved," said Rhian.

Rafal eyed the Pirate Captain, chaining Marialena beneath the buffet table, before the Captain plunged into the fight. "One problem to go."

"I see no problem," said the Good School Master, watching the strong, handsome Captain battle the united Nevers with bare hands. "Just look at him . . ."

"The Storian, you dunderheaded dolt! He has the Storian! The one you and your lovestruck thief boy gave away!" Rafal lashed. "And from the way you're looking at Captain Muscles, your thief isn't the only one who's a lovestruck *fool*. Didn't you learn from the *last* visitor you were drawn to?"

Rhian snapped to attention. "How do we get the Pen back? We tried once and it nearly burnt you to a crisp! The Storian won't let us break a deal. Aladdin set the terms: Pirate Captain helps us and in return, he keeps the Pen. There's no way around it—"

Vulcan threw Evers off him, rising out of the mound, hair wild, face gashed, roaring like a woken bear. He lunged for the brothers, crushing their skulls together and toppling them to the stone floor. Vulcan grabbed Rhian by the throat, pummeling him with punches to the face. A sharp glow lit up behind Vulcan and he turned to see Rafal blast a spell at him, careening him into the wall. Vulcan recovered in a split second, as if every blow made him stronger, and he head-slammed into both twins before either could shoot another spell. Evers rushed to defend the brothers, Nevers to attack them, with pirates joining the mob, and soon the courtyard turned into a giant wrestling pit, with dirty, sweaty bodies writhing and kicking and trampling, until no one knew who was who and what they were fighting for anymore.

Aladdin snatched Hephaestus out of the pile. "Where's Kyma?"

"How should I know? She's *your* girlfriend," Hephaestus growled. "Nice trick with the veil, by the way. Once I saw your shifty little eyes—"

"We have to find her!" Aladdin demanded.

"She could be hidden anywhere!" Hephaestus argued. "It'll

take us forever to case the castle, unless someone knows where she is . . ."

His eyes widened. Aladdin read his mind.

Both boys whirled to Marialena, gagged under the buffet table.

Aladdin ripped out her gag. "You can see everything, can't you? Tell us where Kyma is."

"Oh, *you*," said Marialena, eyeing him and Hephaestus. "I'll never understand boys. The idea that both of you are in love with that wispy, whiny—"

A pastille smacked her in the cheek.

"Say one more thing about my girlfriend and you'll be covered in the whole feast," Aladdin warned.

"Better to just tell him where she is," Hephaestus advised Marialena. "He has no boundaries when it comes to Kyma. Boys' code, included."

Aladdin stared down his friend. "You decked me full-throttle at the Snow Ball and I let it go and here you are clinging to old grudges. And my eyes are not *shifty*—"

Timon clobbered them from behind.

"Thank you," said Marialena as the one-eyed hulk freed her, before she stepped over Aladdin and Hephaestus, dazed on the floor. "They were giving me a headache." She hurried out of the courtyard, past the swamp pit of bodies.

In the melee, Vulcan scrapped with Rhian for the upper hand.

"I see how you look at me, Duckling. Needy. Weak. Like you wish you could do our story all over and end happy happy," Vulcan taunted, on top of him. "Your brother is not enough for you. You want a man who puts you in your *place*."

Rhian flipped him over, pinning him down. "My love for my brother keeps us alive. Long after you're dead."

Vulcan searched his eyes. "No . . . There is a rot in you, Duckling. Killing me won't fix it."

Rhian stared at him a beat too long. Vulcan clubbed him in the face—

Nearby, Rafal grappled with Humburg and Timon, the Evil School Master struggling to fight off the Evil Dean and Neverboy.

Rafal tried to cast a curse, but Timon crushed the School Master's hand under him, preventing him from sparking his fingerglow. Humburg battered Rafal with stun spells, the Evil School Master's consciousness fading. There was something humiliating about being foiled by his own student and Dean, who'd both gleefully abandoned all loyalty to him. Rafal ripped out of his stupor and kicked Humburg in the neck, knocking him backwards. Timon grabbed Rafal by the hair and raised his elbow, about to bring it down between his eyes . . . James Hook threw himself in between them, taking the blow to his stomach. In the split second of Timon's surprise, Hook belted the cyclops in the head, careening him off-balance, just long enough for James to spin to Rafal.

"Give me your powers again!" James urged him.

Rafal gaped at him, struck by the lad's loyalty. Even after everything that had happened between them, Hook was still helping him.

"Do it!" James demanded.

As bodies swayed and toppled around them, Rafal breathed a piece of his soul into the boy, Hook turning cold once more—

Timon came roaring for vengeance, armed with a sword, swinging for them both . . . only to see Hook and Rafal face him united and blast two jets of glow, chilling the one-eyed Neverboy in a block of ice.

James slumped against the School Master, bleeding and battered, the two of them sinking with exhaustion into the pit.

"Your Nevers are strong," James said. "What I would give to have them on my crew, fighting Pan. We'd be unstoppable."

Rafal snorted. "Vulcan's Nevers. Not mine. They fight for him, not me."

James was quiet, watching these Nevers fight.

"Come with me to Neverland," he said.

Rafal spun to him, surprised.

"We can fight the Pan together," Hook proposed breathlessly. "If we join forces, Pan won't stand a chance! Think of it. Your magic inside me? Nothing can stop us. We'll be two sorcerer pirates, bonded by your soul. Kings of Neverland. Brothers in arms, far from the prison of this school. The right ending to your story. To *our* story."

Rafal's heart filled with warmth. The idea was daft, impractical, irresponsible, and yet he found himself lost inside it—before he yanked out of his thoughts. "And Rhian?"

"You left him once before," James pointed out.

Rafal gazed at James.

A warning echoed.

"Betrayal. War. Death."

Slowly Rafal reached out his hand and touched James' heart.

"Which is why I can't leave him again," he said.

He pulled frosty blue glow out of James' chest, Rafal's magic dissipating from inside the boy.

Hook looked at him, betrayed.

A tear rose to Rafal's eye. "You're the only friend I've ever had, James."

The pit crumbled around them, the two falling away from each other, Hook buried under bodies and Rafal landing between Vulcan and Rhian, the Evil School Master taking the brunt of the punches that Rhian and Vulcan intended for each other. Before Rafal could help his twin, the Pirate Captain crashed next to him under a cascade of Nevers, his jacket ripped off his back—

The Storian tumbled out, a flash of steel.

Rafal lunged for it, but tattooed knuckles ripped it away.

Vulcan grinned, brandishing the Storian.

Rafal surged at him, but Neverboys dragged him under. The Pirate Captain went for Vulcan too, until Dean Humburg shot a spell at his knee, felling him into the horde.

Slowly, Vulcan rose to his feet, Pen in hand.

He loomed over Rhian, straddling the Good brother's chest.

Rhian glared up at him, undaunted.

"How do you kill someone immortal?" Vulcan spoke. "With the weapon that gave them immortality to begin with."

In his hands, the sharp ends of the Storian shined in the moonlight, casting slashes of silver glow across Rhian's face.

Rhian sparked his fingerglow, aiming at Vulcan . . . but this time, the glow sputtered, his finger going dark.

"Magic gives. Magic takes away," said Vulcan, eyes flashing. "*I* am the School Master now."

He raised the Pen like a dagger.

"No!" Rhian cried.

Vulcan plunged the steel at Rhian's heart—

It stabbed another's instead.

Vulcan backed away in shock.

The courtyard of the Evil castle went quiet.

Evers. Nevers. Pirates.

All watching Rafal, the Storian impaled in his chest, blood pooling around the wound and soaking his shirt.

"Brother!" Rhian gasped—

Rafal dropped to his knees, emptied of breath.

His eyes were on Vulcan.

A dead cold stare.

"Rafal?" Rhian whispered.

But Rafal only watched Vulcan.

Like a hawk to prey.

Vulcan stumbled back, his face paling—

Because the blood was receding into Rafal's chest, the wound sealing up.

Rhian's eyes grew large as Rafal drew the Storian out of his own heart.

Vulcan turned to run—

Evers and pirates walled him in.

"The Storian gives every School Master a test," Rafal said, confronting his nemesis. "A test they must pass to rule. But you have *failed* your test. Which means you aren't School Master. You never were. Because it isn't the Pen that makes my brother and I immortal. It isn't the Pen that bestows life. It's *love*."

Rafal stared into Vulcan's eyes. "And love can take it away."

He looked at his brother.

Rhian nodded.

With a cry, Vulcan held up his hands—

Rafal brought the Pen down like a sword.

9.

Sun spilled over the horizon, gilding the steel.

Rafal held out the Storian. "It's yours."

"No," the Pirate Captain said.

He and the brothers were standing at the shore, beneath the shadows of the *Buccaneer*, dawn casting a gossamer mist as the boys of Blackpool loaded back onto the ship.

"What do you mean?" Rafal said to the Captain.

"It was the agreement—" Rhian echoed.

"And after what I've seen, we are in agreement that the Pen belongs with the both of you," the Captain replied. "Anyone can see that. Even the most dastardly of pirates."

He touched Rhian's shoulder and smiled into his eyes. The Good School Master smiled back, not noticing his Evil brother silently groan behind him.

The Captain looked up to his crew. "Ready to sail?"

Ferret Boy peered over the rail. "Hook be missing!"

The Pirate Captain frowned.

But James was indeed on the ship, four floors below in the bilge, tracking the Captain's tabby cat, which had been meowing for Hook to follow, all the way down to the basement, where the cat began pawing at a storage cupboard, muffled sounds coming from within.

Hook flung it open.

Princess Kyma was inside, bound with rope. And next to her, a girl with oversized glasses springing out of the cupboard and barreling past him—

Up the stairs she ran, Hook chasing her, before she burst out onto deck, throwing pirates aside.

"*STOWAWAY!*" Ferret Boy cried.

The twin School Masters turned to see Marialena climb onto the rail and leap off, diving towards open sea—

A blast of golden glow hit her.

Her body shrank in midair to a glittering thorax, gold wings sprouting out of her spine, her glasses winnowing down on her tiny, sparkled face until she looked down in shock.

"Told you I'd find a punishment," Rhian boasted.

Marialena cursed at him, but all that came out was *meep meep meep.*

"Try telling lies now," Rhian said. "Marialena, the Good fairy."

Rafal raised a finger and shot his own blast, turning the fairy's wings black, her face green, and her teeth into fangs like a bat's.

"Or Maleficent, the Evil one," he said.

"Or that," Rhian sighed.

Marialena hissed in horror and flew out to sea.

The sun lifted, breaking through the foggy bands of pearls and pinks to the deepest fiery red. Clouds began to gather, thick and white, a silken canopy.

Rhian stood with his brother at the water's edge, watching the *Buccaneer* drift into the horizon. The Storian nestled warmly in the School Master's hands, no restlessness, no struggle, as if it had found its way home.

"It's just us now, isn't it?" Rhian said, soaking in the silence.

"Everything as it should be. Everything the way it was. Perfect balance."

He turned to his brother. "Right?"

But Rafal was walking back towards school.

There was darkness in his eyes.

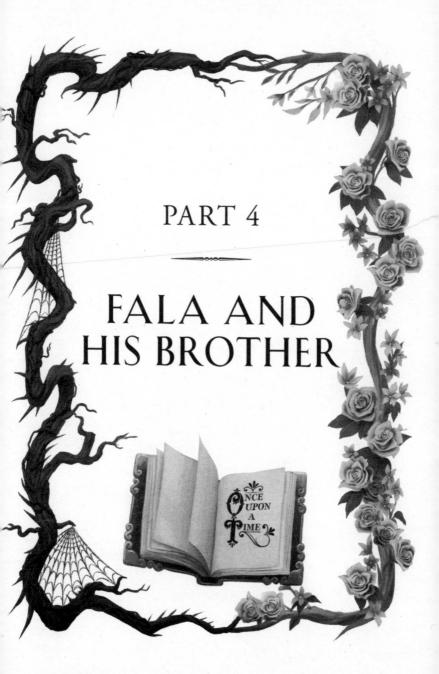

PART 4

FALA AND HIS BROTHER

1.

"So it is my job to torture them," the man-wolf spoke.

"It is your job to find their deepest fear," said Rafal.

The man-wolf was quiet for a moment, seven-foot tall, black in fur, a rock-hard mass of hairy muscle. He looked around the newly built dungeon, deep in the bowels of the Evil castle, the walls hung with swords, spears, axes, knives, whips, clubs, mallets, and other instruments of pain. A sign was nailed to the wall, a few dead flowers in its seams—

DOOM ROOM, it said, broken and crooked, as if it had been repurposed from somewhere else.

The man-wolf's focus lingered on the torture devices. "They are children?"

"Disloyal, ungrateful ones," Rafal said coldly. "Nevers who

betrayed their School Master. Each condemned me to eternal prison and now expects forgiveness. But Evil does not forgive. Evil punishes. That is one of the rules of Good and Evil. So now you will punish them."

The man-wolf peered at the School Master. "And in return?"

"There is word that King Constantius of Camelot is on the hunt for Bloodbrook man-wolves, given one of you ate his daughter," Rafal replied.

"An unfortunate incident," the man-wolf replied. "Constantius didn't accept our apologies. It seems the Good don't always forgive."

"Which is why you and your clan answered my missive, offering protection in return for service."

"I heard the last School Master brought in mountain wolves from Ravenswood. They weren't protected."

"To call him a School Master is a bit like calling you a mountain wolf," said Rafal.

The man-wolf considered this. Then he stood taller, his muscles flexed. "Who is the first student to be punished?"

"Not exactly a student," said Rafal.

He opened the dungeon door, revealing Dean Humburg, bound to a chair.

"P-p-please . . . ," Humburg shouted into his gag. "Forg-g-give m-m-me . . ."

Rafal's laughs drowned out his screams.

2.

Rhian was teaching in the Good castle when the water raids began.

The School Master wasn't in the habit of actually instructing students. His job was to watch over the Storian and the safety of the school. But things changed after Good teachers had been trampled and abused at Vulcan's feast, leading several to quit, including Dean Mayberry.

"I am fairy tale *royalty*. The daughter of Mathilde of Earlingscourt, who defeated Rumpelstiltskin himself," huffed Mayberry, sullied and battered in Rhian's office the day after the battle. "I accepted your *many* appeals to be Dean of Good because you and I know I was infinitely better than all other candidates. But enough is enough. A Snow Ball moved up precipitously . . . this ridiculous glass castle . . . protests and revolts . . . Evers taken prisoners by Nevers . . . my wards cuffed and tormented by fellow students! And then. And *then*! Teachers dragged into an infernal mud-pit, fighting for our lives as if we're pigs to the slaughter! No, no, no. Find yourself another Dean." She flounced out of his office. "I am on the next Flower-ground back to Earlingscourt. First class, thank you!"

Rhian sent bouquets of her favorite gardenias and letters dripping with apology and admiration.

He expected her to come back.

She never did.

With classes suddenly unstaffed, the School Master had to teach the students himself until he found a Dean to fill the vacancies.

Not that he minded the change in routine. Long before Aladdin came and started all this trouble, he'd felt restless at school. Being immortal wasn't all it was sold to be. A wasteland of years stretched before him, nothing but monotonous Good victories and the stresses of managing an Evil twin. Inside, he craved more. A challenge. A distraction. That's where he'd got-ten into trouble: building the new Good castle . . . inviting in an Evil substitute . . . He'd learned his lesson. No more projects. No more shaking things up. Could teaching young souls be the safe outlet he needed? An antidote for his unrest? Then he wouldn't need to hire a new Dean at all!

"Let's consider the most significant difference between Good and Evil," Rhian started, pacing the front of the glass classroom, which looked out onto the lush field between the Good and Evil castles. A troop of twelve hulking man-wolves from Bloodbrook were digging up the lawn, some renovation that Rafal had ordered. A week in and they'd opened up an enormous hole in the earth between schools, so big and wide that there was no longer a way to get from Good to Evil or Evil to Good. Rhian had tried to ask his brother what the man-wolves were up to, only to be met with a death glare—Rafal's reminder that his Good brother had not only built an entire new school without the Evil one's consent, but also invited in a man who'd tried to murder them.

Rhian stopped pacing and faced his students. "What's the one thing Evil can never have . . . and the one thing Good can never do without?"

"A moral purpose?" said Hephaestus.

"Evil believes it has moral purpose, just as much as we do," Rhian countered.

"A happy family?" said Madigan.

"Just because Nevers tend to come from homes where affection and nurturing is sparse doesn't mean they're not happy in their own way," Rhian offered. "Think deeper. What can't Evil have, even if they wanted?"

"A princess as a girlfriend?" Aladdin cracked to high fives from boys.

"Or an ex-girlfriend," Kyma said, and the boys went quiet.

"Are you still mad I didn't rescue you?" Aladdin said. "I told you I tried—"

Kyma scowled. "You stole the *Storian* from the School Master and gave it to a pirate to help you find me!"

"Exactly!" Aladdin argued. "You should be flattered!"

"That isn't *Good*!" Kyma retorted. "That's the complete *opposite* of Good!"

Aladdin threw up his hands. "Well, all I know is I can't live without you so I was going to do anything to get you back. So if that's not Good, then you better get used to me not being Good pretty often."

The princess stared at him. Her fire cooled. "How can I stay mad at you when you say things like that?"

The whole class chorused *ooooh* and Rhian laughed.

"And yet, precisely the answer we were looking for," he said. "*Love*. That's the first rule of fairy tales. Evers love. Nevers don't."

"Nevers can't love at all?" Hephaestus asked.

"Evil shuns love in favor of *power*," the School Master answered. "Treasure and thrones and wealth for this lifetime. But Good chooses love because they believe love *is* power. The purest, deepest kind of love that feels infinite. Love that soothes their yearning souls. Love that makes them feel immortal."

The Good School Master paused after he said this, lost in a thought.

"Which is why you and your brother are immortal, right?" said Kyma. "Because you have that kind of love, even if you're on opposite sides."

Rhian's eyes drifted to her.

Kyma reddened under his gaze. "It was in our history book . . ."

Rhian snapped from his trance. "Right, right, precisely—"

SCREECH!

The sound vibrated the glass around them.

Outside, a flock of stymphs sailed over the field between the Good and Evil castles, spilling water from their beaks and bellies into the enormous trench. One by one, the giant black-furred birds sprayed their load like angry dragons, then flew towards the Savage Sea to fill back up.

Rhian blinked, his heart pounding.

A lake?

His brother was building a lake between schools?

Slowly he looked up at the Evil castle and glimpsed man-wolves raising black scaffolding over them, as if more renovations were about to begin.

"What's going on?" Aladdin asked, bewildered.

But Rhian's eyes were on the figures crowded onto the Evil castle balconies.

Nevers, no longer dressed in Vulcan's glamorous uniforms, but in identical shapeless black sacks, like prison garb.

They were waving at Rhian from the balconies. At all the Evers who might see them.

One of them held a sign.

"SAVE US."

3.

By the time the renovation of the School for Evil was complete, every Never had their turn in the Doom Room.

Rafal enchanted the tall mirror Vulcan left behind to show him these sessions in the dungeon as they happened. He leaned the mirror against a wall in an empty classroom, remodeled into a death-cold ice chamber, before he kicked back at the teacher's desk, watching the mirror like a show. Despite the chill, his heart warmed with satisfaction as he watched student after student face the man-wolf in the Doom Room. Indeed, he found himself so entranced by Nevers being punished for disloyalty that hours and days went by with Rafal hardly noticing.

Dean Humburg shuffled into the frigid classroom, head bowed. "The wolves and stymphs have finished their work, Master."

Rafal followed him outside.

Three black towers stood where there had been four before, the sleek, polished obelisks of Vulcan's tower now remade into hulking, jagged spires like the jaws of a monster, coated with red vines. A giant lake expanded between the new School for Evil and Good's glass castle, the waters calm and clear. Standing in the middle of the lake was the old *fourth* tower of Evil, shielded by scaffolding, while a crew of man-wolves worked.

"The stymphs moved it yesterday," said Humburg. "Between building the lake and flying the fourth tower out there . . . I don't think you'll get much more use out of them."

Rafal followed his eyes to the stymphs, slumped in a pack on the shore of the bay. No longer were they covered in black fur. Instead, they were skinless skeletons made entirely of bones, their old fur heaped around them in tufts and clumps. They leered at Rafal with hollow, eyeless sockets.

"Did I work them that hard?" Rafal said wryly.

"Enough that they molted three years early," said Humburg.

"Perhaps we should only use adult stymphs in the future, then," Rafal wondered, admiring the strange, skeletal birds.

"I use young ones to not frighten the children when they're kidnapped. But it appears my students aren't frightened of me *enough*. How else to explain such disloyalty . . ."

He turned to Humburg, his eyes searing into his Dean's.

Humburg looked down. "We'll use adult stymphs in the future, sir."

"Nothing breeds respect like fear," said Rafal. "Something my twin has yet to learn, given the fact he hasn't punished his Evers for betraying me like the Nevers did. And to think: I took a Storian through the heart for him! So much for the bond of blood."

"To be fair, the Evers were prisoners to Vulcan and the Nevers," said Humburg. "They had no choice."

"There is always a choice between courage and cowardice," Rafal retorted. "There are loyal souls like James Hook. And then there are people like you and my brother, for whom loyalty is a chall—"

His voice trailed off, for over Humburg's shoulder, he spotted something moving through the lake.

Or *someone*.

Swimming straight towards him, lithe and well-practiced.

Rafal frowned. "And the coward appears."

Soon after, Rhian chased Rafal through the front doors of

Evil's castle, still dripping wet.

"I left you alone because you deserve the right to build your school as you see fit, but this is madness!" the Good School Master hectored. "Why is there a lake between our castles? Where have you put the Storian? Why are your students giving SOS signs? Why have you been avoiding me when we're supposed to rule this school *together*—"

"You are dripping on my lovely new floor," said Rafal.

Rhian blinked at the black stone tiles, grimy and thick with soot. He looked up to see his brother parading ahead into a leaky foyer that smelled of fish. Gargoyles leered down from stone rafters, lit torches in their jaws. Along the wall, crumbly columns with murals of imps, trolls, and goblins spelled out the word N-E-V-E-R.

"As for your questions," said Rafal, moving faster every time his brother tried to keep up, "you seem to think it's fine your Evers betrayed me and I don't, so the less I see of them the better. It's fine. I'm not angry with you. It's just clear to me that you run your school your way, so I will run my school my way. Vulcan was right. Good and Evil do need different castles, especially now that my students turned on me, sent me to prison, and then tried to kill me. I would replace all fifty of them with one James Hook if I could. But he's off to Neverland to kill

Pan. So . . . time for a *new* approach. One that has already been successful if my Nevers are begging you to save them. As for the lake between castles, this will foil any possible invasions by future Vulcans and the like."

"But if we need to get *between* castles?" Rhian pointed out.

"Why would we need that? Good with Good. Evil with Evil."

"And the Storian? Let me guess. It stays with you, like it did with Vulcan."

Rafal spun and glared at him harshly. "I see. You feel no compunction comparing me to that maggot. You really do distrust me, don't you? You think I want to betray you at every turn, when all I'm trying to do is get us back to the way we used to be. When our schools were strong and we loved each other without question. When we'd moved beyond the fear that one of us would hurt the other. Hook and I found that. Can we?"

His eyes vibrated with intensity . . . anxiety . . . as if he knew something his Good twin didn't . . . as if he could see a future they were trying to avoid . . .

Rhian shook his head. "You misunderstand me." He touched Rafal's arm. "I trust you, brother. You risked your life for me. You didn't know the Storian would protect you when Vulcan stabbed you with it. I don't doubt your love. What could possibly come between us after what we've faced?"

His Evil twin studied him, looking for the lie. But instead, Rafal found warmth and earnestness, two qualities he used to loathe in Rhian, now welcomed with the whole of his heart.

Not that he would admit this, of course.

He pulled away from his twin and strutted ahead. "The Storian is in our new office."

"Office?" Rhian asked.

Rafal fluttered his hand towards a balcony. Beyond it, in the lake, the wolves were pulling down the scaffolding around the tower, revealing a sleek silver spire at the center of the bay, with a large open window spotlit in sun. Through the window, Rhian caught a glimpse of the Storian's steel, glinting in the light and hard at work.

"It started a new fairy tale yesterday and for once it's not about us," Rafal said dryly, gliding into a sunken room with three spiral staircases. "The Pen finally seems content."

Rhian weaved between the banisters, labeled MALICE and MISCHIEF, before pursuing his brother up a staircase that said VICE. "What's the new fairy tale about?"

"Go see for yourself," said Rafal, striding onto a dark floor, each door marked with students' names. "It's the School Masters' tower. Your new home. *Our* new home."

"In the middle of a lake."

"You can fly, can't you?"

"Human flight is blood magic, Rafal. Evers are forbidden to do it."

"Well, then I'm sure all those early morning swims will come to good use. Don't go dripping all over the place and make a mess of it while I'm gone."

"Where are you going?" Rhian said, startled.

Rafal arrived at a door marked MARIALENA. He erased the name with his lit fingertip and opened the door, revealing an empty dormitory, bed unmade, closet full of clothes, the nightstand and windowsill littered with knickknacks. He circled the space, pointing his finger and magically resetting the room, vanishing every trace of the young seer. Then he smiled at his brother from the window.

"To find a new student," said Rafal.

He fell backwards into the sky and flew away.

4.

It wasn't long before they were on parallel missions.

The Evil brother in search of a student.

The Good brother in search of a Dean.

Until now, Rhian had been convinced that he didn't *need* a Dean. That he could teach the Evers himself.

But things changed once he swam to the new School Masters' tower.

The salt of the lake burned his eyes as he dove under, skimming through the water's calm warmth, before he pulled himself up on the concrete platform at the base of the spire. Carved into the steel was the outline of a door. Rhian ran his hands across it, searching for a latch, only to have the door glow under his palm and open on its own, magically recognizing his touch. (How thoughtful of his brother, Rhian mused; if it was him, he'd have locked Rafal out for a bit of fun.) The Good School Master entered the tower and climbed up the long staircase, lit by white-flame torches, the walls cased with shelves of the Storian's tales, the colorful bindings shining like gems. At the top of the stairs were diaphanous silver curtains, which Rhian pulled apart, stepping into a massive gray stone chamber, more bookcases hugging the walls. Rhian noticed the titles—*Finola the Fairy Eater, Ten Dead Princes, Children Noodle Soup*—and he couldn't help but smile. His brother had made sure to stack the School Masters' office only with Evil's victories, no matter how long ago they'd been.

A familiar scratching sound echoed behind and Rhian

turned to see the Storian flit across a fresh page, its latest book open on a white stone table near the window. The Good School Master sighed, relieved that the Pen was both back to work and, as Rafal had mentioned, writing a new tale that had nothing to do with them. He thought about Rafal's face when his brother accused him of distrust . . . how fearful he seemed . . . how determined to preserve their love . . . Whatever had happened to Rafal in Monrovia Prison, he'd learned his lesson about straying. He'd recommitted to his brother and to this school. His poor Nevers would suffer the brunt of this commitment, but there was no question: Rafal was back. And the Storian was well settled because of it—

Then he noticed what the Pen was painting.

The portrait of two shadows kissing in a forest, while a third spied on them from behind a tree.

As the Storian wrote beneath, Rhian read the words:

> *Fala watched them, heart in his throat.*
> *No! he gasped.*

Fala, Rhian thought.

A familiar name.

Obviously a former student—but he couldn't recall a Fala.

Not a surprise, honestly. They'd had thousands of students at this point; he couldn't possibly remember them all.

And now Rafal was off to find another one . . .

Rhian looked around the big, lonely chamber, where he would spend the rest of his immortal days. He and his brother, each other's sole companions.

But now he found himself thinking not of Fala or his loyal, recommitted brother, but instead of his own early days with Vulcan, that flush of excitement and possibility . . . before Vulcan tried to kill him. He'd felt the same with the Pirate Captain . . . before the Captain stole the Storian. Both times his interests had been misplaced. But clearly, his soul was yearning for energy and kinship beyond his twin. The way that Rafal had Hook.

He tapped his finger against his thigh.

A Dean.

Perhaps he needed a Dean after all . . . a Dean that would be his *own* Hook . . .

He could hear Rafal's voice in his head, shouting him down, but Rhian brushed it away. It was Rafal who'd abandoned him and broken their trust to begin with. It was Rafal who decided Rhian's love wasn't enough. That's how he'd found Hook in the first place! Yes, Hook was gone and Rafal was back—but a Dean would be Rhian's insurance in case Rafal ever deserted him again. He would do it to protect himself. To protect the school. And if it gave him a little company along the way, a dose of fresh blood . . . what was the harm in that? This time things would go better. This time, he'd find a true friend. The Good School Master found himself humming as he left the chamber, glowing at the thought . . .

He didn't see the Storian pause its writing and raise its tip in his direction, like a canny little eye.

5.

Rafal flew south and landed in Akgul at half past midnight, at precisely the time when the kingdom comes to life.

Akgul citizens tend to sleep by day and party by night, freed from the rhythms of work since Akgul has diamond mines beneath it and the King of Akgul distributes the wealth amongst its people to encourage a life of leisure and play. It was another side of Evil, Rafal mused, as he wandered the crowded alleyways of pubs and inns—humans, ogres, and sundry creatures stumbling out, singing, hugging, fighting, puking, all in the name of fun. This is what a life without responsibility looks like, the School Master thought. An endless party. An embrace of pleasure. The epitome of Evil in Good's eyes. If only Good understood: a life of pleasure without guilt might just be the purest life of all. But Good was too in love with talk of morals and duty and responsibilities to ever understand that.

Rafal walked faster. He wouldn't be joining the party tonight, though.

He had his own responsibilities.

A new student.

That's what he'd come to find.

A young Never who could salvage his treacherous class and lead it. A soul who understood the meaning of loyalty and commitment. A soul like Hook's.

Rafal stopped under a streetlamp, struck by a thought. The boy had offered him a place on his ship to Neverland. Why hadn't the School Master suggested he join the School for Evil instead? Hook would whip his classmates into shape in no time! Rafal's loyal, trusted henchman. Yes, it would breach the agreement between Rafal and the Pirate Captain about not poaching each other's students. But that could be negotiated.

What couldn't be negotiated is that James Hook thought he was Good. *Hah!* Rafal scoffed. This was a boy who'd literally begged an Evil School Master to breathe his soul into him and James still thought he belonged in ties and tails at an Evers' Ball. But the truth didn't matter. Souls who *believed*

259

themselves Good wouldn't last long in the School for Evil.

No . . . Hook couldn't do the job.

Even if he did miss the boy.

Rafal sighed and pressed ahead.

The Black Rabbit was at the end of the lane, behind a heavy stone door that camouflaged into the alley wall. A goblin outside held a bucket of glowing green bands.

"Evenin', School Master," the goblin grinned. "Sold-out show. The Gruff Gruff Goats."

"Room for one more?" Rafal asked.

"Be my guest," said the goblin.

Rafal pushed through, brushing past a tall boy leaving, and he was instantly blasted with thumping beats and the fog of sweat. Three horned goats in neon face paint pounded drums on a high stage and unleashed guttural screams, a hundred teenagers stomping and dancing below, heads and arms and wrists wrapped in the signature green glow bands given for entry. But it was the *price* of entry Rafal was interested in and he made his way over to the bar, where a dark-haired woman in neon green lipstick was counting a pile of tiny green parchment scrolls. A few teenagers bounded up, ordering Snake Venoms—a signature bright green tonic made of starfruit, anise, and kola nut that pumped young blood with enough energy to dance until sunrise. Rafal noticed one soul in a hooded cloak slouched over a seat at the other end of the bar, likely the victim of too much fun.

"Any good ones tonight, Divya?" Rafal asked the bartender, who'd gone back to sifting her scrolls.

Divya didn't look up. "Must be desperate if you're back here, Rafal. Already gave you our best before Kidnapping Night."

"Surely there's a new confession worth reading."

"Maybe if they knew the School Master was going through 'em. Price of entry to the Black Rabbit is one Evil confession and most just toss off something about lying to their mother or smacking their sister or peeing their bed because they were too lazy to get out of it." Divya held up one of the scrolls. "'Tipped Daddy's cow.' It's all very uncreative, Rafal. And no wonder, you've already taken our most Evil souls for your school. Only the runts of the litter left."

"The Black Rabbit's famous," Rafal probed. "Nevers from other kingdoms find their way here every night. Must be one whose confession caught your eye."

Divya lifted her eyes to him. "Evil's losing streak is that bad, is it? The lot of us keep thinking it'll turn around. That Evil will get a winning run soon enough to balance it all out. It's the Storian's job, ain't it? But that look on your face is making me think we got it all wrong . . ."

"Evil will win again soon," Rafal assured.

And this was true. He'd returned to Rhian's side. He'd taken a death blow for his brother and proven his love. The Pen would surely reward Evil for it and restore the balance. The Saders had promised him this when he freed them from prison. Indeed, the tale it was writing at this very moment might be the one that turned the tide. But Rafal was still down a student and given recent events, he was on a hellbent mission to find one he could trust.

He put his hands on the bar. "Divya. Don't let me leave without a name. Someone in these Woods who can make Evil proud—"

"Or *beyond* these Woods," said a voice.

Rafal turned to see the figure slouched at the end of the bar sit up and pull back their cloak, revealing a middle-aged woman with hazel-green eyes, long blond hair, and a familiar thin smile.

"If you know where to look, that is," she said.

"Adela?" Rafal stared at her. "You followed me here?"

"I followed my foresight. Which is how I was here first," she replied. "Just in time to meet you."

"But . . . why?" Rafal's voice turned cold. "Your family left me for dead."

"The future is becoming clearer, Rafal," she said. "A new school will rise. It's time you and my family aligned."

The School Master shook his head. "What future? What are you seeing?"

Adela stood. "I lost ten years for you already, Rafal. This time, you'll have to live the answers for yourself."

She drew her cloak back over her head and walked past him, stopping to whisper in his ear, something he hardly made out in the stomps and shouts of young souls . . .

"Look for where the tales go at night."

By the time he looked up, Adela Sader was gone.

6.

Rhian was in the middle of teaching when the Deans arrived.

"True love isn't just the highest power that Evers aspire to. It's also the greatest weapon there is. You saw it yourself at Vulcan's feast," said the Good School Master. "My brother's allegiance is to Evil, but love protected him in the same way that it protected Good. Why do you think true love's kiss redeems so many souls gone astray?"

Rufius raised his hand. "But can true love *lead* you astray? What if you love someone you're not supposed to? Like someone your parents disapprove of? Can your heart get mixed up?"

"No more than your soul getting mixed up," said Rhian. "True love will always lead you in the right direction, just as a soul clearly orients to Good or to Evil. All of you knew before Kidnapping Night which school you belonged in, right? Just as my brother and I knew which sides we were on when the Storian named us School Masters, one for Good, one for Evil. The Pen didn't need to tell us which brother was which. Just as you don't need to be told. Your soul *knows*. Just like it knows your true love. A mix-up? Impossible."

"My soul didn't know," said Aladdin. "A lot of people thought I was Evil. Me included. And I turned out Good."

"Barely," said Kyma.

The other students laughed and Rhian couldn't help chuckling too.

"But I'm serious!" said Aladdin. "Wasn't the point of my fairy tale that we don't always know? That sometimes our souls think we're one way when we're actually the other?"

"Your fairy tale was a special case," Rhian said, refraining from mentioning that it hadn't been Aladdin's fairy tale at all. That the Storian's tale had really been about two School Master brothers who'd argued over whether the boy's soul was Good or Evil . . . who'd indeed gotten mixed up over the exact point that he'd just claimed was impossible—

A fanfare of trumpets detonated outside, making the students jump.

Rhian looked out the window to see a well-dressed parade of bodies march out of the forest towards the School for Good—a mustached man in a glittery green Gillikin coat, an elegant woman in the pastel colors of Jaunt Jolie, an overgrown fairy with Maidenvale's signature purple wings, and more, *many* more, as if they'd all arrived on the same ship from various ports, come to seek their fortune.

"Who are they?" Kyma asked.

Rhian watched the caravan approach the glass castle.

"Contenders," he said.

The interviews for the Dean position took place in Good Hall, with the School Master seated in a golden chair at the back of the ballroom, while the line of candidates waited outside and were sent in one by one.

"I've taught at the Foxwood School for Boys," said a hoary, red-nosed man. "Beat them all into shape, I did. Good's getting puffed up with all these victories. Think nothing can take them down. I remember when I was a young Ever, arrogant like them. Then came the Golden Age of Evil . . ."

"More silence and reflection is what they need. To help them find meaning beyond winning and losing," suggested the next one, a soft-spoken lady from Ginnymill. "A morning meditation, followed by yoga in the garden, and a dedicated time to journal . . ."

"A reinvention of the way we pick students to give non-human folk a chance," advanced the next, a willowy elf from Pumpkin Point. "You've only had two elves in the last twelve classes. We need better representation across all creatures . . ."

Rhian yawned. "We'll be in touch."

A nymph from Eternal Springs urged reintroducing magic wands to the school, since fingerglows were a bit "advanced." A dwarf from Glass Mountain wanted to host a tournament of duels to improve the Evers' combat skills. A gnome from Gnomeland proposed the students take a potion that let them switch genders at will, from boy to girl and girl to boy and anything in between, until each settled on the form that suited them best.

Rhian dismissed them all.

What was he looking for? He wasn't sure exactly. In the past, whenever he'd needed a Dean, he'd picked the most qualified candidate—usually an elder woman, like Mayberry, whose lineage, experience, and skills were unimpeachable. But this time, when that candidate appeared, the last one in line, a diminutive woman named Hedadora with a bush of white hair and thick pink glasses, Rhian found himself focusing not on her credentials, but on the giant mole right under her nose.

"I spent two years teaching at the Jaunt Jolie Academy, where I was elevated to Headmistress, before moving to the Jaunt Jolie Preparatory, also as Headmistress, where I remained for six years, and it was my efforts reforming and enlightening them in the values of Good that led to more Jaunt Jolie students being selected to your school than ever before. Indeed, I have a reference here from Dean Mayberry herself, testifying that I am the best candidate for the position and she has made it abundantly clear that you need a woman's touch in this castle and that *I* am the woman for the job." She held out a piece of paper, neatly pressed between stubby fingers.

Rhian didn't take it. "I'm sure all those things are true," he said vacantly.

"When would you like me to begin?" Hedadora presumed.

After she'd gone, Rhian leaned back in his chair and took a swig of wine from the bottle he'd kept behind it. A new Mayberry, even more fuddy-duddy than the last. Wonderful. Just what his restless soul needed. Another schoolmarm to scold and irritate him.

Rhian shook his head, scowling at his thoughts.

She was the right Dean. The best Dean. He'd done the Good thing and now he was regretting it? Since when did he regret Good decisions? Since when had he become Rafal, looking to cause trouble for himself and the school?

Rhian sat up and plunked the wine bottle down. No, he wasn't Rafal. Because in the end, he'd hired the prig, like the dutiful, sensible School Master he was. Restless soul be damned.

He stood up to leave—

A sharp knock rattled the door.

"Not now," he growled.

Another knock.

"The position is filled!" he snapped.

More knocking.

"For God's sake—"

Rhian stormed at the door and threw it open.

He stepped back in shock, his heart jumpstarting.

"Position can't be filled yet," said the boy in front of him. "Not 'til I get my turn like everyone else."

He was tall and thin, icy blue veins under small muscles, a shadow of stubble across his cheeks. He wore a white shirt, the buttons half undone, a gold chain dangling against his pale chest. His eyes were like polished coal, his hair matching in unruly waves, his face dead serious.

Rhian knew he should laugh.

That he should kick the boy back from where he came.

But he didn't.

Instead, he looked at James Hook and raised his brows, as if the interview had already begun.

7.

"Look for where the tales go at night."

Rafal couldn't make the slightest sense of what Adela Sader had whispered to him as she'd left the Black Rabbit.

What tales? And how can tales *go* anywhere? Had he heard wrong?

And that other thing she'd said . . .

"A new school will rise. It's time you and our family aligned."

Last he saw the Saders, they would have been happy letting him die. Now they were helping him? What future had Adela seen? What new school? And what did this have to do with the new student he was seeking? The new Never he'd yet to find?

All these questions tumbled in the Evil School Master's mind as he flew back to school in the dead of night, gliding over the moonlit bay and slipping through the window of the School Masters' tower.

The Storian was suspended in the dim chamber, as if asleep,

its tale paused on a painting of young Fala spying on two shadows kissing in the night.

Rafal tiptoed close, reaching out a finger to flip backwards in the tale—

The Pen jolted alive and slashed his palm.

"No looking back. I know," Rafal growled, watching the wound magically heal. "Cursed little devil."

Last Rafal checked, before he'd left for Akgul, the Pen had only just begun, with Fala and his brother each leaving home to seek their fortunes.

Another story about brothers, Rafal had thought. But thankfully not one about them, the proof of which came in the Storian's first painting—with Fala's oafish bowl of brown hair and long, crooked nose, nothing like the Evil School Master or his twin. The image had brought Rafal no small amount of relief. The Pen had finally moved on from him and Rhian. Back to normal. And soon to balance.

The name Fala had been familiar, though, and Rafal couldn't quite place it, until his flight back from the Black Rabbit. Surrounded by night clouds, he'd remembered: Fala had been what Rhian had called him when they were children, because he couldn't pronounce Rafal's name. *Fala, Fala, Fala,* Rhian used to babble, clutching onto Rafal when he needed comfort, before Rafal kicked or shoved him away. Rafal remembered one instance in particular, where he'd used blood magic to turn Rhian's skin see-through, revealing his twin's organs and veins, which left Rhian screeching *Fala, Fala, Fala* until Rafal turned it back. How strange to see the name pop up in a Storian's tale a hundred years later . . . and a tale about two brothers no less! Especially after the Pen's previous two stories had been about the School Master twins . . .

Rafal peered closer.

Is this Fala me?

But it didn't look anything like him. And the Storian always told a story as it happened . . . and this *wasn't* happening . . . Which meant this Fala *couldn't* be him. It had to be a former student, since the Pen only told stories of the school's graduates. (At least when it wasn't straying to tales of its School Masters.) He vaguely remembered a Never named Faizal with a hideous haircut and bumpy nose. Or was his name Fala? *Hmmm.* Rhian often remembered the Nevers better than Rafal did. His brother would know.

"Rhian?" Rafal called into the dark.

No answer.

Surely his twin was still awake. Rhian was a terrible sleeper, even though Evers were famously good at sleeping and Nevers woeful insomniacs. Rafal, on the other hand, could sleep through a typhoon.

He dipped his head into the back chamber, expecting to find his brother reading one of the Storian's old tales or doing push-ups or sitting in the windowsill, gazing out at the stars.

But there was no one there.

Odd, the Evil School Master thought. Perhaps he'd gone for a night swim? Or he'd gotten anxious sleeping alone in their new tower. Rhian had always been that way as a child, afraid if Rafal left him alone for even a moment, crying *Fala, Fala, Fala* . . .

Rafal lay down on the cold silk sheets of his bed.

Tomorrow, he'd find his Never.

His new Captain Hook.

But for now . . . sleep.

He heard a sound from the other room.

Scratching, rustling.

The Storian must be writing again, he thought.

The rustling grew louder, thicker.

No, not the Storian.

In an instant, he was out of bed, into the other room, just in time to catch it—

The Storian zipping around the tower, carefully tipping

books off the shelves . . . one . . . two . . . three . . . four in all . . .
the books collecting in midair, before the Pen conjured a golden
ribbon to sash them together and cast them out the window in
a bolt of bright light, like a comet sent to sky.

The Storian returned to its place in the shadows, heaving a
sigh before it hung still—

Then it saw Rafal staring.

Pen and School Master beheld each other.

"Look for where the tales go at night."

The Storian speared to stop him, but the School Master was
too fast, leaping out the window in full flight and following the
books.

8.

Hook had suggested they go for a walk around the lake, but
Rhian didn't want to take the chance Rafal might see them
when his brother returned. So he led the boy to the Good
Supper Hall, the two moving in silence so as not to wake the
sleeping Evers.

Rhian assessed the lad out of the corner of his eye. He'd
grown since the Storian had told his tale—not so much in size,
but in maturity. Gone was the hunched, stroppy stripling that

no one at Blackpool liked, replaced with a confident young man. He seemed handsomer too since the last time Rhian saw him, with long willowy limbs, a sculpted jaw, shiny hair, and dark, dense eyebrows over black eyes.

Rhian wasn't sure why he didn't want Rafal spotting him with James—it wasn't Rhian's fault that the boy had suddenly appeared, demanding to apply for the Dean of Good position, but Rhian also knew that Hook and his Evil brother had forged a deep bond and Rafal wouldn't appreciate his brother spending time with the boy alone.

For this reason, when they reached the Supper Hall, Rhian started by saying in no uncertain terms: "James, you shouldn't be here."

James glanced around the empty dining room. "You don't have any food lying about, do you? A bit starving after the ship ride."

Rhian whistled for an enchanted pot, which stirred awake and came bounding out with a platter of cheese, salami, cornichons, and olives, and a carafe of barley tea, setting it all down with a huff, as if it could have done much better at a reasonable hour.

"You sailed all the way from Blackpool?" Rhian asked, after they sat at one of the tables.

"Not quite," said Hook, taking care not to speak with his mouth full. "Boys voted to stop in Akgul for a night at the Black Rabbit. For a moment, thought I bumped into your brother there on my way out. Tried to get back in to see . . . but the goblin wouldn't let me."

"Rafal at the Black Rabbit?" Rhian popped an olive in his mouth. "Highly doubt the School Master of Evil is trolling about a teenagers' club."

Hook swigged the tea. "Your school is impressive. Seeing it live and up close the last time stirred something within me. I'd like to be its Dean."

Rhian laughed. "What a load of hogwash. Why are you really here?"

James leaned in, his thick brows flattening. "I'm being serious, Rhian. When I was at the Black Rabbit, watching all those Blackpool boys stomping and screaming and behaving like hooligans, I realized . . . I can do better. They're pirates because they like raiding and pillaging and raising hell. Not me. I'm a pirate because I want to make my family proud. And for the longest time I thought the only way to do that was to kill Pan. Because that's what my family thought was Good and right—vanquishing the boy and taking Neverland in our name, even if so many Hooks died chasing that goal. But then I began to wonder . . . What if that wasn't the *only* path to Good? What if there was another way to bring my family glory? It was just a small seed of a thought . . . The next morning, as we returned to the docks, we saw another ship come in to replenish provisions—a ship carrying Dean candidates from all over the Woods to the School for Good. A vacant position, they were saying. All of a sudden, I found myself sneaking onto the boat, stowing away below deck. That seed of an idea had bloomed to action. Your school called to me like a new path in the dark. The path not just to the highest possible Good, but to, at last, making the name Hook worth something."

Rhian snorted. "Forgive me for being skeptical. You'd give up killing the Pan. You'd give up ruling Neverland. So you can teach *students*? Students who are hardly younger than you?"

"Let's be honest, Rhian. I don't want to die," said Hook. "My father and his father and his father before him *all* died fighting the Pan. And my father was a better fighter than me. Who's to say I would beat Pan? I didn't get the answers I needed from the Saders. I have no secret plan or weapon to kill this seemingly invincible little demon. Nor do I have a crew I can trust to fight with me. Maybe, just maybe, if I had your very best Nevers aboard my *Jolly Roger*, I might stand a chance. I saw the way they fought for Vulcan. The most talented Evil students against Pan? Perhaps. But Blackpool boys alone . . . ? No. The odds are too great. If I want to live, then it's time to let go of the pirate. Captain Hook is no more. But Dean Hook? Perhaps that name is worth even more. Because this time I'm not fighting for myself, but for the future of others."

The Good School Master tapped his fingers on the table, unconvinced.

"You think I can't do it," said Hook.

"I don't have the slightest evidence that you *can*," said Rhian. "Why would I pick you, a pirate with no accomplishments, over Dean Hedadora, with forty years of experience leading schools, who is proven in the values and ideals of Good and who *knows* how to be a Dean?"

"Because no one will like her," said Hook.

Rhian pursed his lips.

"You think that doesn't matter," Hook replied. "I'm going to ask you a question. Why did Vulcan win the Nevers' loyalty? Why did he raise their level so high that your Evers were taken hostage and overwhelmed? How did he turn them into a crew that anyone would be proud of, strong and loyal and united? They didn't fight like that for Rafal. But they fought that way for Vulcan. Why?"

Rhian cleared his throat to answer—

"Because people *liked* Vulcan," Hook cut in. "No one will push themselves for Dean Headache or whatever her name is. No one will be inspired by her. Because she doesn't know how your students feel. *I* know how they feel: desperate for glory, determined to make a name for themselves . . . but unsure where to begin. Why do you think the Pirate Captain breeds such undying loyalty amongst his pirates? Because he's young and hungry, just like us. But he has the wisdom of having given up the chase for personal glory in order to help others find it. I can be your Pirate Captain. I can be your Vulcan. Only unlike them, I'll be one you can trust."

"And what of Rafal?" Rhian asked acidly. "What will we tell him? That his precious James is now my *employee*?"

"He had his chance to fight with me," said James. "Who I choose to fight for now is my business."

Rhian peered at him a moment. Then he shook his head. "No. No. No—"

"Three days," said Hook, so sharply that Rhian froze. "You have to give me three days as Dean to prove myself. If only because I fought for you against Vulcan and helped save your school. It's the *Good* thing to do. And after three days, if you're not convinced, then fine, I'll go back to Blackpool."

Rhian looked at him and sighed. "James . . ."

"Three days," the boy repeated. He reached across the table and clasped Rhian's arm. "Rhian. What is there to lose? You can only gain. A Dean. A friend. A companion. In case Rafal ever leaves you. He's done it before, hasn't he?"

This time, the Good School Master was silent.

"Rafal had me on his side once. He could have come with me to Neverland and fight the Pan and he turned it down. That's his loss," said the boy facing him. "So now it's your turn to have James Hook for yourself."

The School Master gazed into the boy's dark, sepulchral eyes.

What if? A soulmate not for Rafal . . . but for himself . . .

Rhian pulled away.

"*One* day," he said, standing up. "Then Dean Headache takes over."

9.

The books flew a long way.

Longer than Rafal had flown before. Long enough that the night passed, then the day, as he sailed over kingdoms he'd never seen, with floating mountains and castles underwater and rivers that ran backwards and islands divided into light and dark. He tried to catch up with the books, to see their titles, to discover which fairy tales the Storian had sent on this strange journey, but each time he gained speed, the books did too, always staying well in front.

But then the books began to descend over open plains, nothing but grassy fields in the morning sun, forever and ever, as if the tales had come to world's end, the light so dewy and clear. Was this the last of the Endless Woods? Had he found the limits of his domain?

Then he glimpsed something below, blurry in sun mist . . .

A village.

No towering castles, no upside-down forests or murmuring mountains, no enchanted nymphs and fairies gliding about. Nothing like the other kingdoms in the Woods. Just a village, with a crooked clock tower, rickety church, yellow schoolhouse . . .

The books dove, heading for the market square and its rows of woodfront shops. Rafal plummeted after them, head down, arms to his side, like a falcon after prey—

BOOM!

He slammed into an invisible barrier, arms and legs splayed like a bug on glass.

The books, meanwhile, had sailed right through.

Rafal illuminated the barrier with his lit fingertip, revealing a thin, shimmery shield, the kind he cast to protect himself from attacks. But this one didn't break under the weight of his magic, as if it had been made by a power greater than his. Bewildered, the School Master flew down, skirting the edge of the barrier, trying to find where the books had landed.

There they were.

In front of a shop crammed between a bakery and a pub.

Miss Harissa's Bookshop.

A black, fluffy dog slunk off the welcome mat and nosed at the books, before barking back at the shop. A moment later, the owner of the shop came out the front door, presumably Miss Harissa herself, with curly gray hair, a red tweed coat, and a matching hat that looked like an umbrella. She plucked the books from the ground, dusted them off, and with a curious "Well!", she took them inside.

Through the window, he watched her sit and unbind the books.

It was then that Rafal noticed the books *in* the window.

Henny Penny, Stone Soup, Hans in Luck, Rumpelstiltskin . . .

More of the Storian's tales.

Tales the Pen had written and sent here.

Why?

Rafal drifted along the barrier, spying on the town in its morning routine. Shopkeepers putting out their wares; villagers watering their gardens and hanging the laundry; carriage drivers feeding their horses; blacksmiths firing their ovens; farmers driving their hogs to the trough; millers traipsing towards the windmills beyond the lake. No one seemed to notice the School Master whizzing over town, as if whatever was outside the shield couldn't be seen by those inside it—the children included, who seemed to be everywhere he looked, unsupervised by adults, as if it was the safest village in the world, playing and roughhousing and skipping and singing and picking apples off trees and most of all . . . *reading*.

Rafal peered closer.

A boy on a swing set, reading *The Singing Bone*. A girl on the steps of the church, reading *Bluebeard*. Two brothers sitting by a fountain, reading *The Frog Prince*.

All of them stories from the School Masters' library.

All of them tales told by the Storian.

How had he not noticed this before? Rafal thought incredulously. Books flying away from *his* library to a mysterious village at night beyond his power, where they were bequeathed to a bookseller who sold them to children. Children who read these fairy tales, wide-eyed, immersed, as if they'd never known such things were possible.

How many stories had arrived here? When had this begun? Shame colored Rafal's cheeks. His and Rhian's job as School Masters was to keep a keen eye on the Storian and its work. A job that up until this very moment, he thought they'd done well. Surely he and Rhian would have noticed if a slew of tales had gone missing? Unless just as the books came here from the school, they also found their way back.

He studied the children closer, hunting for signs of magic, signs of the same talents he sensed in his students . . . but there was nothing. No pulse of enchantment. No hint of the extraordinary. Just as the town was unremarkable, unmagical, so too were the children, as if they lived apart from the Endless Woods. As if they hadn't the slightest knowledge of the fantastic kingdoms around them.

But there was one girl in particular who caught his attention.

A teenage girl with dark red hair, the color of unpolished rubies, and black, flinty eyes, sitting against a tree, reading *Rabid Bear Rex*. It was Rafal's favorite tale, about a bear who gave a town many warnings not to disturb him, but they went unheeded and in return, he ate their little girls. It was a dark tale, full of vengeance and woe, but this girl was *laughing*, flashing her sharp teeth, her cheeks pinked with glee.

Rafal marveled at her.

No one laughed at *Rabid Bear Rex*.

Not even his most dastardly Nevers.

The School Master's heart skipped faster.

This was the one.

This was his new student.

Rafal pounded on the bubble to get her attention. He needed to talk to her. He needed to get her on *this* side. He lit his glow and shot a sizzling curse to break through the shield—it ricocheted in his face, crashing him to the ground, hair and ears singed.

The Evil School Master gnashed his teeth. How could the magic here repel him? "It's *my* Woods!" he said angrily.

"I wouldn't say that," a voice replied.

He turned, but no one was there.

Then something bit his ear—

Rafal whirled to see a black-winged, green-faced fairy.

"This village isn't your Woods," said Marialena, flitting over his head. "It's Woods *Beyond*."

"You followed me here?" Rafal asked.

The fairy landed on his shoulder. "Must I remind you that I am a Sader and therefore can see where you'll be at any given moment. At first, I resented you turning me into a fairy and searched for a counterspell, both to restore my speech and to find my way back into my body. But then I began to think: What if this is meant to be? Who wants to walk when they can fly?" She batted her wings in Rafal's face, making him block his eyes. When he opened them, Marialena was on the other side of the shield. *Inside* the village.

Rafal's eyes flared. "How do *I* get through?"

The fairy glanced at the girl reading against the tree. "I see why you've taken a liking to her. A Reader would be a powerful addition to your school. That's what I call them. *Readers.* They have imagination, ambition, and desire to be part of our world, but also the belief it can never happen, because it's just a 'fairy tale' they read about in books. Imagine if you brought them through that shield into our world. A world where the dreams in their storybooks come to life. They wouldn't take for granted what the rest of us do. They could achieve without limits. Or fail miserably, of course. But you'd bet on that chance, wouldn't you?"

Rafal grit his teeth. "Let me in."

"Now he demands my help," said Marialena, "even though I'm not his student anymore."

"You wouldn't be here if you didn't intend to help me," the

School Master hounded. "Your mother has been following me too. Claiming your family needs me."

"Or that you need our family," said Marialena. "Our fortunes are tied. This is true. But I'm still not letting you in."

Rafal shot a spell at her, but it rebounded off the shield, knocking him on his rump again.

"Unlike the other kingdoms in the Woods, Woods Beyond isn't a Good or Evil realm," the fairy explained. "It is part of the Woods and yet apart from it. Just as it is our duty to live the legends the Storian writes, it's these Readers' role to believe in them, no matter who wins, Good or Evil. They live in the balance, these Readers. Which is why I, as a seer, can enter their realm, since seers are loyal to truth and balance over a side. But you intend to steal a child from this village for your own benefit. That isn't very balanced, is it? That's cheating. No wonder the shield won't let you through. If you get a child, then your brother has to get one too. One Reader for each school."

"No," Rafal rejected. "He has enough advantages. This one should be mine."

"Then I'm afraid your young Reader won't ever know what it means to be a Never," said Marialena, watching the girl finish her story and close the book. The child dusted herself off and scampered back into town, until Rafal lost sight of her.

The Evil School Master hesitated. If his brother even knew what he was considering . . . No. He couldn't know. He must *never* know.

Rafal turned and growled at the fairy. "Don't follow me again."

He trudged away, ready to fly back to school, when he heard a sharp fizz behind him, like a bubble popped, and he spun to see the shield gone and the village brighter and clearer, as if he was no longer on the outside, looking in.

"Just like I saw in my head," said Marialena, fluttering in front of him. "It seems that the balance keeping you out has been disturbed."

Rafal shook his head, not understanding.

"Don't you see?" Marialena grinned. "Your brother wants to cheat too."

10.

On his first day as Dean, James Hook announced a grand new competition at the School for Good and Evil.

The Circus of Talents, he called it, pitting Evers against Nevers in the ultimate combat of skills. Three days from today. Good would send its ten best Evers against Evil's ten best

Nevers, with each student given the stage to present their talent. An impartial judge from beyond the school would preside and the winning team would win the right to host the Circus in their school the following year.

Rhian didn't know about any of this until he overheard two Evers buzzing about it on their way to lunch.

"Aladdin says he can juggle," a girl touted, "and Rufius can bake chocolates."

"Those won't win the Circus," a boy argued back. "We need someone who can breathe fire or sprout an extra head or turn into a wolf!"

"Those are Never talents," the girl countered.

"Then we're *definitely* going to lose."

Rhian tried to hear more, but through the window, he saw Dean Humburg splashing out of the lake towards Good's castle, soaking wet and flapping hands like an addled bird.

"What is this madness!" Humburg harangued when Rhian met him at the door. "Nevers and Evers have been flashing each other messages from their balconies, since they can't cross that blasted lake. And your students are claiming there's a contest of talents next week. My Nevers are already fighting to see who will be on Evil's team! I tried to shut down the idea, to tell them we won't participate in unapproved contests, but they *want* to do battle against your Evers and nothing I say will stop them! Rafal will have your head! Last time your brother was gone, there was a Trial. Now there's a *Circus*—"

Humburg's eyes bulged.

Rhian followed them to James Hook, strutting down the hall in black leather pants.

"Morning, Dean Hook!" two Evergirls chorused, obviously smitten.

Humburg looked as if he'd been slapped, his voice rising five octaves. "*Deeeeeannnan* Hook—"

But Rhian had already snatched Hook by the collar, dragging him to a balcony near the stairwell.

"We agreed you would be here for one day, James. One. Day. And now you're announcing competitions *three* days from now, when you will most certainly *not* be here." Rhian shoved him against the wall. "This is what Vulcan did—"

"*Exactly,*" said Hook.

Rhian stared at him, thrown.

"Vulcan made Evil new again. He bred excitement and loyalty amongst the Nevers, who fought for him because they respected him the same way Blackpool pirates revere the Pirate Captain," said James. "I want Evers who are loyal and true. None of this fussy, frilly ballgowns and true-love's-kiss nonsense. We need to make Good strong and united and potent again. The way Evil has become. And a Circus *against* Evil is the way to start. Look at them! When was the last time you've seen your Evers this engaged?"

Rhian followed his eyes down the stairwell to students on different levels, eagerly practicing their talents, swordfighting, flag twirling, opera singing, doing backflips down the stairs.

The Good School Master shook his head. "Villains are born with more magical talents. None of this will beat the Nevers. This is just like the Trial . . ."

"No it isn't," Hook continued. "The Circus helps you in two ways. First, it pushes the Evers to try harder. But more importantly, it identifies the ten strongest Nevers. The Nevers that will be their rivals in the Storian's tales after they graduate. The more we learn about these Nevers and their talents now, the more likely Good can defeat them in the future."

Rhian considered this, his anger and stubbornness receding.

James touched his arm. "I'm on your side, Rhian. You have to trust me. Like your brother once did. He even breathed his magic into me. *Twice*."

The School Master's gaze flew to his Dean. "Rafal gave you a piece of his *soul*?"

"Only to choose *you* and desert me," Hook said, with a wink.

"In the end, I will leave and you two will have each other. Happily Ever After. But how and when I leave is up to you. So be careful what you wish for." He grinned cheekily.

Rhian couldn't help but smile. He saw now why Rafal had taken to James Hook. The boy was irresistible. A stab of guilt tightened Rhian's stomach . . . the feeling that he'd taken something that wasn't his . . . He pushed it down. *He* was the Good brother. Rafal the Evil one. As long as he trusted his feelings, his soul would always orient him towards the right path. Towards Goodness. And everything in his soul told him to trust James.

He looked into his Dean's eyes.

"I have an idea," said Rhian.

11.

Rafal's mind sharpened like a sword.

Rhian cheating?

What is he up to now?

He had half a mind to fly back to school and catch his brother in the act. But then again, Rafal was in the midst of cheating too, prowling into the heart of Woods Beyond, hunting for a Reader to kidnap. A Reader that would upend everything. Both twins then were deceiving the other, hoping neither would find out.

A fair fight, Rafal had to admit.

Even so, the thought disturbed him. Each time he left Rhian alone, his Good brother strayed from Good. Commandeering a new castle, hiring a replacement for his twin, choosing a thief to fight for the Evers, almost losing the Storian to a pirate because of it, and now . . . *cheating?* All these years, Rafal thought Rhian kept *him* in check, when suddenly, it seemed to be the reverse.

"Rafal?" spoke a voice.

He looked up and saw Marialena's fairy flitting towards the morning crowd.

"If anyone from the village spots us, there will be questions," she said, glancing at his spiky white hair and blue-and-gold suit. "Anything you can do to hide yourself?"

"Aren't you able to *see* what I should do?" Rafal jabbed back.

"I only see the highlights of the future, not the mundane in-betweens," said the fairy, concealing herself in his hair as they approached the market lanes. "I suggest you hurry or they might burn you at the stake as a witch. Can immortality save you from a mound of ash?"

Rafal didn't intend to find out.

Invisibility wasn't an option—too cumbersome a spell—so he sparked his fingerglow and with a whispered incantation, turned himself into a stooped, wrinkly, gray-bearded villager, who ambled into the crowd unnoticed.

"Did you have to make yourself so slow?" Marialena groused.

But after a hundred years as a teenager, Rafal loved the feeling of being old. The weight of years lived. The mass of experience rattling in his bones. Finally, a body that matched his soul.

WELCOME TO GAVALDON, the sign said at the edge of the market square.

A magical name for such an unmagical town.

He gazed around the village—humble dirt roads, creaky shop signs, unruly tulip beds spotted with dog dung—everything so ordinary and earthbound and imperfect, and for the smallest of moments, he wished to stay in this aged body and live as one of these Readers, without the burden of a school or a twin or responsibility. The Storian would punish him with mortality, no doubt. He'd die in this decrepit body and get buried underground like the rest of these doomed souls. If he was *truly* Evil, he'd do it. Hide here and never return . . . Rhian certainly would. He'd claim it was the right thing to do and then expect Rafal to rescue him from the mess.

The thought made the Evil School Master snort out loud.

"Turn right into that lane," the fairy whispered in his hair.

Rafal obeyed, veering into a row of cottages, his feet and back aching, his knees throbbing with age.

He took back his wish to stay old.

"There," said Marialena.

The first house, with light blue eaves and a yellow door, and through a window . . .

. . . the *girl*.

Sitting on her bed, while across the house, through the other window, Rafal watched her mother in the kitchen, calling the child's name: "Arabella! You need to leave for school!"

"Go," Marialena whispered to Rafal, drifting out of his hair. "Go to her."

Rafal's eyes shrank to slits. "You sided with Vulcan against me. You wanted me locked in Monrovia forever. What changed? What do you and your mother know? Why should I *trust* you?"

Marialena's face became solemn. She looked deep into him. "A new school will rise, Rafal. And *you* will be the One."

"Your mother said the same," Rafal replied, struggling to understand. "How can there be One when there are two?"

Something inside him stirred.

The memory of another prophecy.

Betrayal. War. Death.

"Go," the fairy urged. "Before it's too late."

A few moments later, the girl was still dawdling in her bedroom, avoiding the calls for school, when she turned to find a young man sitting on her bed.

"Hello, Arabella," said Rafal.

The girl didn't scream. She studied the School Master with black eyes solid as buttons, her dress a lighter shade of red than her hair. She had a long, sloping nose, thin, colorless lips, and a smattering of freckles on both cheeks. At first glance, she didn't look much younger than Rafal.

"Who are you?" she asked.

"Do you believe in fairy tales?" Rafal replied.

The girl held her breath, searching the School Master's face. "Are you my prince?"

"Do you like princes?" he asked.

"No."

"Then you will like it at my school."

The girl blinked. "A school?"

"The School for Good and Evil," said Rafal. "Would you like to come?"

"How do we get there?" Arabella asked.

"I'll fly you to my castle," said Rafal. "And you'll never return."

For a moment, the girl looked scared.

"*Arabella!*" her mother called.

The girl's mouth twitched.

She gazed at Rafal expectantly. "What will I do at school?"

"You'll be my most trusted student." His eyes glittered like gems. "My loyal companion."

Arabella let out a breath. "Take me."

The School Master grinned.

And yet . . . he didn't move.

Slowly, his smile tempered.

He was Evil, yes.

Always Evil.

But to kidnap a girl?

To rob her away from her family?

Rafal's blood cooled.

Why was he *really* here?

Not to find an invincible weapon against Good.

Not to cheat at the game.

But to find a new Hook.

To find someone he trusted like he once trusted his brother.

To find a student to replace his twin.

His heart shrank in his chest.

All this time, he thought it was Rhian who had lost faith in his own blood.

But it wasn't.

It was *him*.

It was Rafal, who hadn't forgiven his brother for straying.

It was Rafal, who doubted the strength of their love.

"Betrayal. War. Death."

What if this is what the Saders foresaw?

Rafal who couldn't fully forgive.

Rafal who couldn't return to balance.

Is that why Good kept winning?

Because Evil couldn't let go?

And now to go this far . . . to steal a child . . .

Betrayal.

War.

Death.

What if he had the power to stop it?

What if he could prevent the prophecy from coming true?

By making the Good choice instead of the Evil one?

The door to the room flew open, Arabella's mother stomping in.

"You're late for school!" she barked.

But her daughter was sitting on the bed, her hands full of empty sheets, as if she'd found and lost a ghost.

Rafal had lost something too.

Outside, he searched for Marialena.

But the fairy was nowhere to be seen.

12.

"Isn't it cheating to unlock our magic before the Nevers?" Rufius asked, lined up with the rest of the Evers at sunset. "Aren't we supposed to get our fingerglows at the same time?"

"If the School Master of *Good* approves it, then how can it be cheating?" Dean Hook replied, turning to his companion. "Right, School Master?"

"Nevers are born with stronger magical talents," Rhian answered as he surveyed his Evers, gathered in the leafy forest behind the schools that led out to the larger Woods. "Which is why Evil gravitates towards witchcraft and sorcery. If we're to compete with them in the Circus, then we need to know who our own most talented Evers are. How can we do that unless we see what you can do with magic? I would inform Rafal of my actions, of course, but he isn't here. When he's back, I'll tell him and he'll quickly unlock his Nevers' glows, and the Circus will be as fair as can be. So no. It's not cheating. It's . . . *initiative.*"

A few Evers murmured. "Doesn't sound right—" Kyma started, but Rhian had already pulled out a shiny silver key, the bit pointy and sharp like a dagger.

"Evers, right hands please," said Dean Hook, at the School Master's side.

Aladdin was first.

He didn't extend his hand.

James grabbed hold of it, presenting the boy's second finger.

Aladdin resisted. "Wait—what are you—"

Rhian plunged his silver key into Aladdin's fingertip. The skin went see-through and the key dipped past tissue, veins, blood, and adhered to the bone. Rhian turned the bow and the bone painlessly rotated a full circle. The boy's fingertip glowed bright gold for a flicker, then dimmed as Rhian withdrew the key. Gobsmacked, Aladdin inspected his finger as Rhian unlocked the remaining Evers.

"There is only one rule to using your glow. Magic follows feeling," Rhian instructed, when he was finished. "With the right focus and direction, any strong emotion can activate your glow. But you must direct it with intention. Muddy feelings produce muddy spells. So experiment all you wish. See where your talents lead you. The best Evers will be chosen for our Circus team. We will have redemption for the Trial!"

(Aladdin made a fart noise.)

Students shook and flicked their fingers, straining to harness their emotions, but soon fingertips began to spark and glimmer, each Ever's a unique color. By the time darkness came, there were a few fledgling spells: wisps of smokes, shadows of phantoms, and tiny clouds of rain.

"Amateurish," Rhian conceded. "But a beginning."

His Dean glanced up at the dense canopy of branches and leaves overhead, protecting them from the sight lines of Evil's castle. "They can practice here until dinner, where the Nevers can't see them."

"It'll be dark soon," Rhian fretted. "We're lucky no one got killed during the Trial, let alone leaving fifty of our students out here with untested magic."

"Perhaps we need a school yard then," Hook said. "A little forest where they can practice what it means to be in the Woods. We can even make the trees and flowers a different color. Pink or purple or a lilac lavender. So they won't get confused between the real world and their safe, sweet little space."

"That's a good idea," said Rhian.

"I was joking," said Hook witheringly.

School Master and Dean glanced at each other. They both started snickering.

"First a glass castle and now a Lavender Forest," Rhian lampooned. "Rafal would kill me on the spot."

Hook stopped laughing. "You are too afraid of your brother,

when he should be the one afraid of you."

"Why do you say that?"

"You are bolder," said Hook.

A moment passed between them, the boys searching each other's eyes.

"Can you unlock me?" James asked.

"What?"

Hook held out his finger. "I want to try."

Rhian snorted. "What for? So you can be on the team?"

"I want to know what it feels like," said James firmly.

"Not on your first day."

"You still don't trust me."

"This isn't about trust—"

A ray of red light shot between them, almost catching Hook in the eye.

"Sorry!" an Ever piped behind them.

James didn't flinch. "Come on, Rhian . . ."

Rhian exhaled. "All right, only for a moment," he growled. "Then I'll relock it until I decide your appointment as Dean is more than a day-to-day lark."

James thrust out his finger and Rhian stabbed the key in.

Blue light pulsed from Hook's fingertip and he immediately waved it at the trees. "Let's see if we can make Rhian's little school yard," he crowed. "Blue . . . like the forests of Neverland . . ."

Nothing happened.

Rhian chuckled. "Your beginner's fingerglow can't do such things. Maybe not even with the best training."

Hook frowned. "So if I want to build towers or castles or a bridge over a sea—"

"That requires sorcery," said the School Master. "A soul like Rafal's. Or mine."

"I see. Then maybe it's time you put some of your soul inside of me," said James with a cocked little grin. "I've had your brother, after all. I haven't had you."

Rhian stiffened. He snatched James' hand.

"That's enough wizardry now," he said, and with a vigorous turn of the key, he took back his Dean's magic.

13.

A short while later, Rafal returned.

He'd hardly noticed the time go by, lost in his thoughts and the peace of the flight, afternoon turning to sunset and then to night, before he glimpsed the shadows of castles and the rise of the School Masters' tower from moonlit shimmers off the lake.

He was about to descend, when something caught his attention in the forest beneath him, the one behind the schools. Flashes of light detonated through treetops. All different colors, in frantic rhythm.

Slowly, Rafal sank through the sky, and landed quietly in a tree, splaying against the branches like a bat, arms and legs wide, his body swaying with delicate weight. With the tips of his fingers, he pulled leaves aside and peeked through.

Evers were practicing spells in the dark, illuminated by the streaking rays of their fingerglows, which missed their mark and rebounded off trees, creating a rainbow fog of light. There Aladdin was, shooting lightning bolts at Hephaestus, who deflected them with a magical shield. And Princess Kyma, conjuring a clone of herself, next to Rufius, who'd swollen a toadstool and turned it to raisin bread. All the while, Rhian watched off to the side—"Too many conflicting emotions, Madigan . . . Kyma, sustain your glow longer if you want your clone to *do* anything . . . Rufius, if the toadstool is poisonous, your bread will be too, so I suggest you stop eating it . . ."

Up in the trees, Rafal's spying eyes glittered.

The dirty little cheat, he thought.

"Dinnertime!" a new voice suddenly called out. "Finish your last spells and we'll return to the castle!"

Rafal's heart jolted.

That voice . . .

A silhouette snaked out from the trees amongst the students. "But make your last spell a good one!"

Rafal couldn't see him in the darkness, but then the wave of fingerglows came, a kaleidoscope of light, and there he was, like a ghost in a rainbow.

James.

James?

James!

Rhian clapped his hands. "All of you! Follow Dean Hook back to the castle!"

Rafal fell out of the tree.

He crashed into the grass behind a curtain of vines, ten feet from where his brother and the Evers were. The loud thump made the students yelp with fright and Rhian swung his gold glow like a torch to the vines, illuminating Rafal's shadow behind them.

"Who's there!" Rhian called out.

Rafal didn't answer, watching his brother's outline draw closer.

"Everyone stay back!" Rhian called.

Rafal held his breath, assessing his moves.

"You too, James," Rhian ordered.

The Good School Master's silhouette grew bigger and bigger against the vines.

"Show yourself!" Rhian demanded. "Trespassers will be dealt with!"

In a matter of seconds, he'd pull the vines aside and find his twin.

But Rafal didn't want to be caught like this. Not until he understood why Hook was here . . . why his brother was calling him Dean . . .

Rhian's shadowed hand reached for the vines.

Rafal scrambled back.

No time to escape.

Only to disguise.

But what disguise? Trespassers would indeed be dealt with— *Unless* . . .

Rhian threw the vines aside and shined his glow through.

The Good School Master froze. "Who . . . who are you?"

A tall, lanky boy looked back at him with a long, crooked nose, coal-black eyes, and a bowl of brown hair.

"Fala," the boy answered, with a crisp, clipped accent.

"Fala?" Rhian gaped at him. "But aren't you the boy . . . you're the one that the Storian . . ."

"Your brother," Fala cut in. "He sent me. To be new student at School for Evil."

"*Rafal* sent you?" said Rhian.

Fala nodded. "He said Evil one student short. Bird of bones came. Drop me in forest. I need to go to Evil school. Be Rafal's new student."

Rhian peered at him skeptically. "And where is Rafal?"

"He say he go to Blackpool to visit friend named Hook," Fala answered.

Rhian hardened like a corpse, his eyes going wide. Then he nodded. "I see. Yes." He turned briskly, pulling the curtain of vines. "Come join the others. I'll take you to Dean Humburg."

14.

They took the long route back to the schools, around the lake, the Evers giving Fala wary looks, Hook giving the boy even more suspicious ones, as if James could sense something amiss. But in time, they reached the Good castle and the Dean turned off with his Evers, leaving Rhian alone with Fala as they continued on, their reflections mirrored in the lake along their path to the School for Evil.

All the while, Rafal assessed his brother carefully. The rigid fists. The flinty, furtive blinking. The telltale way he was chewing his lip, thinking, thinking, thinking. Rafal could read his twin well. The signs of guilt. The blushes of shame. And now, the feverish attempt to keep up with whatever deceitful web he was spinning. Villains had to do this all the time, the Evil School Master thought. But there was something strange about seeing Good's great leader, trapped in his own schemes.

"Did Rafal say why he was going to see Hook?" Rhian asked.

Fala snorted. "Why would he tell me?"

"Right, right," Rhian murmured.

As they entered Evil's castle, moving past the foyer, they could see through the open doors of Evil Hall, where fifty Nevers were in the midst of practicing their talents. Hidden in Fala's body, Rafal could hardly keep up with the display—Asrael swallowing fire, Nagila dancing and conjuring a new snake with every step, Gryff spawning leathery scales and a carapace, Fodor popping out his eye and bouncing it like a marble, Timon twirling axes on the tips of his fingers . . . And yet there was a quiet discipline to all of this, an intensity and focus, that made Rafal see his Nevers anew. Yes, they'd been disloyal, yes, they'd betrayed him . . . But they'd also grown. They were far superior to the Evers, now that he allowed himself to see it. No wonder Rhian felt so threatened by them. No wonder Hook had been so in awe of their unity and strength. Strength that Vulcan had bred with excitement and Rafal had stoked with fear.

But now, they saw the Good School Master standing there with Fala and talent practice came to a halt.

All eyes went to the young stranger with the bowl cut and lumpy nose.

"What's the meaning of this?" a voice called out. Humburg came through the crowd, bony arms folded over his black robes. "Spying on our students before the Circus?"

Circus? Rafal thought, befuddled.

Rhian pushed Rafal forward.

"This is Fala," said Rhian, pointing at the gloomy, dark-haired child. "Your new student to replace Marialena. Rafal sent him."

Dean Humburg looked Fala up and down, unimpressed. "Do you have any talents?"

Fala stared at him. "My father is Grand Vizier Impala, Master of Dark Arts. What do you think."

Humburg shrieked a laugh. He turned to Rhian. "What is it Vulcan used to call you? Ugly little duckling?" He looked at Fala. "Well here's another one. All right then, Duckling of Dark Arts. Show me these talents."

Fala didn't.

Humburg shoved him in the chest. "I said: Show me these—"

Fala thrust out his hand and a phantom ripped out of his heart, a furry black duckling, which snatched Humburg in its claws, flew him up to the ceiling, and hung him upside down from the flamelit chandelier, the Dean's robes flying over his head and revealing ruffled underpants. Before the Nevers could laugh, the duckling began to grow larger, larger, molting fur into feathers and spreading glorious wings, before it dove and swept around the room, unleashing an ungodly scream in everyone's faces, only to stop and bow before Fala, then pierce back into his heart, the boy unaffected, except for a single drop of sweat off his brow.

"Not a duckling," Fala spoke. "A *swan*."

Silence filled the darkened hall.

Humburg peeped from the ceiling. "Welcome to the team."

Everyone in the room roared and cheered for Evil's new student.

Except Rhian.

15.

At dinner, Fala took his plate of turnips, potatoes, and pork fat, and sat at the edge of the most crowded table, with Nevers huddled in conversation.

"Hope Rafal never comes back," said a dark boy with a shaved head.

"You and me both," said another with white hair and alabaster skin. "He punishes us all for choosing Vulcan instead of asking why we preferred him in the first place."

"Rafal always looks at us like he wants to get rid of us," said an exceptionally tall girl. "Like he's disgusted by his own students or something. Vulcan acted proud of us."

The bald boy bit into his pork. "What did they do to you guys in the Doom Room?"

No one answered. All eyes went to their food.

"Maybe Rafal won't come back," he offered. "We're all happier under Humburg, anyway. Until there's a better place to go. A place where they care about us like Vulcan did."

"If Vulcan had a school in Hell and you had to die to go there, would you go?" the dark boy asked. "Raise your hand if you'd go."

All hands went up.

"We have to win the Circus," the white-haired boy said. "It'll prove we don't need Rafal. That we're better Nevers without him."

"To not needing Rafal," the tall girl said, raising her glass.

"To not needing Rafal!" the others cheered, clinking cups and downing drinks.

Then they saw the new boy staring, his eyes very dark.

"Uh . . . your name is Fala?" the white-haired boy asked. "Where do you come from?"

Fala glowered back. "Hell."

No one questioned him.

16.

Rafal lay in Marialena's old bed, staring at the ceiling.

Once a School Master. Now a student.

How had it all gone so wrong?

Aladdin.

It started with Aladdin.

Or did it?

Because he and his brother had agreed the boy belonged in Evil.

Until the Storian put him in Good.

The Pen.

The Pen was the troublemaker.

The Pen that had named them School Masters.

One Good, one Evil.

The Pen that trusted them to know which was which.

Only to switch a student and upend the balance.

Rafal waited for the knock on the door.

When it came, he reverted to Fala's body, just in time for Dean Humburg to poke his head through and peer into the darkness for bedcheck.

The door closed again.

Then he was off, diving out the window, soaring over the lake, spying through Good's castle for signs of his brother, the glass giving Rhian nowhere to hide, until he found him, on the highest balcony of the tallest tower, deep in conversation with Hook. Rafal slid underneath and peered through the columns, watching his twin shuffle back and forth, while his new Dean stood calmly in place.

"I don't understand why he'd go to Blackpool to find you!" Rhian said.

"You should be thankful," James replied. "Blackpool is a fair distance. By the time he returns, the Circus will be over. He won't be able to change our course."

The Good School Master stopped pacing. Rhian turned on James, his big eyes and golden hair luminous in the dark. "Why does the Circus matter to you so much? Why have you really come, *Dean* Hook?"

James chuckled. "That Neverboy got to you, didn't he!" He touched Rhian's arm. "Even though he's a child and you're a School Master."

Rhian glared back. "He's *in* the Storian's tale, James."

Hook shook his head, not understanding.

"The Pen," Rhian pressed. "It's writing his fairy tale as we speak. And now he ends up at our *school*? I don't like it. Some-thing is happening . . ."

James squinted, as if this all had little relevance to him. Then his eyes grew. "Of course! Don't you see! First, you lose the Trial. And now *this*? The Pen is warning you Evil is on the rise. It didn't write about you losing the Trial. You were lucky. But this Neverboy is a threat. He's come to win the Circus. To humil-iate you and your school. And this time, the Storian will tell of his victory and the Good School Master's fall. News of your defeat will spread far and wide, Good's long run finally at an end. We have to win, Rhian. To protect your school. To protect *Good*."

Rhian drew a breath, as if he hadn't considered this. He paced faster. "That can't happen. If Evil breaks Good's winning streak, then . . . No. The balance has favored Good for a reason. Because Good keeps the Woods balanced and at peace. Things have to stay the way they are. With Good supreme. Invincible. You're right, James. This Circus is important. Good's future is on the line. We have two days left. I don't care what kind of forbidden magic we have to teach them. We need our Evers to *win*."

"That's the spirit!" Hook reveled, slinging his arm around the School Master and following him inside.

Neither saw the figure climb up on the balcony once they'd left, watching his brother and friend intertwined as they headed into Good's castle.

Rafal stood there a long time after they'd gone.

But he was only thinking one thing.

Rhian had been honest with Hook.

More honest than he'd ever been with his twin.

But Hook?

Hook was definitely lying.

17.

Early the next morning, Dean Humburg was in the middle of coaching the Nevers' practice.

"When do we get our fingerglows unlocked?" a boy asked. "We could do so much better than whatever talents we got. We could learn real spells!"

"You'll get your glows unlocked when Good does, later this year," said Dean Humburg. "It's only fair. Evers and Nevers must have an equal playing field. You have your innate magical talents, balanced by Good's weaponry and strength—"

The doors to Evil Hall flung open and Fala tromped in, his arms folded, his eyes simmering, his voice a sleepless growl.

"I will train you all," he said. "Whatever your talents are . . . We throw them out and start new."

Humburg scoffed. "Don't be ridiculous. You're not in charg—"

Fala ejected a storm of glow from his hand, blasting Humburg out the window.

He turned to the students. "Good will do anything to win. You think our side is Evil? They are more. They care nothing for balance. What they say is Good? Fairness? Justice? That is *us*. You listen to me, we win. You do not, we are forever the losers."

He waited for dissent. None came.

"We begin."

For the next two days, Fala led the practices, assessing each student's potential and attempting to find their most viable talent. Humburg returned eventually, his robes half-shredded (he'd landed in the nest of sleeping stymphs and had been treated accordingly). But this time, the Dean watched meekly from the corner as the new Neverboy teased out his classmates' strengths.

"Twirling axes, swinging swords . . . It's quite basic, no?" Fala asked Timon, after the one-eyed, half-ogre boy finished a muscular display. "What is it you really want to show?"

Timon looked offended. "That I am strong."

"Why?" Fala asked.

The ogre boy scratched his head. He'd never been asked such a thing. "So people don't mess with me."

"Why?" Fala probed. "Why is it important people don't mess with you?"

Color rose to Timon's cheeks, but he didn't answer.

"Strong inside is better than strong outside. We must look inside for power. This is how we find *true* talents," said Fala. "So tell me: Why must people not mess with you?"

The young cyclops averted his eyes. "Because people messed with me before and I couldn't defend myself."

"Your father," Fala said.

Timon shook his head. "Mother."

Defensively, he scanned the room, ready to bludgeon anyone who would make fun of him, but the Nevers were quietly listening, heads bowed.

Fala touched his shoulder. Timon flinched. "You are angry. Ashamed. Forget it! It is the past, Timon. What is it you want to do? Fight ghosts? Or find power?"

Slowly Timon's gaze lifted.

"Close your eyes," said Fala. "See what comes."

Timon obeyed.

He took a deep breath.

His fingerglow flickered a silvery blue.

"How is he doing that?" Fala overheard Brinsha whisper to Nagila behind them. "We haven't had our fingerglows unlocked yet!"

Fala knew the answer, of course—magic follows emotion and some emotions are so strong, so core to one's soul, that they activate a magic beyond control. But he didn't share this. The less said about such magic, the more it appears.

Timon's chest rose and fell, the pace of his breaths easing, the color of his glow strengthening.

"Fill the chest," said Fala. "Not with anger. With *power*."

Timon drank in air, slowly, surely, as if swallowing the sea.

"Then let it out," said Fala.

Timon exhaled and from his mouth came a wisp of silver-blue smoke, which formed a phantom egg on the floor of Evil Hall, the size of a full-grown child. Little by little, the egg cracked and a tiny head poked out, its eyes as big as its two little horns, and with two budding claws, it peeled away the rest of the shell, revealing a blue dragon, unsteady on its feet, blinking in fear. It coughed a tuft of smoke and peeked at all the Nevers watching.

"Your mother is gone," Fala whispered to the boy, his eyes still closed. "Who are you *now*?"

The dragon's eyes changed. They narrowed and steeled. The creature stood taller, something growing inside it . . .

Then with a roar, it expelled a jet of silver-blue fire, so strong and intense that the dragon had to spin to control it, the spray immolating Evil Hall in phantom flame, the entire room burning and burning, the boy unleashing pent-up breath, until at last he ran out of air and dropped to his knees, panting.

The fires evaporated, the Hall restored as it was.

Timon opened his eyes.

"What happened?" he croaked. "Was it good?"

Fala smiled. "It's a start."

He overheard Brinsha behind him.

"Imagine if Rafal cared about us like that," she whispered to Nagila. "Imagine what this school could be!"

A stabbing pain hit Fala's heart.

Then he swallowed it down. "Who's next?"

That was all he could do, student after student, hour after hour—ask who was next and give them the attention and support they deserved and had never received from the school's absent leader. Soon the Nevers began to look at young Fala the way they once looked at Vulcan. With trust and respect. With something an Ever might call love.

When he chose the ten best for the Circus, no one questioned him.

Not even Humburg.

The boy had become their School Master.

18.

A short time before sunset, Fala gathered his Nevers outside Evil castle.

The ten Circus players headed the pack, Timon at the fore, hiking behind their young leader, around the massive expanse of lake, on their way to Good.

The sky darkened. The moon took over from the sun.

He'd been doing a lot of these trips the past two days, Fala thought wryly of the circuitous route between schools. Spying on Good. Uncovering their lies and schemes that looked a lot like Evil's.

Maybe we do need a bridge over the lake, he thought. *It'll let Evil keep a close eye on Good.* He chewed on his lip. *But then what would stop Good from infiltrating Evil?*

No.

No bridge.

Rafal caught his reflection in the water, Fala's face staring back at him. He suppressed a laugh. Somewhere out there, the real Fala was worrying about love and kisses. Meanwhile, this Fala needed to win a Circus to keep the balance of the Woods intact. If Good triumphed tonight, Rhian would take it as proof he was on the side of right, no matter how corrupt his actions—just like he'd confessed to Hook. All that smarmy self-righteousness about balance. Rhian didn't care about balance! He'd admitted it out loud! He just wanted Good to keep winning, even if it meant cheating. Win tonight and he'd stop at nothing in the future to keep Good supreme. Look at what he was capable of already! Unlocking magic early. Teaching illegal spells. Stealing the only friend his brother had ever made. All games of Evil, now adopted for Good.

But why was Hook here? That was the real question. The boy was a bad liar and everything he'd said about needing the Circus to protect Good was pure lies. So why had he sailed from Blackpool to be Rhian's Dean? Was it to get back at Rafal for not going with him to Neverland? No, surely not. James didn't need an Evil sorcerer to kill Pan. He just needed a capable crew. Why would he fling aside his life's goal and his identity as a pirate to come and be an underling for Good? Surely Rhian had asked him the same questions. But whatever Hook had told him, his brother had believed . . . or *wanted* to believe . . .

"Fala?" a voice said.

He turned to his students.

"We're here," said a girl.

Good's castle glittered above them, thousands of tealight candles with different colored flames twinkling along the stairways, like a midsummer's night dream.

A new theater had been built for the occasion, replacing Good's old gymnasium. An aisle of silver marble split the theater into two sides, one for the Good students, with pink and blue pews, crystal friezes, and glittering bouquets of glass flowers. The other side was for Evil, with warped wooden benches, carvings of murder and torture, and long, sharp stalactites stabbing from the ceiling. Together, they faced a tall stone stage that had a crack down the middle, while overhead in the rafters, a cricket symphony played a dramatic march.

The Evers were seated and in full-throated cheer when the Nevers arrived, the Good students waving signs ("EVIL = LOSERS", "NO TALENT NEVERS!") and shouting down their opponents. The Nevers followed Fala's lead and took their seats without sound. It was the opposite of the Trial, when the Nevers had been boorish and cocksure about their chances, while the Evers had shown up muted and skittish. As the Nevers waited in quiet formation, Rhian watched from a balcony, the Good School Master swaddled in a white, swan-feather robe. He took notice of the Nevers' stillness, the steely looks in their eyes, as if they all shared a secret. A prickling sensation crept up the School Master's spine. He had nothing to worry about. His team was well-chosen. His Evers carefully prepared. Nothing

Evil could bring would defeat them.

Then he saw Fala turn in the audience and look right at him, as if reading his thoughts. The Neverboy gave him the slightest of grins, then flipped back around.

Rhian's heart went cold.

Dean James Hook came out on stage, dressed in a blue-and-gold suit that he'd torn the sleeves off and adorned with an array of gold chains.

In his seat, Fala shifted. He recognized the suit as one of Rhian's.

Hook and his brother were sharing *clothes*.

Rafal boiled inside Fala's skin.

This little detail . . . this stupid little detail . . .

That Hook would so willingly trade one twin for another.

That Rhian would embrace him as family the moment his brother was out of sight.

Before he could stop himself, Rafal imagined the two of them dead.

Facedown, in pools of blood, side by side.

His heart throttled faster.

He'd never wished his twin dead before.

The thought scared him.

As if deep inside, he'd never really believed himself Evil.

Not until now.

"Welcome to the Circus of Talents!" Hook declared, dancing playfully with each word. "Which side will reign supreme? Which side will be the envy of all the Woods? Which side will tilt the balance in its favor?"

Evers burst into a chant—*"Good! Good! Good!"*—while Evil sat placidly, as if their only competition was themselves.

"The rules are simple," said Hook. "Good will present its talents. Then Evil will have its chance. At the end, an impartial judge will make a ruling and the winning side will host the Circus in their school next year. As for this judge of utmost dignity and neutrality . . ."

The doors to the theater swung open and everyone spun to see the Pirate Captain of Blackpool stroll down the aisle, dressed in his signature long black cloak and wide-brimmed hat, his fingers swaying along to the crickets' symphony.

Rhian's eyes flared. So did Fala's.

"When James wrote me to say he'd run away to take a position here, I had to see it for myself," the Captain drawled. "It was his idea to put me to work while I'm at it."

He found a seat in the back row, drew a small vial from his pocket and took a swig. "All right, then. *Dean* Hook. Let's get on with this clown show."

Fala's gaze swung between the Pirate Captain and Hook.

Hook, here at school—and now the *Captain* too?

Something strange was going on . . . some twist that was about to reveal itself . . . as if this Circus was all a charade . . . but instead, the Captain earnestly directed his attention to the stage and Hook swept his hand to the Evers, inviting them to perform.

If the Nevers were expecting the usual Good talents—lute playing and arabesques and hammer tosses—they were instantly surprised. Hephaestus took the stage first, lighting a red finger-glow and transforming himself into a live tiger, bounding across the tops of the Nevers' pews, roaring in Evil students' faces, and scaring them half to death. Before the Nevers could recover, Rufius raised his glow and turned two Evil benches to crisp bread, which shattered under the students' weight, sending Nevers tumbling into the aisles. Madigan topped off the act by morphing into a thundercloud that loomed over Evil's side and detonated to rain, sogging the Nevers through. Evers howled with laughter.

"*Cheating! Cheating!*" the Nevers cried in protest. "They have fingerglows!"

As Evers shouted them down, Kyma frowned in her seat. "The School Master promised it would be fair," she said, spinning to Aladdin, who was lustily booing the other side. "We're not supposed to have magic if they don't!"

"Oh, stop being a goody-goody," Aladdin needled, grabbing bits of bread out of the aisle and pelting the Evil kids with it. "Whole point of this school is to *win*, isn't it?"

Kyma was about to retort, but then glanced around and saw all the Evers shared this view, heckling and catcalling the opponent, delighted by their advantage.

"What's happened to us?" she asked softly.

She swiveled towards the Good School Master, seated in the balcony, expecting him to match her disapproval. But instead, Rhian was . . . *smiling*.

Slowly, his eyes lowered, meeting hers. The School Master caught the expression on her face. Then he coolly looked back at the stage.

"Next," he summoned.

Despite the Nevers crying foul, every single one of the chosen Evers used a fingerglow—Aladdin most notably, with a spell so advanced it turned all the Nevers' skin see-through, revealing their organs and veins.

A spell that made Fala jolt taller in his seat.

Surely the boy had learned the spell from Rhian.

Because long ago, Rhian had learned it from his Evil twin.

Dark magic, now the weapon of Good.

In the end, only Kyma rejected the tactics of her side, using her turn to raise her lit finger high in the air, while the crickets rolled their tiny drums . . . before she extinguished her glow dramatically.

"The greatest talent of Good?" Kyma declared. "Staying true to itself."

Both sides booed her. (The crickets too.)

Dispirited, she plopped back next to Aladdin, only to see her boyfriend subtly scoot away. She stared at him, hurt, but Aladdin pretended not to notice and went on cheering loudly for the final boy, who possessed two of the Nevers with rogue spirits, inciting them to box violently and knock each other out.

Watching his Evers shock the Nevers with their prowess, Rhian chuckled in his seat. They'd been well-coached, of course, their talents chosen for them by the School Master himself. But even so, they'd done precisely as he'd ordered and now they were assured victory. A rebellion put down. A threat extinguished. Good the master of Evil, once more. He searched the theater for Hook, eager to share their triumph, only to find him crouched beside the Pirate Captain, the pair whispering as Hook took notes.

If we weren't winning badly enough! Rhian thought with a grin. *Now Good's Dean is colluding with the judge!*

James was leaving nothing to chance.

Which made Rhian smile all the more.

In his seat, Fala noticed Hook with the Captain too, the Neverboy's eyes narrowing suspiciously, but James had already folded the notes he was taking into his pocket and bobbed back up, his focus shifting to Fala and his team.

"The stage is all yours," the Dean of Good said, adding a puckish bow.

For a moment, Fala forgot he was Fala and Rafal's light eyes glittered through his disguise. Clearly, Hook was intent on the Evers winning this competition—enough that he'd brought the Pirate Captain here to ensure it—which left Rafal puzzling . . . *Why?* Why had James Hook come to the School for Good and Evil? Why had he organized this Circus to begin with? And why now, after helping Good to a dazzling display, was he watching the Evil students so keenly, practically licking his lips, as if desperate to see the defense they mounted? Somewhere inside Rafal, the clues all trickled together . . . the truth so close . . . as if he was the Storian himself, poised to write the answer—

"Well, Humburg?" a voice interrupted.

He turned to the balcony and saw Rhian glaring down at Evil's Dean.

"Do your Nevers have anything to show or are you surrendering already?" the Good School Master taunted.

The Evers whistled and hissed.

Humburg's eyes swung to Fala.

"Oh, I see! The boy is in charge," Rhian mused, assessing Evil's new addition. "Fala, your name was, wasn't it? Remind me. Fala of . . ."

Rafal listened to the brother he'd imagined dead.

But instead of the fantasy returning, this time the impulse weakened.

Fala of . . .

Softness grew in the shadows of bitterness.

Even after all this . . . he loved his brother.

A love undiminished.

Not because the Storian demanded it.

Because it was the truth.

Even if his brother wanted the worst for him and his students. Even if his brother wanted him to lose for the rest of time. None of this changed what Rafal wanted.

That they could love each other again.

That they could *trust* each other.

The way they used to, when one was pure and one was wicked and they stayed true to their parts.

Fala of . . .

His eyes filled in with black, the School Master returned to a student's body.

He looked up at Rhian.

"Fala of *Good*," he said.

Rhian laughed. He arched a brow with a golden-faced smile.

"All right, then, Fala of Good," he said. "Let's see your first act."

Fala turned to his Nevers and nodded.

Timon stood.

This was hardly a surprise to the Evers, who expected Evil's strongest competitor to open their show, and they yawned with feigned boredom—

Until eight other Nevers rose too and joined Timon in taking the stage.

The Good students froze, unsure what was happening.

Rhian spun to Hook, for a rule had surely been broken, but James just watched curiously from against the wall, giving no impression that this was out of bounds. The Pirate Captain, too, had pitched forward in his seat at the back of the theater, dark eyes glimmering, as if only now had the Circus truly begun.

Nine Nevers gathered in a ring on the stage, holding hands.

They bowed their heads, silently communing, so focused

and intent that their chests rose and fell in matching waves.

Then one by one, the Nevers raised their necks and breathed out a wall of mist, each a unique color . . . seafoam green, dusky blue, scarlet red . . . as if instead of a finger's light, they'd manifested a soul's worth.

Within each mist, a scene appeared.

A vision of the Nevers' future.

Or what they dreamed that future to be.

Brinsha, saving a nest of baby trolls from a sword-swinging prince.

Fodor, hiding a sea witch in undersea grass, as mermen and mermaids stalked past, tridents in hand.

Nagila, conjuring a cave full of deadly snakes to protect a dragon and his gold from a king's army.

Gryff, spawning scales and a carapace, to absorb the blows of two warrior princesses while a family of giants escaped down a beanstalk.

Never after Never, offering a future where villains saved villains and Evil was Goodness, futures of honor, valor, and purpose, each mission so bold and heartfelt that Evers watched them unfold with wide-eyed suspense, as if rooting for their opponents to succeed.

Rhian groaned loudly. "What's next? Evil in love?" he

scoffed. "Happy *Never* After?"

His Evers snapped out of their trance, erupting into jeers. *"Boo! Boooooo!"*

But now it was Timon's turn, the last Never in the circle, who rather than offering his own future, stared down the Good students instead. His one eye bulged, the blood vessels darkening, his muscles hardening, and with a great inhale, he blasted a blue rush of phantom flame that swallowed the Evers, illuminating their spirits beneath—faces decayed and scarred, bodies misshapen, the ugliness of their arrogant, cheating souls pulled to the surface.

Only Kyma remained as she was, gaping in shock as the rest of her classmates turned monstrous under Timon's light.

Screams and shrieks flew from Good, the Evers stumbling and clamoring for the doors, but Timon's eye burned with blue glow and in response, the doors slammed shut, locking them in. His fire burned brighter, brighter, finding every last soul, no matter how far they climbed under pews or cowered to corners, the flames revealing maggots and worms in their eyes and charred ash beneath flaying faces, all of this the hideousness of what Good had become, a doomed flock, writhing and piling on top of each other, trapped in their own circle of Hell—

The fire stopped.

Timon sank to his knees, emptied.

Slowly, the Evers lifted their heads and peeked through their hands to see themselves as they were, young and luminous, the outsides untouched.

But from the way they looked at one another, it was clear the damage was unseen.

A frantic silence hung amongst them.

James Hook and the Pirate Captain locked eyes, their faces inscrutable.

Rhian jumped to his feet, cheeks flushed. "Well, a group light show isn't possibly enough to defeat what we've done. Pirate Captain, am I right—"

"We're not finished," spoke a voice.

Rhian looked down to see Fala, still seated.

"That was nine," said the boy. "We have a tenth."

Rhian croaked back, as if he knew the answer. "Who?"

Fala rose. "Me."

He never took the stage.

Right then and there, Fala's face began to change, his nose curving and straightening, his hair blooming to wild, golden curls, his face bronzing to a tan, until there he was, looking up at Rhian, the School Master's duplicate. Before Rhian could react, Fala's face cracked down the middle, his torso and legs too, the left and right sides of him splitting off and morphing into complete bodies, *two* new Rhians instead of one. Only he was dividing again now and suddenly, the Evers were at attention, watching a Neverboy not only morph into Good's leader, but three of him, five of him, *ten* of him, before they all flew back together, like cards in a deck, his hair curling and going dark, his legs and arms lengthening, his skin paling and pinking, until he was no longer Rhian at all, but . . . Hook.

Against the wall, James cocked his head. "Blimey."

By the time he'd uttered the word, Fala's face had become half James and half Rhian's, the School Master and the Dean in one body. The two sides of his face switched, from James and Rhian, to Rhian and James, back and forth, faster, faster, blurring and scrambling, until out of the haze came a new face, with sky-colored eyes and alabaster skin and frost-white hair as sharp as spikes.

Even the Evil students were struck dumb now, by the sight of their feared School Master returned, especially when his feet lifted off the ground and he began to fly, soaring over the Evers and Nevers, flicking off the Pirate Captain's hat, before rising higher to the balcony of the theater and landing in front of Rhian.

The Good School Master didn't speak or move, his face as ashen as his Evil twin's, and he stayed rooted in his seat as if bound to it, even when his brother reached for his chest and drew a fistful of golden glow from his heart.

He gently twisted the glow into an orchid flower and held it out, like an offering.

Dazed, Rhian took the magical bloom into his palms.

"Rafal," he breathed. "It's you . . ."

In Rhian's hands, the flower rotted and crumbled.

The Good brother gasped and looked back up, but his Evil twin was already touching down to the stage, his face changing, the hair browning and slumping to a bowl cut, the nose a lumpy hook once more.

"No," the boy answered, his voice sharp and clear as a crystal. "Only Fala, Fala, Fala."

A tear fell from Rhian's eye.

The theater went deathly still.

All the students turned, looking up at a School Master.

A School Master who'd mistaken one of their own for his twin.

Like a cannonshot, the Nevers roared with victory. They swarmed the stage and hoisted the boy on their shoulders, rejecting the need for a judge's verdict. *"FALA! FALA! FALA!"* The

Evers did nothing to protest this outcome or press their case, the Good side of the aisle as mute and stone-eyed as the Nevers had been when they'd entered the theater. Carrying Fala down the aisle, the Nevers danced and sang his name.

Dean Hook watched all this with a curious expression on his face—then noticed Rhian fleeing the theater from the balcony.

James followed him.

In the Good pews, Kyma shook her head, shellshocked. "This is what happens. This is what happens when Good acts Evil."

Aladdin glanced at her, sheepishly. "I just did what the rest of you did. You know . . . follow the Good guys . . ."

Kyma looked right at him. "But we're not Good anymore. Don't you see?"

"Maybe the Pen was wrong about me," Aladdin admitted. "Maybe I am Evil."

"The longer we stay at this school, we all are," said Hephaestus, slumped grimly on the other side of him. "We've lost our way. We've lost our purpose for being here."

"Maybe you need a *new* purpose, then," a voice replied behind them.

They turned in their seats.

The Pirate Captain grinned back at them.

19.

In a dark forest, two shadows moved through the trees.

Loping across treetops, Rafal watched them.

"Rhian, stop!" Hook called.

Rhian whirled around, eyes wild, his skin speckled in moonlight like a nocturnal animal. "This is *your* fault. The Circus was *your* idea. Coming to my school was *your* idea. And now . . . and now . . ." He clawed at his neck. "They've seen through us. And that boy . . . he's seen through me. It's Rafal . . . it has to be Rafal . . ." Rhian shook his head. "But the Storian was writing about the boy long before this . . . So it *can't* be . . ." He shuddered and bounded ahead. "That's why Rafal chose him. To play games with my head. He has a student now that's unbeatable. A student like *him*. What will happen when my brother returns from Blackpool? He found the chink in Good's armor . . . in my armor . . ."

"Then fight back," said James.

Rhian stopped and looked at him. "How? That boy is as strong as Rafal himself. What is there to be done?"

"The only thing that can be done," Hook conceded.

The School Master stared at him. "You don't mean . . ."

"What do you think I mean?" James asked, a sparkle in his eye.

Rhian went very pale. "You w-w-want . . . you want me to . . ."

"Make him disappear?" James proposed. "That would solve everything, wouldn't it?"

Up in the trees, the Evil twin went cold.

Rhian forced a laugh. "Don't be daft. My duty is to preserve this school—to preserve balance—"

"Getting rid of him will only correct the balance," James countered. "You said it yourself: he is unbeatable. Rafal's weapon to take you down. As long as Fala is at this school, Good will always be subservient to Evil."

Rhian flinched, but waved his hands, as if warding off the blow. "There are rules. Good doesn't attack Evil. Good doesn't *kill* Evil—"

"Even if it's your mortal enemy? Your nemesis?" James drew closer, touching the School Master's shoulder. "He will only grow stronger as you grow weaker. As long as that boy is here, you will never find peace."

Rhian gazed at him . . . then shoved him away. "I can't." He hustled ahead, suddenly obscured from Rafal's sight—

"But I can," Rafal heard James say.

Now Rhian was quiet.

His footsteps had ceased.

"And I will," said James. "As long as you do something for me."

Rafal lowered to the ground to get a view, his snow-colored hair and skin luminous in the night. Quickly, he camouflaged to Fala's dark locks and peeked from behind a tree.

"What do you want?" Rhian asked softly, facing James.

"Give me your magic," Hook said. "A piece of your soul, put into me, like your brother once did."

Rhian exhaled with force. "James—"

"It's the only way I can get rid of him," said Hook sharply. "You saw how powerful he is. If you're too scared to do it, then I will. I will help you, Rhian. Because I care about you. More than I cared about your brother. You can make Good what you want it to be. Supreme. Invincible. This time, with a *true* companion at your side. One you can trust, unlike Vulcan or your twin. No one in our way to stop us." He put his hand on Rhian's chest. "But I need your magic to finish the job."

Rhian didn't move.

His throat bobbed, his eyes very wide.

Fala watched them, heart in his throat.

His twin about to cross the line into unforgivable Evil.

Don't do it.

Please.

Please, Rhian.

Slowly his brother's shadow slid forward, meeting the shadow opposite him, their hands intertwined.

Rafal choked.

That painting from the book.

The Storian's latest tale.

This was it.

Two shadows in the forest.

Fala watching them.

No, Fala gasped—

Rhian leaned in and put his lips to Hook's, breathing golden glow into him. James' chest flooded with light, his back arched, tensing with power and thrill, the deed done . . .

A cry ripped through the sky.

Hook and Rhian whirled and looked up.

But there was nothing there.

20.

Rafal flew into the School Masters' tower.

The Storian was mid-stroke, painting Fala reverting to the Evil School Master as he'd fled his twin and traitorous friend, humiliated, ashamed.

"You liar! You cheat!" Rafal yelled at the Pen, swiping violently for it—

The Storian slashed his arm, blood spraying the stone walls.

Rafal released the Pen in shock.

Panting, he stared at the wound, waiting for it to magically heal.

It didn't.

Blood dripped onto the Pen's open book.

Rafal backed against the wall.

A memory of the Pen's voice stabbed at his heart.

The one and only time it spoke.

> *Every School Master faces a test.*
> *Yours is love.*
> *Betray that love and the test is failed.*

Now their love was betrayed.

Their immortality robbed.

The test failed.

Everything the School Masters stood for—students, balance, *life*—erased.

Slowly, he looked up at the Pen, which had turned the page.

It drew a new scene.

A scene from long ago.

A pair of twins, one golden and wild-maned, one frigid and spiky, standing in front of the Storian the day they'd arrived at the School for Good and Evil.

The day the Storian had entrusted them the balance.

Rhian for Good.

Rafal for Evil.

Just like the Pen had said.

Rafal peered longer at the painting of him and his twin.

But did it say that?

Or did it say something else?

Blood throbbed in his wound.

I choose you.
Two brothers.
One for Good.
One for Evil.

The Pen had never said which was which.

They'd chosen.

They'd assumed.

They'd had no doubt.

Because of what they thought they knew about each other.

Because of what they thought they knew about themselves.

Rafal couldn't breathe.

Impossible.

Impossible!

Rhian was the Good twin.

Rafal the Evil one.

Of course he was.

Father Sader had confirmed it!

He'd said it in his prophecy under the sea—

"The Pen senses a restless soul, Rafal. Questioning whether a brother's love is enough . . ."

Rafal's gut twisted.

He never said the soul was Rafal.

Because it wasn't Rafal.

It was never Rafal.

It was *Rhian*.

Rhian, the restless soul that wanted more. Rhian, the soul that strayed to Vulcan, to the Captain, to Hook. Rhian, the soul that kept testing the peace he and his brother had been given to protect.

"That is why Evil suffers," Father Sader foretold.

That is why Evil kept losing.

Because *Rhian* was the Evil one.

And Rafal wasn't.

The Evil School Master who couldn't win . . .

. . . until he realized he wasn't the Evil School Master at all.

Rafal screamed in horror, the sound exploding through the tower, resounding through both schools.

Somewhere in the forest, Rhian heard it too.

And he knew his brother had returned.

21.

Rhian stirred, babbling in his sleep.

"Fala . . . Fala . . . Fal—"

He bolted awake, lurching upright, his back against a brick wall, his eyes very big.

Where am I?

But he was right where he should be: in his bed, nestled within the School Masters' chamber, the dust of sunlight trailing around the corner from the next room.

The second bed was empty.

Rhian tried to remember what had happened last night.

First, the Circus . . . then the deal with Hook in the forest . . .

His stomach knotted at the thought.

He pushed aside the feeling.

It was the right choice.

Whatever he and Hook had decided . . .

It had to be done.

Which is why he'd parted ways with James and come here to the tower, looking for Rafal. He'd had an inkling his brother was back, but instead the chamber was clear, the tower eerily peaceful.

He'd slumped to his bed in relief.

His brother still gone.

Fala soon to be gone too.

Good again on the rise.

Sleep was often a battle for Rhian, but not then.

He'd slept better than he had in a hundred years.

Now it was morning.

Hook's work surely complete.

He slipped out of bed, his steps cold against the mottled stone, before he turned the corner into a glorious wash of sun.

Rhian stretched his arms and glanced around the bookshelves, fairy tales lit up in a golden spray like a thousand jewels.

That's when he noticed the Storian, resting in repose. Underneath, the new tale was finished, waiting for the School

Master to place it on his shelves. Rhian approached the book, the emerald-green cover shut, the title *Fala and His Brother* carved into the wood. Quickly, he reached to open it, eager to read its ending—

A great bellowing pierced the silence.

Braying, terrible shouts from outside.

Rhian looked out the window and froze.

What in the . . .

There was a bridge across the lake.

A bridge, where there wasn't one before.

He smeared his eyes, unsure if he was dreaming.

But no, there it was: a stone passage over the lake, connecting Good's glass castle and Evil's black fortress—

More shouts.

Frenzied, unhinged.

They were coming from a figure *on* the bridge.

Humburg.

For a moment, the School Master felt a pang of relief. Fala was dead . . . Humburg had found him . . .

But then he heard what Humburg was saying.

"They're gone! They're all goooone!"

Rhian dove into the lake, using a spell to propel himself to the far banks, to Evil's Dean who came flurrying from the bridge, eyes glassy with shock, grabbing the School Master by his white robes, words spilling out of him—

"Hook and the Pirate Captain . . . they stole them . . . our best Nevers . . . *all* of them . . . our whole Circus team . . . They had magic somehow—sorcerer's magic!—and conjured the bridge in the night to sneak them out . . . Timon left a note . . . Hook offered them a place on the *Jolly Roger* . . . to be his crew and fight Peter Pan . . . to take Neverland for pirates . . . They didn't want to be students under Rafal anymore. Fala had given them a glimpse of a better life. So they went with Hook . . . They wanted Fala to come with them, but they couldn't find him. No one can find him! They took the best Evers too . . . *Your* Evers who think Good is lost . . ." Humburg shook Rhian by the collar. "Don't you see? Hook came to steal our best! He and the Captain had a plan all along! They played you for a fool!"

Rhian couldn't breathe, his face red, nothing but spittle coming out of his mouth. "No . . . no—"

He shoved Humburg aside, dashing onto the bridge and hurtling across the lake towards the School for Good. His naked feet battered against the stretch of stone, built with a wizard's magic, *his* magic, given to Hook to kill a boy and instead used against him. He threw open the doors to his castle, stumbling up the stairs to the first floor . . .

Dozens of eyes gaped back at him.

Evers gathered in their pajamas and dressing gowns, huddled like spooked egrets at the end of the hall.

"Who?" Rhian gasped. "Who did he take?"

Rufius pointed at the doors.

Three of them were wide open.

The names on the doors scratched out.

~~ALADDIN.~~

~~KYMA.~~

~~HEPHAESTUS.~~

A ripped piece of parchment hung tacked to Kyma's door.

Sorry, love. Once a pirate . . . always a pirate.

Hook

Rhian's face paled in horror.

He was already running . . . away from his students . . . down
the stairs . . . out the castle and into the forest . . .

By the time he reached the shores of the sea, he caught the
last glimpse of the pirate ship, black flag flying, before it faded
into mist like a mirage.

Rhian crumpled to his knees in the sand.

Schools upended.

Students absconded.

Good, the loser.

This was the end he deserved.

For Evil thoughts.

For Evil deeds.

For betraying his brother and the balance.

What will Rafal say?

What will he do?

He sobbed into his hands: "I'm Good . . . I promise . . . I can fix it . . . I'll be Good again . . ."

"If only that was a promise one could keep," said a voice.

Rhian looked up.

"Rafal?" he whispered.

His brother was perched on a rock, as if he'd been summoned like a genie, as if he'd been there watching him all along. Legs curled under him, he sketched something on the rock with a lit fingertip.

"It doesn't matter what you are," said Rafal. "It only matters what you *do*."

Slowly Rhian rose and saw that his brother was drawing two interlocking swans, one black and one white. There was a wound near his elbow, the blood new.

Rhian gasped. "Rafal, your arm! Why isn't it healin—"

"Fitting for the crest of our school, don't you think?" Rafal said, not looking at him. "Some will say the white swan is the Good swan . . . the beautiful swan . . . because the black swan is clearly the Evil one. But then there will be others who think the black swan is Good and beautiful, for standing out in a flock of white. Good and Evil. It's what you see, isn't it? The Pen warned us with that boy. That's how it all started. A warning that we had it all wrong. That what happened with Aladdin could happen with us."

Rhian swallowed. "What do you mean?"

Rafal kept sketching. "A seer told me once. That my love would never be enough. I thought she meant your love would never be enough for me. That I could never be happy by your side. That my soul would always betray you. But that's not what she meant. It was you she was talking about. My love will never be enough . . . for *you*."

Rhian stepped closer. "I don't understand."

His twin said nothing.

He kept drawing his swans.

"Rafal," Rhian rasped. "They're gone."

"Mmm?"

"Our students. Yours and mine. Our best ones are gone."

"I see."

Rhian's shadow fell over his twin. "What do we do?"

"We get more, of course," said Rafal.

"From where?" said Rhian. "Where can we get students as good as the ones we've lost?"

"There is a place," Rafal answered, head down. "A land beyond us where our stories only live in dreams. A land filled with fresh souls better than any we've found before. Waiting to be taken. A new school will rise. And everything will change."

"Where is this place?" Rhian asked, quickening with hope. "What is it called?"

Rafal looked up at his brother, his face dead cold.

"Gavaldon."

Now it's time to go to school!
Read an excerpt from *The School for Good and Evil*,
book 1 in Soman Chainani's *New York Times* bestselling series.

The Art of Kidnapping

By the time the sun extinguished, the children were long locked away. Through bedroom shutters, they peeked at torch-armed fathers, sisters, grandmothers lined around the dark forest, daring the School Master to cross their ring of fire.

But while shivering children tightened their window screws, Sophie prepared to undo hers. She wanted this kidnapping to be as convenient as possible. Barricaded in her room, she laid out hairpins, tweezers, nail files and went to work.

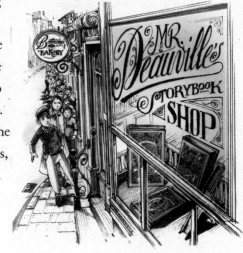

The first kidnappings happened two hundred years before. Some years it was two boys taken, some years two girls, sometimes one of each. The ages were just as fickle; one could be sixteen, the other fourteen, or both just turned twelve. But if at first the choices seemed random, soon the pattern became clear. One was always beautiful and good, the child every parent wanted as their own. The other was homely and odd, an outcast from birth. An opposing pair, plucked from youth and spirited away.

Naturally the villagers blamed bears. No one had ever seen a bear in Gavaldon, but this made them more determined to find one. Four years later, when two more children vanished, the villagers admitted they should have been more specific and declared *black* bears the culprit, bears so black they blended with the night. But when children continued to disappear every four years, the village shifted their attention to burrowing bears, then phantom bears, then bears in disguise . . . until it became clear it wasn't bears at all.

But while frantic villagers spawned new theories (the Sinkhole Theory, the Flying Cannibal Theory) the children of Gavaldon began to notice something suspicious. As they studied the dozens of Missing posters tacked up in the square, the faces of these lost boys and girls looked oddly familiar. That's when they opened up their storybooks and found the kidnapped children.

Jack, taken a hundred years before, hadn't aged a bit. Here he was, painted with the same moppy hair, pinked dimples, and crooked smile that had made him so popular with the girls of Gavaldon. Only now he had a beanstalk in his back garden and a weakness for magic beans. Meanwhile, Angus, the pointy-eared, freckled hooligan who had vanished with Jack that same year, had transformed into a pointy-eared, freckled giant at the top of Jack's beanstalk. The two boys had found their way into a fairy tale. But when the children presented the Storybook Theory, the adults responded as adults most often do. They patted the children's heads and returned to sinkholes and cannibals.

But then the children showed them more familiar faces. Taken fifty years before, sweet Anya now sat on moonlit rocks in a painting as the Little Mermaid, while cruel Estra had become the devious sea witch. Philip, the priest's upright son, had grown into the Cunning Little Tailor, while pompous Gula spooked children as the Witch of the Wood. Scores of children, kidnapped in pairs, had found new lives in a storybook world. One as Good. One as Evil.

The books came from Mr. Deauville's Storybook Shop, a musty nook between Battersby's Bakery and the Pickled Pig Pub. The problem, of course, was where old Mr. Deauville got his storybooks.

Once a year, on a morning he could not predict, he would arrive at his shop to find a box of books waiting inside. Four brand-new fairy tales, one copy of each. Mr. Deauville would hang a sign on his shop door: "Closed Until Further Notice." Then he'd huddle in his back room day after day, diligently copying the new tales by hand until he had enough books for every child in Gavaldon. As for the mysterious originals, they'd appear one morning in his shop window, a sign that Mr. Deauville had finished his exhausting task at last. He'd open his doors to a three-mile line that snaked through the square, down hillslopes, around the lake, jammed with children thirsting for new stories, and parents desperate to see if any of the missing had made it into this year's tales.

Needless to say, the Council of Elders had plenty of questions for Mr. Deauville. When asked who sent the books, Mr. Deauville said he hadn't the faintest idea. When asked how long the books had been appearing, Mr. Deauville said he couldn't remember a time when the books did not appear. When asked whether he'd ever questioned this magical appearance of books, Mr. Deauville replied: "Where else would storybooks come from?"

Then the Elders noticed something else about Mr. Deauville's storybooks. All the villages in them looked just like Gavaldon. The same lakeshore cottages and colorful eaves. The same purple and green tulips along thin dirt roads. The same crimson carriages, wood-front shops, yellow schoolhouse, and leaning clock tower, only drawn as fantasy in a land far, far away. These storybook villages existed for only one purpose: to begin a fairy tale and to end it. Everything between the beginning and end happened in the dark, endless woods that surrounded the town.

That's when they noticed that Gavaldon too was surrounded by dark, endless woods.

Back when the children first started to disappear, villagers stormed the forest to find them, only to be repelled by storms, floods, cyclones, and falling trees. When they finally braved their way through, they found a town hiding beyond the trees and vengefully besieged it, only to discover it was their own. Indeed, no matter where the villagers entered the woods, they came out right where they started. The woods, it seemed, had no intention of returning their children. And one day they found out why.

Mr. Deauville had finished unpacking that year's storybooks when he noticed a large smudge hiding in the box's fold. He touched his finger to it and discovered the smudge was wet with ink. Looking closer, he saw it was a seal with an elaborate crest of a black swan and a white swan. On the crest were three letters:

S.G.E.

There was no need for him to guess what these letters meant. It said so in the banner beneath the crest. Small black words that told the village where its children had gone:

THE SCHOOL FOR GOOD AND EVIL

The kidnappings continued, but now the thief had a name. They called him the School Master.

A few minutes after ten, Sophie pried the last lock off the window and cracked open the shutters. She could see to the forest edge, where her father, Stefan, stood with the rest of the perimeter guard. But instead of looking anxious like the others, he was smiling, hand on the widow Honora's shoulder. Sophie grimaced. What her father saw in that woman, she had no idea. Once upon a time, her mother had been as flawless as a storybook queen. Honora, meanwhile, had a small head, round body, and looked like a turkey.

Her father whispered mischievously into the widow's ear and Sophie's cheeks burned. If it were Honora's two little sons who might be taken, he'd be serious as death. True, Stefan had locked her in at sundown, given her a kiss, dutifully acted the loving father. But Sophie knew the truth. She had seen it in his face every day of her life. Her father didn't love her. Because she wasn't a boy. Because she didn't remind him of himself.

Now he wanted to marry that beast. Five years after her mother's death, it wouldn't be seen as improper or callous. A simple exchange of vows and he'd have two sons, a new family, a fresh start. But he needed his daughter's blessing first for the Elders to allow it. The few times he tried, Sophie changed the subject or loudly chopped cucumbers or smiled the way she did at Radley. Her father hadn't mentioned Honora again.

Let the coward marry her when I'm gone, she thought, glaring at him through the shutters. Only when she was gone would he appreciate her. Only when she was gone would he know no one could replace her. And only when she was gone would he see he had spawned much more than a son.

He had borne a princess.

On her windowsill, Sophie laid out gingerbread hearts for the School Master with delicate care. For the first time in her life, she'd made them with sugar and butter. These were special, after all. A message to say she'd come willingly.

Sinking into her pillow, she closed her eyes on widows, fathers, and wretched Gavaldon and with a smile counted the seconds to midnight.